A
RISK ON
FOREVER

N.S. PERKINS

Book Cover Design by Murphy Rae

Editing by The Word Maid

Formatting by Meet Cute Creative

À mes parents, qui m'ont donné tout et encore plus.

1

ADELAIDE

"*P*lease, I can't lose this job."

Even I could hear the desperation in my voice, but I didn't care. This could not be happening. Not to me. Not right now.

Antonio, my boss, dragged two fingers over his thick mustache and exhaled loudly. "Look around, Addy."

I did as he asked, noticing the same small coffee shop with nonmatching chairs and round tables I'd contemplated for the last two years. What was I supposed to see?

"There's no one here," he added, answering my unspoken question. "I'm really sorry, but we just can't afford you anymore."

I closed my eyes, willing the threatening tears to go away. It wasn't his fault; this was meant to happen at some point.

When I trusted myself to look in control, I gave him a curt nod. "Do you need me to finish today's shift?" Not that I'd started it. Antonio had cornered me as soon as I came in, casually destroying my life with a few simple sentences.

He winced. "If you don't mind, I think I'll be all right by myself today."

I didn't have the strength to say anything, so I shrugged.

I'd rather start looking for another job as soon as possible anyway. With a tight smile, I walked out of the shop. If I'd tried to say goodbye, I would probably have broken down into sobs, and what good would that have done?

With my head hung low, I headed to the small park on the other side of the street and sat on a cool metal bench.

Standing in front of Antonio, I'd been able to keep a semi-straight face, but once I started thinking about everything losing my job entailed, panic arose in my chest. The image of the bank statement I'd looked at this morning seared my mind. The nighttime singing gigs wouldn't cut it.

God, what would I tell Louis?

It wasn't like my little brother would understand what losing my job meant for him, but if I couldn't pay the rent at the end of the month, he'd know something was up.

Maybe by some miracle, I'd come home later today and my father would be out of bed, ready to start looking for work all of a sudden?

Yeah, right.

I hugged my knees as a heavy wind blew around me. A storm was brewing. Hopefully, it would fall as rain instead of snow.

My eyes stung, but I again pushed the tears back. Everything would be okay. It wasn't the first time I'd lost a job. I'd find something new. I *had* to find something new. I'd beg if it came to it. We would make it through this.

Everything would be okay.

Swallowing the lump rising in my throat, I picked up my phone. I knew what I'd likely find on Craigslist; I'd been monitoring job postings every other week for an opportunity, in vain. The difference was, now, I wasn't looking *just in case*.

For a few years, there had been a shortage of jobs in Portland, Maine, that didn't require fifteen years of experience or a college diploma. Finding the open barista position had been nothing short of a miracle.

I leaned back on the park bench as I scrolled through the ads I had already seen a thousand times. Third grade teacher at the Portsmouth Elementary School. Registered Nurse at the New England Hospital. *Experienced* dog walker in Ogunquit.

I huffed at my phone before continuing to scroll, and that's when a title caught my eye. I stopped dead in my tracks as I read the ad again. *Looking for full-time caregiver. Must have experience working with people with major mobility limitations. For more info, call 207-424-5795.* It'd been posted two days ago.

This was it. A *true* miracle this time. Pressing my phone to my chest, I looked up and gave a small dip of the head to the gray sky. My mom was watching over me today.

Just as I was getting ready to call the number listed, I saw a piece of text I had missed before. *Interviews for the position will be held for anyone interested on Monday, March 25th, from 8 to 9:30 a.m.*

I glanced at the time on my phone. 8:28 a.m. The address given on the ad for the interview was in Cape Neddick. A forty-five minute bus ride away, *if* I was lucky. I might be too late, but I had to try to make it. My family's livelihood depended on it, and that wasn't even an exaggeration.

Jolting up from the bench, I dashed to the bus stop, getting there just in time to catch the 8:30 to Cape Neddick. When I finally sat down, I looked down and repressed a groan. I'd gotten dressed as unprofessionally as I possibly could have this morning. My black cotton leggings had a large hole over my right knee, my t-shirt had a small grease stain chest level, and my black Chucks were covered in dirt from the time I'd played soccer with Louis in the rain. Antonio never cared about what I looked like behind the counter. As long as I was there on time and smiled at the few clients who came into the café, he was happy. With this employer, though, it might be a completely different story.

The ride to Cape Neddick was pure torture. My right knee kept bouncing, reminding me with each movement of the hole that might be the reason for my demise. I tried to tame my curly brown-black hair in a bun behind my head, but there was no way to hide the frizz framing my face. I looked at the time on my phone every two minutes and huffed every time the driver stayed longer than necessary at a stop. When the bus finally pulled to my stop fifty-one minutes after leaving Portland, I was a puddle of sweat and nerves.

Scurrying out the door as soon as the bus came to a halt, I ran all the way to the address on the ad, my phone's GPS guiding me to it. Luckily, I got there in three minutes, and as soon as I lifted my eyes from my phone, my breath caught in my throat. The two-story home stood on a cliff side and had an unobstructed view of the Atlantic Ocean. The beige-gray shingles covering the house were in pristine condition, as were the white shutters, which practically sparkled from cleanliness. The windows were large and numerous, and I could only imagine the light they let in during a gorgeous summer day. The whole thing was splendid.

After ogling the house for a good minute, I reminded myself I had somewhere to be and rushed to the front door, knocking almost immediately. If I thought about it too long, I'd leave this impressive home and run straight to my apartment.

As I waited for someone to answer, I glanced around. The driveway was empty, so I guessed no one else was here for an interview at the moment. The owners' cars must've been in the garage. The brisk March wind whipped around my head, reminding me I should have left with a thicker coat this morning. I'd forced Louis to wear one, but what applied to others didn't apply to me, it seemed.

After a few seconds, footsteps echoed from inside. I looked up to see a tall man opening the door, and my eyes widened when I took him in. He had black hair that was combed back, although a slight wave was still detectable in it. His eyes were also of the deepest of blacks, so dark that discerning the pupil from the iris was impossible. His skin was tan and a closely

4

trimmed beard covered his jaw. His broad shoulders and chest fit perfectly in his crisp black shirt, tucked in trousers of a matching tone.

Black was definitely his color.

"Are you here for the job interview?"

The deep tone of his voice startled me from my gawking. Heat crept up my neck as I forced a smile. "Y-Yes. I am."

It seemed as if he hadn't taken a good look at me before, but after the words left my mouth, his eyes trailed my body from head to toe. I licked my lower lip. When his eyes made their way back to my face, he did not return my smile. His lips were even pinched. Still, he took a step back and held the door open wider for me to come in.

As I stepped inside, my predictions were confirmed. The house was as beautiful on the inside as it was on the outside. High ceilings, elegant paintings on the walls, mahogany floors; everything screamed of class and wealth. I followed the man— who still hadn't introduced himself—through a kitchen that was all modern appliances, quartz countertops, and white wooden cupboards, before arriving in a living room, where I crashed down to earth and remembered the reason for my presence in this luxurious place.

A lady sat beside a white-tiled fireplace in a large wheelchair. Her head was bent to the right, her ear almost touching her shoulder as if some invisible weight was pulling her down. My neck hurt just looking at her. But even in this awkward position, she gave off a sense of comfort and serenity.

Her baby blue blouse seemed to be made of the finest silk, and her white pants were of the same quality. A simple golden ring adorned her right middle finger. Her honey blond hair was cut to her shoulders and had clearly been blow-dried and straightened before I'd gotten here, no strand untucked.

As I took a step in her direction, her ocean blue eyes caught mine. They shone with a hearty light, but the warmest part about her was her smile. Looking at her, I was taken by how much she reminded me of my own mother. Not that they looked anything alike, but the woman had the same energy; one that warmed like a hot chocolate on a winter day.

I returned her genuine smile as the man sat down next to her, a notepad in his hands. He gestured for me to take a seat on the plush velvet chair in front of them. As soon as I sat, he said, "Tell us your name please." He wasn't impolite or rude per se, but his tone told me everything I needed to know about my chances of success here.

"Oh, of course, sorry. I'm Adelaide Samson. My friends usually call me Addy, though." I flashed a quick smile that probably looked as awkward as I felt.

"I'm Matthias Philips, and this is my mother, Helen. Thank you for coming here today."

I nodded as I looked at the two of them again. They had nothing in common, from the color of their hair to the tint of their eyes.

"Before you tell us about yourself, I'd like to tell you a bit about me," Helen said. Her voice was velvet soft, though her words were slurred.

"I was diagnosed with ALS two and a half years ago. Do you know what this disease is?"

I nodded.

"Good. So, as of now, I have lost the utility of my legs and my arms, as well as some

muscles on the left side of my neck and head. I still have some control over my right hand, which allows me to move around the house with this chair." Beside her right hand was a small joystick.

"What I'm looking for is someone to help me with daily tasks when Matthias is away. I already have a caregiver— Dora—but she can only work a small number of hours per week, and I need someone who can be here on almost a daily basis."

This time the smile that took over my lips was genuine. For

the first time in my life, I felt like I was perfectly qualified for a job. I'd done this for years with my mother. I could certainly do it for someone else, especially if it meant I'd be able to pay rent next week.

"So, Adelaide, what makes you think you're the right person for this job?" Matthias asked, an expression that bordered on ennui on his face.

"Well, I—"

A phone rang. Matthias slid his phone from his front pocket and looked at it before frowning. "Please excuse me for a minute, I really have to take this." He got up and left the living room.

"He's a pilot," Helen whispered. "He has to take his calls when they're from his airline company."

"Oh, I get it. No worries." I glanced at her again. Her smile hadn't faltered since I'd walked into the room.

Her eyes drifted down to my chest. "I didn't know my teenage music tastes were still relevant."

I hesitated before realizing she was looking at my ABBA t-shirt. Pulling on the hem, I said, "Oh, um, this was my mother's." A side of my lips quirked up. "She used to say 'Dancing Queen' had been written for her."

Helen chuckled, then gave me a pained smile, like she knew what the past tense I'd used meant. "I think I would've liked your mother."

A lump grew in my throat, and I tried my best to push it down. Even years later, the sting didn't ease.

Focusing my attention on the floor, I noticed one of her shoes was on the verge of falling off her foot. Without thinking about it, I got up and leaned over so I could put the shoe back in place. I made eye contact with her to make sure she didn't mind before doing it. When I was done, I returned to my chair.

She eyed me, and I think her grin got even bigger. "Thank you, that was nice of you."

"It's nothing."

Matthias chose that moment to come back to the living room, but he didn't go back to his seat. Instead, he stayed on his feet next to his mother, hands in his pockets.

"Well, Adelaide, thank you for coming. We'll call you if we're interested in your services."

My eyes bulged. "Oh, but I didn't get the chance to tell you about my credentials. If you need me to hurry, I can rapidly go over my experience."

"I don't think that will be necessary, but thank you for your time." Then, he gave me his first smile of the day, which screamed fake from a mile away.

I was frozen for a moment. Had I done something wrong? Yes, disapproval had been etched all over his face ever since I'd gotten here, but did he think it was so improbable for me to be qualified that he didn't even give me the chance to talk about my experience?

I turned my head to Helen, who had both eyebrows drawn. At least she didn't seem to agree with his urgent dismissal. I gazed back at Matthias, who was looking at me expectantly, probably impatient to have the scoundrel out of his clean-cut house. I gave Helen one last smile before getting up.

As I walked toward the front door, I couldn't help my shoulders from slumping. This had been too good to be true. A job that I would've been good at, that I would've liked? *Come on, Addy.*

As soon as I stepped out of the house, I pulled my phone out of my back pocket and opened Craigslist again.

MATTHIAS

"*W*hat do you think you're doing?"

I stopped walking and frowned after turning around. My mom was giving me a death glare.

"Going to get a cup of coffee," I answered, my pitch rising as if I was asking.

Helen rolled over to me, her eyes still boring a hole into my face. I took a step back, but she moved even closer, her wheels almost touching the tips of my shoes. "Why would you run her out the door?"

How could I *not*? The girl looked like she had come here straight after hopping out of bed. I mean, what professional would come to a job interview—a *serious* job interview—looking like a slob and without having called beforehand? Anyway, we'd interviewed great candidates before her. There was no reason to keep her here and let her talk about herself only to give her the same rejection afterward. It would only have been a waste of time.

But, God, the second I'd told her she could leave, I felt a pinch to the heart. She was beautiful. The kind of gorgeous woman that could make your jaw drop while dressed in a stained shirt and an old pair of leggings.

When I'd opened the door, words had escaped me. Her skin had looked so soft, I'd had the weird urge to touch it. It was speckled with freckles, over her nose, her cheeks, and even over her chin. Her lips were plump, the bottom one slightly bigger than the other, and when she licked it in nervousness, I felt it straight to my groin. Catching her large hazel eyes roaming over me definitely was good for my ego. Her cheeks were flushed when our eyes met. Maybe she'd felt the same attraction I had?

But it didn't matter; there was no way I could give her the job. I had to remind myself a few times that this interview was for my mother, not for me. And so I'd made the right decision. For Helen. She needed someone reliable. Knowledgeable. Professional. Not some young woman who couldn't offer proper care, as beautiful as she was.

Helen wheeled her chair closer to the patio door over-looking the black-looking ocean, bringing me out of my

9

thoughts. "I want you to call her back. Give her the job." She might not have been able to cross her arms over her chest, but the way she stared at me made her look as serious as if she had.

Had she lost her mind?

"I most certainly will *not*. We've seen plenty of perfect candidates for the position. Candidates with *experience*."

Her eyebrows drew closer together. "How would you know about her experience? You didn't even give her the time to share it with us!"

I took a breath, feeling the beginning of a headache taking place. I needed coffee. And for this conversation to be over. I turned around and walked out of the living room to the kitchen. "I didn't need her to. I knew she wasn't as capable of caring for you as Diane or Monique."

She moved closer to me, not allowing more than a foot between her chair and my heels. "Oh, that's a nasty comment to make, Matthias. I didn't raise you to judge people by their appearance. At least I thought I didn't."

Putting a Nespresso capsule in the machine, I sighed. "Come on, Helen. You know that wasn't what I meant. Just…" I put my hands on the counter before leaning on it. "I need you to be in good hands. In the hands of a professional. I'm sorry if you think that makes me a bad person, but I won't back down. Not for this."

"Well, I won't either. And I've decided it's her I want."

I spun on my heels, glaring at her. "And why is that?"

My mom's eyes might have been the color of ice, but I could've sworn flames were burning in them. "Because she's the only person we saw today who spoke to me like a fellow adult. Who treated me like a whole person, and not just some patient they should pity." Her eyebrows rose, the right one higher than the left. "Diane and Monique, who you seem to be so fond of, all but screamed in my ears and spoke syllable by syllable, as if I were a child. So, yes, Adelaide is exactly the person I want to take care of me."

I shook my head. "No."

"It's not your decision to make, Matthias." Her face softened a little. "I know you're worried about me after what happened, but you're not the one who'll be spending your days with this person. I am. So, frankly, I don't care what you want. It's my decision, and I choose her."

I looked at her blazing eyes and couldn't help the deep exhale that escaped my chest. She had a point. I knew she had. We stared for a long moment, and my face must have revealed my resignation because a smug smile took over her face. She was so sure this was the right decision.

And if I had to agree to this, then I prayed to God she was right.

ADELAIDE

"*H*urry, Addy, I need to pee!"

Leaning my hip against the door, I searched blindly into my purse for my keychain with one hand, all the while carrying two grocery bags with the other. "Yes, Lou, I'm going as fast as I can."

From the corner of my eye, I caught my little brother jumping from one foot to the other, ever-so-elegantly holding his crotch with both hands. "I won't be able to hold it in much longer, Addy!"

I rolled my eyes right before palming my keys. Juggling with them until I found the right one, I opened the door. As soon as he could, Louis ran inside the apartment, toppling the precarious grocery bag I had balanced on my hip and sending three apples tumbling to the ground and rolling down the building's stairs in the process.

I sighed but kept my mouth shut. He *did* say he had to go to the bathroom when I picked him up from school, but I had to make a stop to get what was needed for dinner before getting on the bus back home.

After closing the door with my hip, I hurried to the kitchen to place the bags beside the stack of bills on the counter before Louis had the chance to crash into them once more.

I heard the toilet flush—one of the perks of living in an apartment the size of a dollhouse—a second before Louis came out of the bathroom.

I eyed him as he walked in the direction of the kitchen. "Did you wash your hands?"

He did a one-eighty, headed back to the bathroom, and came back a few seconds later. I gave him a smug grin before ruffling his tousled chocolate-brown hair.

"Can you come to my room now? I wanna show you Marie Antoinette! I got it from Timothy at school today."

Did I know why my little brother called his toy cars the names of 18th century historical figures? No. Did I love it? Absolutely.

"I'd love to, Lou, but I gotta make dinner before. I promise I'll come see it before you go to bed, okay?"

He gave me a frown, his round brown eyes the perfect picture of a sad puppy. My heart cracked a little. "Do you think Daddy will come see it too?"

Now, my heart didn't just crack. It got sledgehammered, shattering into a thousand pieces.

"You know, Lou, Daddy might be tired because he had a big day today." His lips tilted downward even more. "But I'll see if I can convince him to come later, okay?"

He nodded, but the smile I loved so much was nowhere to be found.

"Come on, give me a hug."

I didn't need to say it twice. He practically ran into my arms and crushed me in his. I squeezed him in return. "And later, I'll race Thomas Jefferson against Marie Antoinette, and I'm sure I'll beat your butt." I pinched one of his butt cheeks, which made him shriek, then erupt in giggles. I smiled as I listened to my favorite sound in the world.

Louis turned around and raced to his room. When he was out of sight, I headed toward the living room, where I found my father sitting on the beige futon, staring at the small television in front of him. He didn't notice me. His eyes were riveted on the screen though I was willing to bet he couldn't say what he was watching if his life depended on it. There wasn't even any sound coming out of the television. He probably hadn't noticed.

God, this was pathetic.

It was also why I had to find work as fast as I could. I couldn't keep hoping for him to go out and get a job. Before, I could have. Now, he was just the shell of the man I used to know.

"Hey, Dad."

He jumped before turning his head in my direction, confirming he had no idea about Louis' and my arrival home. "Hey, sweetie, did you have a nice day?" His brown eyes—the same as my brother's—were underlined by dark circles, and although he gave me a thin smile, I doubted he really cared what my answer was.

Don't let it get to you, Addy. It's fine. Everything's fine.

"Yeah, it was okay." No need to worry him or Louis until it was necessary. And, hopefully, that day would never come. "Hey, do you think you could go play with Lou when you have the chance tonight? He really wants to show you his new car."

"Yes, of course, I will," he said, right before returning his eyes to the television.

I took a big breath, fighting the urge to say more, to tell him to go right now. Instead, I turned around and walked to the speaker sitting beside the television, which I connected to my phone. Music was a constant when I was here; it put some life in the otherwise drab apartment.

I pressed the shuffle button on my music application, and

the first notes of Ben E. King's "Stand by Me" came out of the speaker. I automatically shifted toward my father, hoping for a reaction of some sort, but I didn't get any. No smile. No sigh. Not even a freaking twitch of a lip.

I didn't know why my heart toppled over. I shouldn't have expected otherwise.

I let the song play and headed toward the kitchen. After turning the oven on, I took out a green bell pepper from the fridge. Right as I started to cut it, my phone vibrated in my back pocket. I took it out with one hand before placing it between my shoulder and my ear.

"Hello?" I said as I resumed my cutting.

A male voice spoke next, cold and deep. "Can you start tomorrow?"

My Dear,

I still remember the moment I met you as clear as day. I knew right as I laid my eyes on you that you would change my life for the better. And my instinct has never been wrong.

How much you would change my life, though, remained a surprise. And with time, I came to understand that the way you would affect me wouldn't be on the surface, but in the deepest, most unknown part of myself.

The way my life turned out was directly affected by your presence in it, and I wouldn't change it for the world. With you, every little moment was sweeter, every sunny day, brighter.

Even now, as death separates us, the love we had during the time we shared still lives on.

Love,
Helen

2

ADELAIDE

*T*he morning was not supposed to go this way.

Before going to bed last night, I'd made sure to set my alarm clock fifteen minutes earlier than usual. My work clothes were ironed and hung on the living room's doorknob. Louis' lunch was packed and ready to go.

I knew I hadn't been the Philips'—well, Matthias'—first choice, yet he'd still called me. I had no idea why, but the important part was, he had. Needing this job more than anything, I'd sworn to myself I'd do whatever it took to get back in his good graces. I wasn't going to let anything get in the way of showing up to my first day at work on time.

Except, of course, there was always something that could get in the way.

After waking up, I'd folded the living room futon back in place and replaced my pillow and blanket in the closet, my movements controlled by muscle memory. After nudging my father awake to tell him it was morning and I was leaving, I woke Louis up, made him eat his breakfast, and got dressed in record time. I'd followed my usual routine to a T. We were ahead of schedule. Everything was going as planned. Everything was great.

Until it wasn't.

As Louis was grabbing his backpack, his eyes widened and he ran back to his room, not taking the time to remove his rain boots.

"Lou, you know you don't go inside with your dirty boots on," I called at his back. I groaned when I saw the traces he left on the floor. "What are you doing anyway?"

When I didn't get an answer, I removed my shoes and went to look in his room.

Louis was on all fours, lifting his Cars bedspread to look underneath his bed. When he heard me come in, he turned his head in my direction, eyes still wide and breathing frantically. "I can't find Marie Antoinette! And I need her today! Timothy will be mad at me if I don't bring her to school!"

Marie freaking Antoinette could *not* be the reason I lost my job before it even started. I lifted pillows and dirty pants from the floor while Louis opened his backpack and emptied its content on the floor.

After five minutes of frenetic searching, Marie Antoinette was still nowhere in sight, and our time was up.

"We have to go, Lou. I'll look for it tonight after work."

Just as the words escaped my mouth, I realized they wouldn't go over well with him. His lips started to tremble, right before a lone tear fell from his eye, followed by another, then another. Soon, he was a sobbing mess, the one thing my poor heart couldn't handle.

"Oh, it's okay, Lou, don't cry. We'll keep looking." I hugged him, all the while cursing myself for being such a sucker for his tears.

My reassurance slowed his cries, and after another five minutes of searching, we found Marie Antoinette, forgotten next to the gallon of milk in the fridge.

We jogged out of the apartment and I glanced at my watch while slamming the door closed behind me. We were not ahead of our schedule anymore. I rushed Louis down the stairs of our building, then grabbed his hand and pulled him with me as we ran so we wouldn't miss our bus, but it was useless. As we were turning the corner of our street, I saw the bus leave our stop. We were ten seconds too late.

The next bus wouldn't be here for the next thirty minutes. If I wanted to have the slightest chance of getting to work on time, I had to think of another solution, and fast.

"Okay, Lou, we're just gonna have to walk to your school."

He grumbled beside me but didn't complain as I pulled on his hand. We jogged the ten blocks to his school, both of us breathing hard. As soon as I dropped him off, I ran to the closest bus stop and got on just in time to catch the one going to Cape Neddick.

When I made it to the Philips' house, heart pumping and armpits sweating, I looked at my watch while running up the cement front steps. 9:02 a.m.

I lifted my fist to knock when the massive front door opened, beating me to it.

"You're late," came a deep voice above me, the disapproval clear in his words.

I peeked up at Matthias who was dressed as neatly as yesterday. He was wearing a white, wrinkle-free dress shirt and black slacks, his hair styled to perfection, just like his short beard. An impeccable picture of elegance.

And he was glaring, lips drawn and brows furrowed.

"I know, I'm so sorry." I was two minutes late, but it might have been thirty from the glare he was giving me. "My little brother couldn't find his toy car and he started crying and we missed our bus and—"

"I don't care," he interrupted, his voice harsh. Taking a step past the threshold into the cold coastal air, he closed the door behind him. Our height difference became much more notice-able at that moment. My eyes widened at his sudden proximity as my heartbeat sped up even more. I swallowed down my nerves, but they threatened to come back when I caught the seething burn in his gaze.

"You see, this is my mother we're talking about. Not a doll, or a plant, or a dog. My mother." He talked slowly, enunciating every word like he was scared I wouldn't understand them. "I'm basically putting her life into your hands right now. And, while we're being honest, you weren't my first choice, nor my second. But, Helen wanted you, for whatever reason, so here you are." He took another step forward so he towered over me, forcing me to look up. Waves crashed behind the house, playing a lullaby I would've found soothing on any other occasion. "But, let's be clear here. I frankly don't give a fuck about what's going on in your personal life right now. Someone's well-being is at stake here, and that's the *only* thing I care about. Understood?"

My mouth fell open as I stumbled backward. Was this embarrassment or anger welling in my chest? My breathing quickened as shock from his tone settled. Who did he think he was, talking to me like that?

I glanced back at the sidewalk, tempted for a second to turn around and leave right then and there. My ego pulled me —no, yanked me—in the direction of the street, but my internal voice wouldn't shut up.

You need this job, Addy. Keep your mouth shut and nod like he didn't just crush you under his polished leather shoe.

So I did.

Inhaling a large gulp of salty air, I said in a sickly-sweet voice, "I apologize. It won't happen again." I was tempted to add "sir", but I didn't think that would go over well with him, especially since he couldn't be more than a few years older than I was.

He glared at me for an extra second before saying, "Good."

As he turned around to open the door, I glared at his back and mimicked the stupid serious face he'd just made, mouthing a silent 'good.'

I followed him inside, where a glowing Helen was waiting for me. She was sitting in the brightly lit kitchen, her shiny hair perfectly curled around her face.

"Hello, Addy. So good to see you again."

I grinned at her. "Good to see you too."

Matthias went to stand next to her, his hands clasped behind his back, and again, I was hit by how different they were. The energy they conveyed was as antipodal as could be. While her good mood was palpable, the tension in his jaw was unmistakable. I had no idea how such a bubbly woman could have raised a broody man like him, and I had no plans to find out.

My job here was with Helen. Not with him. From what Helen had said, he'd be gone most of the time while I was working, so I wouldn't have to endure him too much. That thought was the highlight of my day.

*A*fter less than an hour, I felt as comfortable with Helen as I would've with a long-time friend. Right after Matthias had left, she'd initiated the conversation, telling me all about the life she'd lived, both before and after having her son. I'd never felt so at home at work.

Dora, her usual caregiver, had left a short while ago, noticing we were doing well without her help. It wasn't like I was new to all of this.

"This home used to belong to my father," Helen said as I chopped cucumbers for a salad. She'd been telling me about growing up in Maine for the past half hour.

"Quite a nice inheritance you got," I said.

She laughed before erupting in a coughing fit. In the half second I swiveled to check if she was okay, I slipped and slashed my finger with the knife. "Shit!" I exclaimed, running to put my finger under the tap.

"Are you okay?" Helen wheeled herself in my direction. "Let me see that."

"Oh no it's fine, just a small cut. No need to bother you with this."

She gave me a stern look. "Addy, I was a doctor for more than thirty years. I think I can handle a cut."

Lifting my brows, I showed her my throbbing finger. After looking at it for a few seconds, she said, "You're right, this looks pretty shallow. There are Band-Aids in the cupboard above you."

I wrapped one around my finger and finished preparing lunch. After I helped Helen eat and grabbed a bite too, we settled into the living room. The gas fireplace cast a warm glow over the room, especially with the gray skies outside. I wrapped a fleece blanket around her, then did the same for me.

"So," I asked, looking at my injured finger, "what kind of doctor were you?" I'd met with a whole array of them with my mother a few years back. If I had to guess, with Helen's calm and sweet personality, I'd say she was in a front-line position.

Helen smiled, her giddy expression revealing her passion. "I was an emergency room doctor when I retired, but I worked for ten years with Doctors Without Borders all around the world when I was younger."

"Oh, wow," I said, eyes widening, "that must've been quite the experience."

"Yeah, it definitely was." She smiled. "It was also the best thing I ever did because that's how I met my son."

I nodded. That explained the difference in their looks.

Even with the blanket, a shiver ran down my spine, so I got up to make us some tea. While in the kitchen, another question arose: where was Matthias' father? Usually, I would've waited to get to know someone better before asking personal questions, but with Helen, it felt different. Like she *wanted* me to ask them and learn more about her. So, when I came back into the living room, two mugs in hand, I asked, "Were you with someone when you decided to—"

"Adopt? No, I wasn't." She chuckled. I helped her have a sip of her tea before sitting down and letting her continue. "I was thirty-seven and felt my biological clock ticking with every new day I spent alone. And, one day, while I was stationed in Greece, this newly-orphaned baby boy was brought to my clinic, so thin and small." Her eyes shone with every word, as if she could still imagine the scene in her head. "I decided then that I didn't need a man to help me raise a child, and I adopted him."

My eyebrows lifted as I imagined what it must've been like to make a decision like that. Raising a child was anything but easy; I knew it all too well. As much as I loved Louis, I couldn't say taking care of him mostly by myself was what I'd wanted for my life. So, to hear she'd made a choice similar to the one I'd had to make a few years ago, I felt an even stronger sense of connection with her.

For the first time in a while, it felt like I was right where I should be.

MATTHIAS

Slamming on the horn of my Audi, I cursed under my breath before leaning my head back on the headrest. Damn Portland traffic. I'd gotten out of the plane from my last trip as fast as I possibly could, but it hadn't helped in avoiding the end-of-day jam on the highway.

She's okay. Everything went fine. You would've received a call if something had happened.

I was a rational human being. I was always able to make sense of every situation. I knew the facts. I was aware of what was more than likely going on, or rather, *not* going on at home.

Still, I worried like a mother hen, which was almost ironic, considering she'd been *my* mother hen for more than twenty-seven years. But, after what had happened last year, there was no way for me to avoid getting all riled up.

The car in front of me slammed to a complete halt, like all the other vehicles on the bridge. I sighed loudly before turning off the radio. Even Vivaldi couldn't help right now.

When I'd left that morning, I'd made sure to tell Dora, my mom's medical aide for the past two and a half years, to teach Adelaide everything she might need to know about my mother's health and needs. I'd also given her the right to fire Adelaide if ever she didn't seem competent enough. Helen might've said the young woman was the one she wanted, and I'd respected her wish to that extent, but I wouldn't be as generous if I received any sign that Adelaide couldn't do the job. I'd take my mom's anger over the alternative.

Outside my window, water stretched as far as the eye could see, glinting under the bright beginning of spring sun. It should have calmed me, this endless view of deep blue and soft waves, but right now, it only reminded me of the distance I imagined separating me and my house. Endless.

After fifteen minutes, the traffic cleared—some totaled car finally towed away—and I was able hurry home, driving ten miles over the speed limit. When I reached the driveway, I realized no other car was there. Weird. I could have sworn Dora had arrived in her red Corolla this morning.

I hurried up the steps and opened the front door, immediately frowning as I heard loud pop music playing over the speakers. I walked briskly to the living room, and my face dropped when I saw my mother sitting in her chair next to Adelaide on the couch, laughing loudly with a popcorn-filled bowl between the two of them.

"So, what did his wife say?" Adelaide said in between bouts of giggling.

"She—" Helen herself seemed to be having difficulty

putting her thoughts into words from how hard she was snickering. "She told me that she had no idea how the cucumber had gotten that deep." Adelaide burst out laughing again, her head tipped back, her chest heaving as she pressed a hand to her lips. When Helen caught her breath, she continued, "She was so red. She clearly knew how that cucumber had gotten there!"

I cleared my throat. They turned in my direction, their laughter fading quickly, as if my presence alone had been enough to dampen the hilarity of the situation. It wasn't that I didn't like seeing my mom this happy—I did—but I didn't think this was what I should expect from a relationship between a caregiver and her patient. Dora had always been nice and polite with my mother, but never had I seen her acting this friendly with her.

Wait a second.

"Where's Dora?" I asked. My voice might have been a bit harsher than I'd intended it to be.

I looked behind me, making sure I hadn't missed her while walking toward the sound of music and laughter. When I turned back around to look at them, Adelaide was on her feet, making her way to turn down the sound of a high-pitched, upbeat song. *Thank God*.

"She left around noon. She saw we were more than okay by ourselves, and she was missing her nephew's birthday party to be here. I told her to go." She shrugged, as if what she was saying truly made sense to her. "I didn't need any more supervision."

I took a step back, my face falling to a deep frown. "So, you're telling me you've been alone with my mother all afternoon with less than three hours of training?" I balled my hands into fists before extending my fingers, repeating the motion once, twice, three times, all the while taking in deep breaths.

"It's okay, Matt, she truly was doing fine by herself. I wouldn't have let Dora leave if I didn't think I was in good hands." Helen gave me one of her warm smiles, but the look in her eyes told me to calm down and shut up. It was the face she used to give me as a child when some other kid wanted the book I was reading at the public library while I was clearly not finished with it, or when I wanted to keep playing the piano but it wasn't my turn to use it anymore.

At the same time as Helen glared at me, Adelaide walked in my direction and came to a halt in front of me, crossing her arms over her chest. Her hazel eyes were slightly brighter today. It might have been the mascara on her dark, furnished lashes that made them appear so. Her white blouse snuggled her curves without being provocative, while her black leggings left little to the imagination. *God, if this were in any other context…*

"As I tried telling you before, this isn't the first time I've done this. I actually have way more than three hours of experience."

When she pierced my eyes with hers, I looked away, examining my mom instead. I didn't need Adelaide's appearance to start clouding my judgment. Helen seemed fine, as they'd mentioned multiple times. Her hair was blow-dried, although more ruffled than if Dora or I had done it. She was wearing a lavender pullover—the one she'd knitted a bit before receiving her diagnosis—with black cigarette pants, and…

"What the hell is this?" I asked before stomping in the direction of my mother. I lifted the hem of her pants to make sure I wasn't mistaken, and when it was clear I wasn't, I could practically feel my blood boiling.

"What. Is. This?" I asked again, this time looking straight into Adelaide's eyes while pointing at what I couldn't believe I was seeing.

"Um…socks?" She even had the audacity to smile sheepishly.

"For someone who's supposedly so experienced with care-giving that she doesn't need training, you certainly didn't have a problem putting your patient's life at risk."

Adelaide was no longer smiling.

"Matt, please, calm down," Helen gritted through her teeth, but I didn't even look in her direction.

"I'm not sure I understand what the problem is," Adelaide continued, giving me a doe-eyed, confused expression.

"Let me explain this to you, oh Masterful Professional. When a patient can't move their legs, not putting compression socks on their feet puts them at risk of forming clots, which may lead to a pulmonary embolism, which may lead to death. Was that what you were aiming for? Killing your patient on your first day?"

"Matthias, that's *enough*," Helen hissed beside me, but again, I ignored her. All my focus was on Adelaide, a mix of confusion, anger, and fear clear on her face.

"I'm... I'm sorry, I really didn't know. My—"

"It's okay, Addy dear, it was an honest mistake," Helen said. "We'll be more careful next time."

I interrupted my mother's comforting words. "No, it's not okay. This was her job, and she screwed it up."

Adelaide lifted her hands in front of her body. "If you could let me explain—"

"Let me repeat this in case I wasn't clear before: I don't care about your excuses."

She took a step back, her eyes widening. I knew I was being an asshole, but if that's what it took to keep my mother safe, then so be it. "You know what? Just get out. We'll be better off without your help."

"Matthias!" Helen yelled, but Adelaide interrupted her.

"It's okay, Helen. I'll be on my way. I... I really wish you the best," she said before taking a step forward and bending to give my mother a kiss on the cheek. When she straightened, she gave me a look that almost made me shiver from its coldness. I kept my face impassable and waited to hear the sound of the front door opening and closing before dropping down on the couch next to my mom.

"What in the world were you thinking, Matthias?" Helen's

voice was soft and cold, an indicator of the tempest that was coming my way. "Who gave you the right to speak to that poor girl like that?" She exhaled through her nose. "I can't believe what just happened. The son I raised never would've acted this way."

I sighed before rubbing my palm down my face. "I'll find someone else. Someone better."

"That's not even the point. You were plain disrespectful to Addy for no reason." She exhaled slowly. "I understand you don't want history repeating itself, but this doesn't give you the right to be a fool."

"Mom, I—"

"And, for the record, she truly was wonderful to me today. The care she gave was excellent, and I don't remember spending a day this pleasant since I've started spending my time at home with caregivers." She closed her eyes and I saw she was trying to hide it, but I still recognized the trembling in her lower lip.

I replayed what had just happened in my head, and... Fuck, maybe she was right. I'd been a dick.

"Helen, look, I'm sorry. If there's—"

"I can't do this." She began moving her wheelchair away from me. "I love you, but I'm so ashamed of you right now, I can't even look at your face."

Her words were like a punch to the gut. I wanted to follow her and apologize again, but that wasn't how Helen worked. She didn't want apologies; she wanted me to make up for my fuck-ups. And as I laid down on the beige leather couch and closed my eyes, one thing was clear: I had fucked up.

Dear,

Through all the time we've spent together, one thing has been unmistakable in your behavior: the way you care for others.

Not one day would pass by when you didn't treat me like I deserved all the love and happiness in the world, and I don't know if I've ever properly thanked you for it. So, here it is: thank you for how wonderful you've been to me.

I won't lie; I've been through a lot of hardships in my life, the biggest one being the one I'm battling as I'm writing. But, having you by my side through these tough moments has allowed me to keep being —to keep feeling—thankful every single day. And, for that, I'll never thank you enough.

Your presence, your help, and your attention have been my lifeline in this storm.

Love,
Helen

3

ADELAIDE

*W*hile stirring the pasta, I shot a quick text to my best friend Stella.

Me: Boss was an asshole. Job was a flop.

She answered with a thumbs-down emoji and a sad face.

Just as I put my phone down, Louis appeared beside me. "What are we eating for dinner?" he asked as he lifted the cover of the pot on the stove. I swatted his hand away, turning sideways to glare at him.

"Lou, you know you can't put your hand near the stove when it's on! You could burn yourself!"

He gave me his remorseful eyes, which he knew I couldn't resist. "Sorry, I was just hungry and wanted to know what we were going to eat."

"Mac'n'cheese," I answered while getting a strainer out of the cramped cupboard.

"Again?"

I closed my eyes for a moment, breathing out through my nostrils. What kind of seven-year-old complained about eating too much boxed pasta?

I didn't have the heart to tell him that we might have to eat a lot more of this for the next few weeks if we wanted to stay afloat. Rent was due in a week, and I was out of a job. *Again.*

When I'd come home earlier today, I'd told my dad about how precarious our situation was, and he'd told me he would try to find a job, but I knew I couldn't rely on his word. Not after getting my hopes up and ending up disappointed more times than I could count in the past.

"Yes, again, but if you finish your plate, I'll let you eat a cookie afterward, okay?"

That seemed to be enough to put me in his good graces again. He gave me a giant grin—minus one of his front teeth—and I ruffled his hair before asking him to set the table. God, how I wished to be young and carefree like that again. Not that I was considered old at twenty-three, but still. To have my biggest problem be eating mac'n'cheese two nights in a row. I sighed.

"Food's ready!" I yelled to my father, who I'd left asleep on the living room couch. Just talking to me for a few minutes had seemed to drain him of all his energy.

It still felt weird to utter those words to him. As if for all my life growing up, he hadn't been the one to cook for me and tell me to come eat dinner, right after giving my forehead a kiss. That might as well have been another lifetime.

As I was plunging a wooden spoon in the pasta, three loud knocks sounded from the front door of the apartment, making my brows furrow. "Hey, Lou, did you ask Josh to come play?"

"No," my little brother said as he grabbed the bowl I gave him. My dad didn't say anything, so I suspected he wasn't expecting any visitors—not that he'd invited anyone over in the last few years. Putting the spoon down on the stained melamine counter, I headed to the door, expecting to see a salesperson or Jehovah's Witnesses. I'd told some a few weeks ago I wasn't interested, but that didn't stop them from coming back with their briefcases and pamphlets. I unlocked the door, opening my mouth to politely tell them off. "Good evening, we're not..." My jaw suddenly went slack.

What the heck?

"Hi," Matthias said, his voice deep and smooth. I looked him over, taking a few seconds to regain my bearings before saying anything. He'd changed out of his uniform, now dressed in a cream knitted sweater and jeans. His hair was also different than earlier today, more ruffled.

What in the world was he doing here?

"How did you find out where I live?" I asked.

His eyes raked over me, causing goosebumps to run down my arms. I bristled and tightened my cardigan, crossing my arms over my chest when he cleared his throat. "Your address was on the resume you sent me after your interview."

Huh, so he'd actually read that.

I stared at him for a moment, until it was clear he wouldn't be telling me more than that. "So, what is it you want?"

He sighed before raking a hand in his hair, explaining its messy appearance. "I wanted to—"

"Hi, I'm Louis Samson! Who are you?" my little brother asked as he extended his chubby hand to a man he'd never seen in his life, pushing me to the side to make room for him in the doorway. I rolled my eyes for the second time in a row at the way Louis' manners worked.

"I'm Matthias. I, uh, work with your...mother?"

"Sister," I corrected, although my focus was on the rest of his answer. Hadn't he just fired me?

"Nice to meet you, Matthias. Would you like to come inside and play with Benjamin Franklin?"

A mix of amusement and questioning took over Matthias' face. "I'm sorry, what?"

"Lou, Matthias cannot play with you right now. Actually, he was just leaving. Go finish your dinner, and I'll play with you later, 'kay?"

He pouted. "But I want to play now."

31

I exhaled, impatience threatening to overwhelm me. "Louis, I said go eat, or else I'll take your cars for the night."

His lower lip wobbled.

Oh, for goodness' sake.

"But... But I—" Louis' voice broke as tears fell down his cheek.

I kneeled in front of him. "Oh Lou, I'm sorry. Just please go inside and we'll play right after dinner, okay?"

Giving me the most heartbreaking sad eyes, he nodded and headed back to the kitchen table.

I got up and partially closed the door behind me. "As you can see, I'm busy, so care to tell me what you're here for?" I asked while crossing my arms in front of my body, working really hard to repress another sigh. I didn't have time for this, especially after the way this butthole had spoken to me.

"I want to...um...apologize." He shifted on his feet. "The way I spoke earlier was not appropriate, and I want to make things right."

I eyed him over. Even in his casual clothes, he made me feel small in my tank top, cardigan, sweatpants, and fluffy bunny slippers. Luckily, I didn't give a rat's ass what this guy thought of me. "You're right, it wasn't appropriate."

He scratched his beard. "Like I said, I, uh—"

"I appreciate it, I guess," I interrupted, turning around. "Have a good drive back home."

"Wait," he blurted out.

Leaning back against the doorframe, I waited with a raised eyebrow.

"Is there any way we could go talk somewhere else? Take a walk, perhaps?"

"No, we're fine right here."

He eyed the stained carpet of the hallway and the cracked paint on the walls, but he didn't say anything about it.

"All right, well, I wanted to ask you if you'd consider coming back to work for us. Starting tomorrow."

My eyes widened. I waited for him to say something else, but he didn't. He simply stared at me, jaw moving back and forth.

"I'm sorry, is this a joke?"

A crease formed between his brows.

"You just fired me," I added, as if the reason for my confusion wasn't clear enough.

His expression was still serious, his black eyes humorless as he dug his hands in his front pockets. "I thought I just apologized for that."

"Well, sorry if I don't forget so easily."

He huffed, which only made me more pissed.

I kicked one ankle over the other. "Why would you want such a careless, stupid person to come work for you anyway?"

"I never said you were stupid."

If I rolled my eyes one more time, they would probably stay stuck that way. "And I'm doing this for Helen," he said. "She wants you, and so I want you too."

"Sorry, not interested." I turned around right before feeling his long, warm fingers on my wrist. I gasped at the touch.

"Please. If not for me, then at least for her."

I stayed frozen for a moment. I did not give a crap about this guy, but Helen? I loved her, even if I'd only met her the day before. Was it fair to make her pay for her stupid son's mistakes?

Also, pasta from a box. For the second night in a row. A third, if I didn't suck it up. I might not have considered the offer if I was alone, but it wasn't just myself I had to take care of. Louis and my father counted on me.

God, my life sucked sometimes.

I turned around to face him again. "Fine. I'll come back, but don't you dare think it's for you. Helen deserves someone who will take good care of her, and that's the only reason why I'm swallowing my pride." I took a step forward and pointed my right index finger at his chest. "And, if you ever talk to me that way again, I won't give you another chance, and you'll be the one responsible for making Helen lose a good caregiver. Is that clear?"

Mouth pinched and eyes burning in fury, he swallowed loudly and nodded once. I looked down to see his hand still gripping my wrist. When he caught my eyes' movement, he promptly removed it and turned to leave.

I rubbed the spot he touched and huffed in frustration, fighting the urge to go scrub it in the sink.

MATTHIAS

*H*eart rate through the roof, I took a break and got up from the rowing machine.

Wiping my face with my towel, I took a look around me. Still alone. Going to the gym at night was my favorite. I liked the peace and quiet.

I'd used the past two hours to think about my visit to Adelaide's apartment. Now that I'd spent a lot of energy, I felt calm enough to call Helen. I dialed her number while taking a large gulp of water.

She answered on the third ring. "Hello?"

"Hey, it's me." Towel around my neck, I took a seat on one of the bench presses.

"Where are you? I thought you'd be back from your errands by now."

Avoiding her question, I asked, "Everything okay with Dora?"

From the sigh she released, I could imagine her rolling her eyes at my question. "Yes, everything is fine. Now, where are you?"

I wiped a hand down my face. "I'm at the gym. I... I went to see Adelaide earlier. She'll be coming back tomorrow."

Helen squealed. "Oh, that's wonderful news, Matthias." When I didn't answer, she added, "Tell me you believe so too."

Another man entered the gym, so I headed toward the locker room, keeping my voice down. "I won't lie, I'm still not sure she's the best choice."

She groaned. "For God's sake, Matthias, not this again."

I put the phone on speaker when I entered the room and put it on top of the lockers so I could remove my sweat-drenched shirt. "You know I'm only this wary because I love you."

"Yes, I know," she replied, her tone a tad softer, "but there is no need to be wary of Addy. She's amazing, I promise you."

There was probably nothing I could possibly say to change her mind, so I went with, "If she makes you happy, then I'm happy."

"Great. So that means you'll try to keep me happy, right?"

My brows furrowed as I put on my clean shirt. "Of course."

"Then I have one more thing to ask you," she said, her voice smug. "It's great that you apologized and got her to come back, but that's not all. You need to make an effort with her too."

I huffed. "I *am* making an effort."

She clicked her tongue. "No, Matthias, you're not." I faintly heard Dora asking Helen a question, to which she answered before coming back to me. "I want you to be nice to her. Give her a chance, not just as an aide but as a person too."

From Helen's tone, it was clear there was no room for argument. And, anyway, did I really want to argue? I was stuck in this situation, whether I wanted it or not. Might as well make the most of it and not be in a shitty mood twenty-four-seven.

Grabbing my coat and closing my locker door, I uttered, "Fine. I'll try."

ADELAIDE

"*S*o, have you thought about what I mentioned last week?"

I laughed through the phone. "Stella, you talk so much bullshit, I can't remember half the things you said last week." If she'd been here with me, I'd have nudged her with my elbow. How I wished she'd been.

An old lady sitting next to me on the bus bench, face half-covered by her wool scarf, glared at me with wide eyes. I mouthed an apology, promising myself I'd lower my voice.

Stella huffed. "Oh, come on, girl, you know damn well what I'm talking about. Coming back here for college?" Here, as in Montreal, Canada. My hometown. "It'd be so much cheaper for you than staying in the States to study."

"Stellz, even if it was free, it'd still be too expensive for me. You know I can't afford college right now. I can barely make ends meet while working full time." I took a pause, grieving for the idea of going to college with her like we'd promised each other in elementary school. With the way things were going, she'd have graduated from med school before I got the chance to even consider going back to school.

She didn't speak, probably sensing I needed a moment to think like only she could. Wanting to lighten the mood, I said, "Besides, I've lost all my French."

She huffed. "Arrête, je sais très bien que ce n'est pas vrai." *Stop, I know that's not true.*

I snickered. She was right, it wasn't true. I'd lost some of it, but I could still consider myself pretty much fluent. I looked out the window. "Well, anyway, as long as Louis needs me here, I'm not going anywhere. Guess you'll just have to find a way to survive without me by your side until then."

Stella guffawed. "Oh, don't worry, I can survive very easily without your awful life advice and poor boyfriend picks."

"Shut up, you prick." The bus turned onto the street a few blocks away from Helen's house. "Hey, I gotta go, Stellz. Call me when your on-call shift ends?"

"Wouldn't miss it. Love you."

"Love you too," I said before hanging up and making my way out of the bus. There was a newfound spring to my step today, probably the result of catching up with Stella. The sun warmed my skin and reflected on the water behind the Philips' house, creating a portrait of serenity. I was also ten minutes early, and, when I glanced down at my black pants and beige blouse, they were still clean and wrinkle-free. Maybe I'd finally find a way not to have Mr. Stick-in-the-Butt give me hell at nine in the morning.

When I knocked on the door, it was Dora who answered, dark eyes crinkled and smile sparkling. I assumed she was in her sixties, gray strands woven in her black braided hair. "Addy, come in!" She spoke slowly and her voice was thick with what I assumed was a Haitian accent.

"Hey Dora." I followed her in. "What are you doing here?"

She continued walking inside the house, not turning to look at me when saying, "Matthias had a flight that left during the night, so he asked me to come until you got here." We made our way from the main hallway to Helen's room where Dora opened the door, urging me to follow her inside. "I gave her a bath when she woke up. I was actually drying her hair when you knocked. Would you like to finish doing it? I have to go."

"Sure," I answered. "Have a nice day."

She smiled at me before heading down the hall and outside. I walked to Helen's en suite bathroom, where I found her in a bathrobe with half-dried hair. As soon as she saw me in the mirror, her face lit up, which made mine do the same.

"Addy! I'm so glad to see you here. I was afraid after

Matthias' little stunt yesterday, you wouldn't want to see me again."

I got closer to her and squeezed both her shoulders with my hands over her chair. "I was afraid I wouldn't see you again too," I answered in all honesty.

She gave me a sad smile. "I'd like to apologize about yesterday." Her eyes avoided mine. "Matthias is just a bit...overbearing."

I sat on the counter facing her, crossing my arms. "He can be whatever he wants, but he doesn't have to take all his problems out on me."

Helen winced.

Crap. I might have overdone it.

Leaning forward, I put my hand over Helen's arm. "I'm sorry. I know it's not your fault."

"No, it's definitely his." Her lips thinned. "He should know by now that trying to play God and control everything won't do him any good." Her eyes went thoughtful all of a sudden. It felt like there was more to the story, but I didn't dig any deeper. I didn't want to talk about the prick anymore.

Pushing myself away from the counter, I grabbed the blow dryer, bringing it to her blond strands and ruffling them with my other hand. When I was done, we went to her walk-in closet and I asked what she wanted to wear before helping her get dressed in a navy sweater and jeans. When I was done, I went to her sock drawer—asking her for directions on how to find it—and while I was putting one of her compression socks on, I froze.

"Why didn't you tell me yesterday when I forgot the compression socks?" It wasn't like I was blaming her for the fallout that had ensued—that was all on Matthias's hands—but I still wanted to understand why she'd kept something that could have been dangerous for her health from me.

She gave me a pained smile. With the way some of her muscles were constantly contracted, it was sometimes hard to decipher all her expressions, but I was starting to get the gist of it. "You were doing such a good job. I didn't feel like pointing out a mistake on your first day."

I frowned, hoping she could see in my eyes how I didn't care if she told me I made a hundred mistakes, as long as I didn't put her in harm's way. I was about to say it out loud when she interrupted me. "Besides, if I would've thought I was in real danger, I would've said something. But I can't recall ever losing a patient over the one time they didn't put their compression socks on, so don't worry about it, all right?"

I'd forgotten about the small detail that Helen knew a lot more about health precautions than I did. Matthias had underestimated her. And, if I was being honest, I had too. If anyone could help me give her good care, it was her. "Okay, well thank you for being so considerate of my feelings, but if I ever do something wrong again, I want you to swear to tell me."

"I swear," she answered with a smile.

The rest of the day went by much too fast for it to feel like I was working. Apart from the times when I helped Helen go to the bathroom or eat, it was like I was hanging out with a friend. I talked about Louis and my old job, and she continued to entertain me with all kinds of funny stories from all the years she worked in the ER.

It was dark outside when the front door opened and Matthias entered. My schedule working there would be pretty weird, considering it depended on Matthias' flying schedule, which was ridiculous. There was no routine whatsoever. Dora would be able to cover for me on some occasions, but she'd told me she didn't want to work more than a few hours a week, so I was pretty much doomed to live my life according to Matthias from now on.

I didn't mind it that much, though. When I was here, with Helen, I didn't have to worry about whether my dad had eventually gotten out of bed for the day, or if Louis had done his homework after school. I felt like a *real* person here, not just someone's guardian or rent-payer.

"Hey, I'm back," Matthias called from what I assumed was the foyer. Helen was in the living room listening to a romance novel audiobook, and I was folding clothes in the laundry room. After stacking clean towels in the laundry basket, I headed out to meet them to say goodbye.

"Well, I'll get going then. See you tomorrow morning, Helen."

Just as I was heading out, Helen called out, "We were actually going to order some Chinese food. Would you like to stay with us to eat?"

Matthias' eyes widened slightly at his mother's words, but he didn't say anything. His black hair was, as always, perfectly styled, and his white uniform shirt only made his black eyes appear darker.

"Oh, I wouldn't want to impose." My stomach, however, had a mind of its own, and grumbled so loud as I spoke, everyone in the room heard it.

"Oh, nonsense, we'd love to have you here with us." Helen was smiling brightly while Matthias had the most neutral face I'd ever seen. It was almost impossible to read him, but if I'd had to guess, I would've said he wasn't so happy with his mother's invitation.

Now, I wasn't one to create drama, but I had to admit I was more than tempted to stay, if only to spite him. And, takeout sounded like heaven at the moment after eating boxed macaroni for the past two days.

"All right, I'll eat with you, but I won't stay long. Don't want to impede on your time together."

"Awesome," Matthias said before getting up from the couch. His expression was still blank, and it confused me to no end. How could someone whose mother was so expressive and gentle be so impassive? As he passed me on his way to the kitchen, my nose filled with the faint scent of his cologne, which was soft, kind of musky, very masculine. I had to admit, it smelled good. I wondered how much that cost.

Matthias called the Chinese restaurant, then told us he'd shower while waiting for the food to be delivered. When he was gone, I turned in Helen's direction. "I have to make a phone call. I'll be right back."

She hummed her answer, her focus back on her book.

I went into the kitchen and called Mrs. Zhu, my next door neighbor. She answered on the second ring.

"Hey, Mrs. Zhu, it's Adelaide."

"Oh, hi! I was just about to prepare the kids' dinner."

"Actually, that's what I was calling about. Would you mind if Louis stayed at your place for a bit longer? I have to stay at work for an extra hour, but I'll still be back before bedtime to pick him up."

"Of course, honey. He and Josh have transformed my living room into a race car circuit stadium, so I'm sure he won't mind having to stay here longer." As she said it, I heard my brother scream like he did every time he won something. I smiled as I imagined him jumping in Mrs. Zhu's living room, both arms in the air.

"Thank you so much. I'll text you when I'm on my way," I said.

"No problem. Take your time."

Thank God for Mrs. Zhu; at least watching Louis wasn't *all* on me.

After hanging up, I went back to the living room and sat on the couch with Helen while waiting. A few minutes later, Matthias came out of the guest bathroom dressed in gray sweatpants and a deep blue t-shirt, his still-wet ebony hair pushed back. I was so surprised to see him dressed this casually, my jaw slackened a bit at the sight. It wasn't that his dress shirts or uniforms didn't fit him well, but this... I hadn't realized he could look this relaxed.

Once the food arrived and Matthias paid for it, we made

our way to the dining room. I automatically sat beside Helen to help her eat, but Matthias said he'd do it. I took a seat facing them, and we all ate in a semi-comfortable silence.

"So, Adelaide," Matthias said after a few minutes. "What is it you do when you're not here?"

I lifted my head from my plate. "I'm sorry?"

He wiped his mouth with his napkin. "What do you do in your free time? Pastimes, maybe?"

Taking care of my little brother? Trying to find ways to pay the bills? Getting my father out of bed? Yeah, I wasn't going to share that with him. Instead, I went with, "I don't have a lot of free time."

"Right." He cleared his throat, then focused back on his dinner. We continued eating in a now uncomfortable silence.

At some point, Matthias got up and disappeared from the room. I was about to ask Helen if she knew where he'd gone when delicate instrumental music started coming out of speakers hidden in the ceiling. The sounds of cellos, violins, and pianos intertwined in a slow melody that felt like a balm to the heart. A few seconds later, Matthias returned without commenting on his need to interrupt the silence.

When we were done eating, I got up to grab the plates, and Matthias helped me bring them to the kitchen. I filled the sink with soapy water as I appreciated the new melody coming out of the kitchen ceiling, this time more upbeat and tumultuous. Expecting Matthias to leave the kitchen, I placed the clean dishes on a rag for them to dry, but he surprised me by picking up a dish towel and grabbing the plates.

We continued washing the dishes, a melancholic cello melody the only sound between the two of us. Sometimes, I caught him watching me before looking away, but he never spoke up.

What? Did he think I was doing this incorrectly too?

When we were almost done, Helen popped her head in the kitchen entrance. "I'm going to go read a bit in my room before

bed. You two take the time to catch up!" She winked—actually
winked—before wheeling herself away.

Matthias looked her way before huffing. "I think my mom
is trying to set us up."

I turned to the side to look at him. He wasn't exactly smiling, but there was a certain glint in his dark eyes that told me
he found the situation funny.

"She must think I have a thing for rude men then," I said
without thinking, only half-joking.

I expected him to cuss me out, but he surprised me for the
second time in the span of a few minutes by giving me a faint
smile instead. "I really was a dick, wasn't I?"

A corner of my lips twitched up. "A huge one.
Enormous."

He stifled a laugh with a not-so-casual cough and a heat
flooded my cheeks. Crap. "That sounded really nasty,
didn't it?"

"Enormously," he confirmed, voice thick with humor.

A surprised chuckle burst from the back of my throat. Me
and my damn verbal diarrhea. I was sure Stella would crack
up too when I told her. I covered my face with the dish, trying
to hide my embarrassment.

"Oh, shoot," I muttered as water dripped over my blouse
and on the counter. I stole Matthias' towel, and while I wiped
the mess, he leaned his hip on the counter, seemingly scrutinizing my every move. When I tilted my head in question to
the sudden severity of his face, he said, "I really *am* sorry about
the way I acted. I'm not usually that blunt or disrespectful, if
you can believe it. I'm just… I'm really protective of my
mother."

I turned to face him, an eyebrow raised. "You don't say!"

He rolled his eyes and didn't smile at my comment, but
again, I could recognize that sparkle in his eyes. "Okay, I
deserved that, but try putting yourself in my shoes for just one
second. I had to basically put my mother's health and life in the

hands of someone who I knew nothing about and whose experience I knew nothing about."

I pulled out the drain in the sink, grabbed the rag, and dried my hands as I leaned my hip on the counter to face him. "Well, if you'd taken the time to listen to me on the multiple times I tried to talk to you, you would've known I took care of my mom when she was sick for many years, and am one hundred percent comfortable caring for a physically disabled person."

His face dropped at my words. I hadn't expected the conversation to go from light to deep so rapidly, but this needed to happen at some point, I guessed. At least now he might doubt me a bit less and trust me more.

"I'm sorry," he said. "I didn't know."

"Obviously."

His head lowered, eyes roaming over the floor before he looked up again. "Can I ask what happened to her?"

I gazed at him, expecting to see the same indifference he'd shown me over the past days, but his face held more emotions than ever. Curiosity. Fear. Pain. Understanding. The last one was what pushed me to answer him. "Heart failure." I swallowed. "At first, it wasn't that bad, she just had to take things a bit slower, but in her last years, she almost couldn't get out of bed."

I inhaled deeply as the image of my mother resting in her bed, oxygen tube around her nose and chest rising and falling rapidly, popped into my head. People always told me I looked like her. We did share the same frizzy dark hair, hazel eyes, and ever-present smile. Even when breathing was a struggle, her face would light up every single time I came into her room to help her eat or get dressed.

"I quit school to take care of her while my dad worked, and I stayed by her side until the day she died."

I took a moment to regain my composure after being bombarded with images of her body lying in a casket. I could still feel Stella holding me up when I'd thought I'd fall to my knees from seeing my mother this way. I almost hadn't been able to recognize her on that day. My mom didn't seem much like my mom without joy transforming her expression.

When the silence became too thick, I exhaled and tried to lighten the situation. "So trust me, I do know what I'm doing with your mother." I forced a smile, but he didn't return it.

"I'm truly sorry, Adelaide. For your mom, and for making you talk about it."

"Thank you, and it's okay." I gave him a quick half-smile. "I actually don't dislike talking about her, but I don't have a lot of occasions to do it. My father never mentions her, and my little brother—the one who asked you to come play with him— doesn't remember her that much, so it feels good to share things about her." I rubbed my hands down my pants. "I'm scared I'll forget about her if I don't."

"Yeah, I get that."

I tilted my head. "You know, you're actually not so bad when you're not being an ass!"

He smirked, just a little. "Yeah, I'll try to keep the enormous dick away in your presence."

I went wide-eyed, then sputtered with laughter. His own face lit up too.

We finished the dishes and I thanked them both for dinner, staying only a few minutes longer.

I laughed to myself as I walked out the door and thought about that stupid joke all the way home.

Have I ever told you about my passion for romance novels?

I've always considered myself a hopeless romantic. Reading about love blooming, especially between two people reluctant to it, has always been one of my favorite things in the world. I liked to read about people getting closer and connections being created. I loved to long for a first kiss and dread the eventual fights in the couple's future.

I might not have had a very extensive love life, but it didn't stop me from wanting to see love blossom around me. All my life, everywhere I saw a spark, I watched in eagerness and waited for it to come to life and expand into a colossal, life-altering, exhilarating love.

And I've always prided myself in having a gift for it. Maybe it was all the romance books I've read in my life, or just good instinct, but you'd be surprised to know about the number of couples I've predicted and helped come to life.

So, if you've ever felt like I've overstepped into your love life, know that it was only because I was looking out for you. Oh, and because I had a gut feeling.

Love,
Helen

4

ADELAIDE

*T*he next morning, I almost fell asleep on the bus on my way to work and jerked awake right as the bus came to a halt at the stop closest to the Philips' house. The ache of sleep-deprived muscles stretched down my knotted back. Every time I'd closed my eyes last night, images of my mother's dull brown hair sprawled on a pile of pillows and of my father kneeling beside a bed, holding a lifeless hand seared my brain, keeping me tossing and turning until my alarm clock rang. It had been a while since I'd talked about my mom out loud, and it must have played with my subconscious.

I still wasn't sure why I'd told Matthias so much yesterday. I hadn't talked about my mom that much after her death, even to Stella, who was like a sister to me. After keeping my feelings about her death away from discussions with my family, I'd gotten used to pushing those feelings down, only inspecting them further when I was alone.

I might not have shared as much with Matthias if he hadn't looked so enthralled and impacted by my words. When I was speaking, it felt as if he understood what I was saying in a way no one else ever had.

I wasn't sure what that meant. Two days ago, I was

convinced the guy was a spoiled, unpleasant man with no redeeming qualities whatsoever, but there was no denying we were on the same wavelength last night. And, he'd made me laugh. A lot. I could try denying it as much as I wanted, but it had felt natural to converse and joke with him.

Once I got inside and greeted Helen, we spent a very quiet morning talking and relaxing. Thoughts of his small grins and deep voice clouded my senses, though I did my best to push them away and focus on what mattered—Helen.

⚜

The sun was reflected by the rest of the snow dusted on the ground outside, giving the living room a luminescent glow. Florence and The Machine's "Never Let Me Go" played in the background as I painted Helen's nails a deep purple.

"What did you think of last night's dinner?" Helen asked, gazing at the drying color. "I loved the chow Mein."

I looked up from my paint job. This was Helen's fourth time asking a question about last evening, and I suspected it had nothing to do with the food.

Instead of answering her question, I asked, "What did you say to Matthias?"

Her eyes widened slightly. "I have no idea what you're talking about."

I grinned. "Come on, Helen. He did a full one-eighty with me yesterday." I pursed my lips. "Well, maybe not completely, but at least a good hundred-degree rotation."

Helen bit her lip. "All right, I might've had a little talk with him."

I returned to painting her thumbnail, faking disinterest. "And what did you talk about?"

"Well," she said, taking her sweet time, "I may or may not have given him a little push to be nicer with you."

48

I huffed. "I didn't need you to do that." I wasn't sure how it made me feel that they'd talked about me while I wasn't there.

"I know you didn't, honey, but he definitely did."

A chuckle burst out of my lips. That was a fact.

"What you've seen of him," she continued, "it's not who he is." Her stare was intense, as if she needed me to believe her. "When he's not concerned for my safety, he's the most amazing man… At least more like the one you saw yesterday."

I bit my inner cheek. He *had* been nice to me yesterday.

"I think you might actually like him very much once you get to know him." Her voice was much too confident for my taste.

I snickered, giving her teasing eyes. "I'll have to argue with you on that."

"Careful there," she answered, her own eyes gleaming in amusement. "Wouldn't want to say things and look like a fool when the opposite happens."

Shaking my head, I laughed and got up. "Come on, now. Let's get these nails under the UV light."

***

It was near the end of the afternoon when Helen and I got dressed to go outside.

Just as I finished wrapping Helen's scarf around her neck, the front door opened, and Matthias entered.

Brows furrowed, I looked at my watch. "You're home early," I said, more like a question than an affirmation.

"Yeah, my last flight got canceled," he answered, unzipping his coat. He stopped in his tracks when he saw us dressed for a trek outside. "Where are you going?"

Helen cleared her throat. "We were just going shopping for a bit."

Matthias lifted one of his eyebrows. "Shopping for what?"

"Um, things," she answered, looking at her bent knees.

Matthias' eyes alternated between the two of us before he said, "Okay, well, I'll come with you."

I shook my head way too vigorously to be considered subtle. "Oh, no, we're fine. It's just a new shop a mile from here. We'll be all right."

Matthias zipped his coat back. "Nonsense, I'll take you in the adapted car." He looked at Helen. "Besides, I haven't seen you a whole lot in the past few weeks."

Helen smiled, so I said, "Okay, then." Now that I knew he was coming with us, I was kind of excited to see Matthias' reaction to where we were going.

Matthias and I followed Helen outside. As she wheeled her chair forward, I leaned toward him and whispered, "Let me guess, you want to supervise me?"

He lifted his hands by his sides and shrugged. "You said it, not me." His tone wasn't condescending, just amused.

I sighed in abandon. I wouldn't change this man overnight.

We got in the car and drove the distance to the shop. Once we arrived and I opened the front door, Helen wheeled herself inside, disappearing between the aisles at the speed of light.

Matthias stopped walking like he'd struck a wall when he gazed around the shop. He turned to me, mouth agape. "This is a lingerie shop?"

I fought hard to repress my grin. "You're the one who insisted on coming with us."

He took in our surroundings, from the pastel-colored bras to the more daring panties, cheeks getting pink. "But..."

"What, you've never seen female lingerie before?"

His answer took less than a second to come. "Of course, I have. I just—" He turned with his brows furrowed and found me giggling. "You're teasing me."

I shrugged, pinching my lips together. "Sorry, it was too easy." Ah, men and their fragile image of masculinity.

He shook his head, a corner of his lips slightly lifting. He looked around us again. "I just don't understand why she needed, to, um, to come here."

I headed toward the aisle Helen had vanished in. "What do you mean?"

Matthias followed me. We browsed the bras and panties, his eyes lingering on a very sexy, fiery red set for a second too long. "Well..." He swallowed. "It's not like anyone is seeing her in her underwear."

"So what?" I stopped and crossed my arms. "Do you think a woman needs a partner to decide to buy sexy underwear?"

He shook his head, skin turning crimson. "No, I —"

"What if your mom just wants to feel sexy for herself? Isn't that reason enough?" I knew he had gotten the point, but I was having way too much fun to let him off the hook.

He closed his eyes and groaned. "Please don't refer to my mom and the word sexy in the same sentence."

I feigned ignorance. "Why? Because you don't want to imagine your mother as a woman who embraces her femininity?"

"Ugh, please stop." He dragged a hand down his face.

Snickering, I nudged his arm with my elbow. The teasing move came to me so easily, I didn't even think about it. "Come on, now. Don't be such a baby." I gave him a smirk before spotting Helen moving toward the fitting rooms. I followed her inside one.

"So," she said, her tone smug, "I saw you and Matt having fun out there."

I rolled my eyes. If only she'd known what we'd been talking about. "Not this again, Helen."

"I didn't say anything!" She chuckled at my accusatory stare. "Just stating facts."

"Sure," I answered.

I helped her change into one of the bras the employee had selected for her. She looked at herself in the mirror before sighing. "Everyone tells you about the wrinkles and bone pains, but no one tells you about the struggle of finding a bra that's both sexy and comfortable when you get old."

I chuckled. "We'll find the perfect one, you'll see."

We did, after a few tries.

Once Helen was dressed again, she said, "While we're here, you might want to try something for yourself. You know, in case you find a special someone soon."

I groaned. She was impossible. It wasn't hard to understand who she wanted this special someone to be. I didn't know how she'd gotten the idea of Matthias and I ever being something, but apparently, once she had her mind set on something, she wasn't letting go. And what was it with this family and their view that lingerie had to be bought for someone else to see?

I headed out of the dressing room and went to find Matthias. On the way, I stopped in front of the red lace set, the one Matthias had eyed longer than the others. I traced it with my fingers, then shook my head and continued walking.

Do you know one of the most important things I have learned in all my years of life? It's to listen to people's advice. I know, I know, sometimes, they don't apply to you, but from my experience, following the advice of the people surrounding me has always been a good decision.

Now, I know what you might think. "Helen, you're more stubborn than a mule. When have you ever listened to my advice?" Well, you're right, I've often done what I wanted regardless of people's suggestions, but I never said I was perfect!

Luckily, you mostly are. During our time together, you've followed most of my advice, and I'm grateful for it. I'm sure you are too!

But, don't think just because I'm not there to physically guide you anymore it means you will be free of my advice! I might have a few more in store for you.

As you'll see, some lessons go beyond life and death.

Love,

Helen

5

ADELAIDE

"*C*ome on, Lou, time to go!"

As I waited for my brother to come out of his room, I bent my neck from side to side, wincing at the movement. The couch hadn't gotten more orthopedic overnight.

I'd gone to bed at 11:30 last night, having had to do laundry and organize the bills on our kitchen counter after coming back from work and picking Louis up from Mrs. Zhu's. Still, I'd set my alarm clock for 6:30 before falling asleep. Even if I didn't have to go to work until 11:00—when Matthias would have to leave—Louis needed someone to bring him to school in the morning.

"Louis, you get your butt here right now or we're gonna be late!"

"Coming!" my little brother said as he came out of his room running, his hair all over the place and only one sock on.

I chuckled at the sight. "At least take the time to put on your other sock."

When he was *actually* ready, I grabbed the lunchbox I'd prepared for him and we headed to school.

When I got back to the apartment, I did the first thing I always did: put some music on. I wanted to pump myself up for work, so I played Taylor Swift's *1989* album. Never failed to put me in a good mood.

I used the free time I had before going to work to clean up the apartment. I vacuumed, mopped, and dusted, all the while moving my hips to the beat and singing along to every single word.

Once I was finished in Louis' room, I was surprised to find my dad seated on the living room couch, staring at the television. I looked at my phone, afraid I'd lost track of time and was late for work, but it was only 9:30. He usually wasn't out of bed before noon.

"Hey Dad," I said while walking toward him.

He turned his head in my direction and said, "Hey," with a smile that didn't quite reach his eyes. I sat down next to him.

"What are you watching?"

His head turned back to the television, and he narrowed his eyes. "Um, I'm not sure."

I hadn't seen him a lot in the past week with my longer work hours, so I took the time to examine him. He was still dressed in the shirt I'd seen him in a few days ago, and although it didn't smell bad, it didn't seem clean either. His hair was getting much too long to be considered stylish, which reminded me that it had been a very long while since he'd gone to the barber. I'd try cutting it myself this weekend.

While I looked almost exactly like my mother, Louis was the spitting image of our father. At least, he used to be. Now, my dad's unshaven face and greasy hair didn't remind me of my little brother at all.

What would my mom have said if she'd been here to see him? To see *us*? Would she have wanted me to shake him by the shoulders and tell him to *wake up*? Would she have been mad that I let him get to this point, that I failed to put him back on track?

He wasn't like this before. My mom never had to push him

to do anything or go anywhere. He used to bite into life. He used to smile.

If only she could tell me what to do.

I got up from the couch, heading out of the living room, but stopped abruptly before spinning on my heels. "Why don't you ever talk about her?"

My dad's head slowly moved from the television to my face. "Talk about who?" His voice was low, his speech heavy.

"About Mom." My voice cracked on the last word. Strange, how I'd talked about her two days ago with Matthias without feeling like breaking down, but simply mentioning her to my father made me weak in the knees.

My dad's eyes widened and became troubled; it might have been the first time he'd expressed any kind of emotion in the last year or so. But before he had the chance to say what was going on in his head, his face regained its neutral, empty expression. "There isn't anything left to say." He returned his attention to the television, his throat bobbing, yet not saying another word.

I continued staring at him for a few moments and stopped when I realized we were now in complete silence. I'd gone through the whole album, and the music had stopped. I grabbed my phone from my back pocket to start the music again, and as I scrolled through my playlist, I spotted "Stand by Me." Her song. Their song.

I wanted him to react. I *needed* him to react, to smile or cry or tell me to stop the music, just *something*. How could I help him if I didn't know what he was thinking or feeling? If anything could make him react now, after talking about her, it was this song.

Without thinking too much about it, I pressed play and kept my eyes on him. And waited. And waited. The first verse blared through the apartment, followed by the chorus. I kept my gaze focused on him through it all, looking for any sign of life.

By the time the song came to an end, like the last time, I'd gotten nothing from my dad. Not a single muscle twitch.

I stopped the music and left for work early.

*P*eeking through the ajar door, I made sure Helen was still sleeping. She'd been feeling tired this afternoon, so I helped her get ready for a nap. I was still getting used to the mechanical lift that allowed me to help her get into her bed or take a bath. I wanted her to be comfortable at all times and was afraid she wouldn't tell me if she wasn't. But with the way she was sleeping, mouth open and snoring like a pug, I figured she was fine.

When I wandered back to the living room, I connected my phone to the speakers and put on my reading playlist, opening a book on the history of aviation sitting on the coffee table. I wasn't a big nonfiction reader, but I needed something to take my mind away for a while.

It had been a day since the conversation with my father, yet I still couldn't stop replaying it in my head. His hollow eyes. His lack of interest in things that used to spark life into him. His unresponsiveness, even to the song that used to hold such special meaning to him.

What could I do? I'd been playing this ignorance game for almost two years now; thinking that if I didn't mention the problem out loud, it didn't exist. But yesterday's conversation, however brief, had made it clear as day there was a problem, whether I wanted to admit it or not. No matter how I tried to explain his behavior, after this long, it couldn't be excused as simple grief anymore. And I had no idea what to do about it.

After an hour, I realized I'd been reading the same page over and over again, never processing what the paragraph I'd gone over was about. I was so lost in thought I didn't hear Matthias arrive home.

"What are you listening to?"

I jumped, dropping the book on the couch. "Oh God, you scared the crap out of me." I got up, straightening my blouse. We might've acted friendly three days ago, but that didn't mean it would always be that way between us. It might've been a fluke, a one-time deal. I was still his employee, after all, and he was still...him.

"Helen's napping in her room," I said before he could ask.

His lips twitched. "I know. I just went to look."

"Oh."

I stood straight, having no idea what to say. Why was this so awkward? We'd been able to talk so freely when doing the dishes, and he hadn't been so bad when we went shopping, yet now, it felt as if an invisible wall had been built between the two of us again. I started toying with the taco charm on my bracelet, the one Stella had sent me for my birthday a few years back in commemoration of the time we'd tried to participate in a taco-eating competition for fun. We'd failed splendidly.

"So, are you going to tell me what you're listening to?" His voice was soft and deep, and I had no idea if it meant he was happy or not.

Then, he smiled softly, all pink lips and warm eyes, and the wall was sledgehammered once more. For good, I hoped.

"Hmm, I'm not sure." I let go of my bracelet and listened closely for a second, trying to identify the soft melody the cello and piano were playing, but couldn't pinpoint what it was. "I just put on a reading playlist." Classical music was the only thing I could listen to when I had to fully focus on something —not that it had worked all that well today.

"Huh."

I raised an eyebrow. "What does 'huh' mean?"

"Just that I didn't peg you for a classical music kind of woman."

Taking a step back, I crossed my arms. Maybe there were

still bricks that needed to be torn down in the wall after all. "And why is that? Because you didn't think I had the depth to like this kind of music? Am I not intellectual enough?"

A deep belly laugh erupted from his throat, and I took another step back. Who did this guy think he was?

Matthias lifted his hands in front of him, flashing me a gentle lopsided grin. "Don't take this the wrong way. I absolutely think you have the emotional intelligence to appreciate classical music. It actually suits you, I think." He chuckled. "It's just that the last time I came in here, you were listening to cheesy pop music."

I sat on the armrest of the couch, arms still braced across my chest as I forced my own grin down. I wasn't about to put him out of his misery so quickly. "So you thought because I listen to Justin Bieber, I can't like Chopin or Vivaldi?"

He bit his lip and lifted his shoulders, which reminded me of Louis' little boy shrug when I'd asked him last week how his white shirt had gotten so dirty in a single day.

"Well, you guessed wrong, boy. I'm a very versatile person."

"I can see that now."

The song playing around us came to an end, replaced by one of my favorites. When I was younger, my mother would work at home sometimes and she'd put on Clair de Lune, humming to the theme. One time, when I was five or six, she'd even taken my hand and twirled me to the rhythm of the music after she'd caught me listening to the song with her.

Matthias took a step forward, hands in his pockets and chin up. "Hmm, Debussy. Nice choice. Although, I probably like the version without the cello best."

I rolled my eyes. "Quite the connoisseur, aren't you?"

He shook his head. "No, I just..." It looked as if he wanted to say more, and I gave him a look that urged him to go on. After opening up to him, I would've liked for him to do so too. But he didn't. Swallowing, he shook his head before grinning.

"Let's say I like to fill my life with beauty, and there's nothing more beautiful than good music."

My jaw fell, right before I mirrored his smile. Maybe he hadn't told me all about him, but it was a start. And I had to admit, something about his personality was growing on me. A breath of fresh air compared to the stuffiness at home. I... I liked it.

I love that you love music as much as I do.

Whenever I feel a particular kind of way, it's like you can sense it and put on the perfect song, the one that can translate what I'm feeling inside into words or in melody. I don't know how you do it, but you've proven repeatedly that you have this special power.

Time and time again, you've selected the song I didn't even know I needed. A fast pace with cymbals and carillons for the good days, when I felt like a young woman all over again. A wistful piano ballad on the occasions the pain overtook everything, where I couldn't focus on anything other than breathing and trying to make it through the rough patch. A soft violin serenade on the hopeful days, when the sun would rise above the water, rays of light bursting through the living room curtains and warming our faces, making us feel as infinite as the ocean.

You have this emotional intelligence that I hope you never lose. Being able to read people without needing them to tell you what's wrong is the greatest of gifts. It has helped me so much through our time together, and I'm sure it will help all the people with whom you spend your time in the future.

As I said, it's a gift. Use it. Give it to the ones who need it.

You've already spread so much goodness around me with it. What's using it to spread even more?

Love,

Helen

6

MATTHIAS

*T*wirling the scotch and ice cube in my glass, I leaned back against my stool and sighed. I'd told her I would trust her from now on, and I meant it. But I couldn't help stressing. It was the first time I was gone this long, leaving Helen overnight with an aide other than Dora since the incident with Krystal. I gritted my teeth. Even thinking of her name made me want to break something.

I'd tried to keep my mind busy. I'd put my earbuds in and blasted Bach's "Goldberg Variations" before my flight. I'd even entertained some kind of conversation with Rosalie, my copilot, during the flight, which I almost never did. Still, I hadn't been able to keep my mind away from what was going on at home.

The hotel had advertised live music at the bar in the evening, which had been my last relaxation resort. The dimmed lights, mahogany walls, and quiet chatter were alluring, but the shrill of the electric guitar didn't help to calm my nerves in the slightest.

I looked at the time on my phone. It was almost nine in Maine. Putting my phone back down, I leaned on the bar counter, raking my fingers through my hair. I was a real basket case. Dropping a couple euros on the counter, I got up and headed toward the elevator. When the doors closed in front of me, I gave in and grabbed my phone, calling Adelaide before I could overthink it.

"Yes, everything is going fine," she said as she picked up on the second ring. Her voice sounded soft and amused.

My lips twitched and I exhaled in relief. I didn't know what I was expecting her to say, but hearing her calm down my fears right away felt good. Still, she didn't lack arrogance. "Hello to you too. And, what makes you think I'm calling about that?"

She chuckled. "I'm starting to know you, Matthias."

Huh. Was she?

The elevator doors opened, and I strolled to my room through the hallway still decorated as if it was the 18th century. "I was actually just calling to tell you about my schedule for tomorrow."

"Uh-huh." I could feel her smiling through the phone. I guessed my lying skills weren't as good as I thought they were. "Where are you, exactly?" she asked, putting me out of my misery.

I scanned my hotel card in front of the lock and pushed the door open while holding my phone between my head and shoulder. "Paris." Once the door was closed and locked, I unbuttoned my shirt and took off my pants before lying over the plush white comforter in only my black briefs and white undershirt.

"Wow, lucky you. I've always dreamed of visiting the City of Love."

"Hopeless romantic?" I asked, putting an arm under my head.

"More like hopeless adventure-seeker."

"Then why haven't you gone yet?"

Voice half-amused, she answered, "You mean between the

time I had to take care of my sick mother and the moment I became the support system for my whole family?"

"Uh…" *Damn, Matthias, wrong question.* "Yeah, sorry, that was stupid of me."

After a second, she muttered something to herself before saying, "No, I'm sorry, that wasn't fair to you. It's not your fault." She exhaled loudly. "I guess I'm just jealous of your… freedom, sometimes."

That made sense.

Shuffling sounds filled my ear, like she was repositioning herself on a comforter. Helen was an early sleeper and early riser, so I wasn't surprised they were already in bed at nine.

"Are you going to visit a bit before flying tomorrow morning?" she asked, changing the subject.

"No, I'll probably just sleep in."

She tsked through the phone. "What a waste."

Didn't seem like a waste to me. Spending two hours in bed versus with overeager tourists taking pictures of every building and imitating French accents was an easy choice to make.

"So, how did today go? Were there any problems?" I asked instead of telling her that.

"Ha! I knew you were worried!" She laughed, the sound clear and light, and I couldn't help myself, I chuckled with her.

"All right, all right. I might have asked myself once or twice if everything was going okay with Helen."

"See, it didn't hurt to ask."

I rolled my eyes even though she couldn't see me, yet for some reason, the sound of her laughter made me think she could feel it through the phone. "Yes, everything went wonderfully well, and you don't need to be worried. Do I tell you how to fly a plane?" I grinned at her witty answer. "I'm *actually* good at what I do."

"I know, I know," I said, nodding.

More shuffling, followed by the click of a lamp. "By the

way, is there a reason you call your mother Helen? I've been meaning to ask."

I smirked at the memory her question brought. "When I was a kid, I was a little shit, believe it or not."

She burst out in laughter, snorting in the process, which made me laugh in response. "I can believe it all right." Arrogance and amusement laced her voice.

"So, when I was eight or nine," I started, "my mom punished me because I got in a fight at school. She took away all my favorite books for a week." Adelaide snickered. "I was so mad, I decided to start calling her Helen instead of Mom, just to spite her."

"Wow, you truly were a little shit. A book nerd little shit, to be precise."

I grinned. "Indeed. So, anyway, it sort of became an inside joke between us through the years, and the name stayed. I think she even likes it now."

"Huh. Somehow, I can't picture you getting into a fight, even as a kid. What was it about?"

Fuck. I hadn't thought about the fact that she'd ask about this. I swallowed roughly, my mouth dry all of a sudden. "I don't remember," I lied. Somehow, my deception skills must have improved in the last minutes because she didn't ask more about it.

We continued talking about everything and nothing, the conversation smooth and easy. After a while, Addy said, "Hey, I just realized you must be so tired. What time is it in Paris?"

I brought my phone away from my ear to look at it. "A quarter past three."

"Oh my God! I'm so sorry for keeping you up! Go to bed, I'll see you tomorrow." The call ended.

Did she just hang up on me?

Huh.

I'd called to do a simple check up on my mom, yet we'd ended up speaking on the phone for over twenty minutes. I wasn't sure how to explain why I'd stayed on the line with her this long, other than the fact that she'd made me smile more in this short period of time than I had all day.

After closing the bedside lamp, I tried to fall asleep, but I couldn't. Instead, I kept replaying our conversation in my head, and somehow found myself wishing it could have lasted just a little longer.

Have I ever told you about my time in Paris?

In my younger years, I stayed there for a whole month while doing an elective clinical rotation during my clerkship. My romantic heart had never been fuller.

The lights, the wine, the food, the architecture... It couldn't have been more perfect. It was the most flawless setting for falling in love, and although I didn't, I saw plenty of people around me who did. Proposals under the Eiffel Tower, stolen kisses in the Jardins du Luxembourg, moonlight promenades beside the Seine, I saw it all.

I'm not sure why I'm writing all of this to you right now. It might be because I was thinking about what I would've liked to see you doing if I'd had more time, and this came to mind: seeing you with your lover in Paris, walking hand in hand in Montmartre and stopping for a café au lait and a pain au chocolat, a smile on your lips and hearts in your eyes.

I hope with all my heart you get to experience it one day, even if I'm not there to witness it. And, even if I won't be able to see it in person, I can imagine it so clearly now. It will have to do.

Love,
Helen

7

ADELAIDE

I was in Helen's kitchen preparing fish tacos—apparently, I wasn't so bad a cook when there was enough food to fill the fridge—when my phone vibrated in my pocket. I picked it up and smiled when I saw *Stella My Favorite Person In The World* written on the screen. Answering and putting the phone between my ear and shoulder, I said, "Hey, girl, what's up? How was your shift?"

She groaned through the phone. "Let's just say I've seen more shit in twenty-four hours than most people do in their lifetime."

I couldn't help the giggle that escaped my lips.

"Shut up," she continued, "I don't even want to think about it anymore." I could swear I heard her shudder. "I need you to make me think of something else."

"Okay, um, well, I have received my first paycheck this week from my new job, and I almost shed tears of joy when I saw the amount."

It wasn't even an exaggeration. Matthias and I had discussed salary very rapidly on the day I'd started working, so I hadn't wrapped my head around what I'd receive for every

68

two weeks of work, but it was... It was more than enough to remove a huge weight off my shoulders.

"So, Mr. Asshole pays well, at least?"

We hadn't had a lot of time to talk in the last two weeks, between my all-over-the-place schedules and her crazy shifts at the hospital, so I hadn't brought her up to date on the Matthias situation.

I grabbed a knife and started chopping some red cabbage. "About that. He's... he's actually not that bad." I might have whispered the last three words.

"Oh really? And why's that?" Even though I didn't see her, I could imagine her knowing smirk and raised eyebrows.

"I don't know, we might have had a rough start, but since I've gotten to know him better, I can say he's a pretty cool guy." I shrugged. "He's grumpy most of the time, but other than that he's fine."

"Uhhhhh-huuuuhhhh. Well, I guess you'll just have to use that big money he's giving you and come to Montreal to tell me all about it."

Putting the chopped cabbage in a metal bowl, I said, "Ha, ha. You wish."

"No, but seriously, though, have you given any more thought about coming here to study next year?" Stella asked.

I released a sigh; she wasn't going to give this up, was she?

"I know, I know, you're tired of me harassing you with it, but you said so yourself, you'll make a lot of money this year. What's stopping you from coming now?"

If I was being honest with myself, I *had* given more thought to the idea. But I wouldn't tell her that; it would only give her false hopes. Because no matter what possible scenario I'd come up with, it always seemed too impossible to come true. Too many variables stood between me and the realization of this project.

"Well, for starters," I said, "Louis. It's not like I can just abandon him. And do I really want to go to college? Maybe it's not meant for me. Plus, there have to be thousands of people more qualified than me."

"Come on, Addy, that's fucking bullshit and you know it."

"I—"

The sound of a cupboard slamming shut startled me so much I screamed and dropped my phone on the ground. I turned around, fists in the air, only to be met with Matthias, dressed as usual in his neat pilot uniform, lips rolled back in an attempt to suppress his laughter. It wasn't working.

"Jesus Christ, you scared the living daylights out of me!" I finally said after seconds of looking at him like a deer in the headlights. "Is that how you always greet people?" To that, he chuckled, throat bobbing and perfectly-white teeth on display. I glared at him before bending down and grabbing my phone, luckily intact.

"Hey, I have to go," I told Stella. "I'll call you back."

"Yeah, bitch, you better, 'cause this conversation isn't over."

"I know. Love you."

"Love you too."

Hanging up, I glanced at him with a smile, though his own grin had disappeared in the last few seconds, replaced by a sad expression of indifference. Turning around to grab a glass in the cupboard, he asked, "Boyfriend?"

"Yeah, right," I huffed.

When he looked at me, an eyebrow raised, I explained further. "No, that was Stella, my best friend."

"Oh," he said as he turned to face the kitchen counter again and poured water into his glass. I wasn't sure if I'd imagined it, but some of the tension in his shoulders had seemed to have dissipated. Weird.

"So, college, huh?" he said, his back still to me.

My eyes widened. How much had he heard?

"Don't worry, I just came in a few seconds before you half-deafened me with your scream. I didn't hear all your personal gossip," he said as if he'd read my mind.

"No, no gossip," I replied, though I could feel the traitorous heat rising to my cheeks. Matthias looked at me smirking, a dimple pitting his stubble-covered cheek, but didn't say anything else. "And yeah, college." I shook my head and inclined my back against the kitchen island. "Well, actually, not for me."

Ignoring my last answer, he leaned on his forearms beside me on the counter and asked, "And what would you like to study?"

Looking at my socks, I swallowed hard. I hadn't told anyone about the plans I'd had for the future since the end of high school except Stella and my mom. And it had been so long since I'd been convinced this dream would come to life, it felt silly speaking it out loud. But the *I'm not sure* lie died on my tongue when I looked up and found obsidian eyes filled with pure curiosity.

"When I was younger, I wanted to go into special education. Work with students with health concerns," I said with a shrug, returning my hands to the bowl of cabbage and grabbing the carrots. It was a pipe dream—something not meant for my reality.

I could feel his eyes on me, my own nonchalance lost in his persistent gaze, and for a moment it felt like he was scrutinizing me.

"I think you would make an amazing special needs teacher," he said after a moment.

I jerked my head up to find a genuine grin on his lips, and a lump started to grow in my throat. That was it. One simple sentence. Ten tiny words. And suddenly it didn't feel so foolish. Suddenly, it felt like if my life had been different, maybe I *would've* been plenty qualified.

"Thank you," I said with a guttural slip of my voice. One, thankfully, he said nothing about.

He nodded before lifting himself from the counter and pointing at my chopping board. "You staying for dinner with us?"

I exhaled, glad for the lighter subject. "I'd love to, but I have somewhere I need to be."

Just like he had a few minutes prior, he looked at me with an eyebrow raised. "Now what could be more exciting than eating cabbage with us?"

Jeez, someone was curious tonight. And I had already revealed one part of myself; I didn't feel like disclosing another. So, I simply answered, "Um, church."

His eyes widened while his lips parted a little. "I hadn't pegged you for the religious type."

Lacking the courage to tell him he hadn't been wrong, I shrugged and went to pick up the coat and purse I'd dropped on one of the stools this morning.

"Guess I'll need to make a bigger effort to get to know you, then," he said casually.

I lifted my head slowly from my bag, feeling his gaze searing through me. When our eyes met, a shot of electricity coursed through my belly. His chest rose and fell, and his eyes lit with an emotion I wasn't able to pinpoint.

Were his cheeks red?

Breaking the eye contact, I cleared my throat. "Um, yeah. Well, I better get going." I grabbed my stuff and left the kitchen to go see Helen.

MATTHIAS

*C*ursing at myself silently, I watched Adelaide leave.
Why the fuck had I said that?

Things were going well. We were talking like... like *friends*, and then something had taken over me, and I'd spoken without thinking. Telling her I had to get to know her... What a stupid and borderline creepy thing to say. And the worst part was, despite the fact that the words had come out by themselves, I realized now that I'd meant every single one of them.

There was something about Adelaide that intrigued me. And it wasn't because she was mysterious; she wasn't. She wore her heart on her sleeve. I'd realized in the past two weeks that even when words failed her, her face and body language always revealed exactly what was on her mind. Maybe that's what I found intriguing, though. Someone who could share whatever they were feeling, whether it be good or bad. I had no idea how someone could be so honest—even if just with themselves—all the time.

Adelaide stopped beside Helen's wheelchair in the living room. Her face lit up as she said her goodbyes. Beaming, she gave Helen a hug and a kiss on the cheek before making her way to the front door.

This was another thing I didn't understand about Adelaide: why would a twenty-something woman think she wasn't good enough to go to college when she was one of the best aides we'd ever had? I'd had to admit it to myself a few days ago; I'd been wrong about her. It was fascinating to see her *care* this way for someone, especially someone she'd so recently met. She had something very few people had. So, how could someone so genuinely good doubt herself so much?

While she grabbed her coat, I joined her in the foyer and put my hands in my pockets. "Do you need me to call an Uber for you?"

She snickered, rolling her eyes. "I'm fine with taking the bus, but thank you."

When she was ready to leave, I opened the door for her. Before she crossed the threshold, I said, "You're very good at what you do."

She looked up at me, cheeks blushing as a corner of her lips rose. "Thank you."

I nodded. "Good night, Adelaide."

She got out the door, but after a few steps on the porch, she spun on her heels. "Why don't you ever call me Addy?"

"You never told me I could," I said as I tilted my head.

After a short pause, she said, "Well, you can."

I grinned. "Then have a good night at church, Addy."

Biting her lip, she gave me a dip of the head and disappeared down the street.

ADELAIDE

*E*ven singing hadn't helped clear my mind. It had never happened to me before.

"Hey, good performance, Addy." Benjamin, our cellist, put his hand on my shoulder while passing beside me, startling me in the process. His light red hair was sticking in every direction, like it always had.

We'd dated for a while after high school, our couple lasting all of six months. He was a nice guy—always had been—but something was missing between us. We'd been friends for a long time, so we knew each other well. He'd been there for me when my mom had gotten sick. I'd lost my virginity to him; a real rom-com story. It should have worked out, it made *sense*, but I didn't feel any chemistry with him. I'd tried and tried, looking for it through every kiss and every intimate touch, but had come up empty-handed. He'd been a gentleman even after I'd broken up with him, agreeing to stay friends.

"Are you okay?" he asked when I didn't answer his previous comment. "You look upset."

"Yeah, I'm fine. Thanks, Ben."

He gave me a gap-toothed grin. "Okay, good. Meet you at the venue?"

Forcing a smile, I bobbed my head yes, then watched him

leave the church, meeting Gabrielle—our violinist—at his car. They both hopped in.

I headed out, the crisp spring wind meeting my face like a whip. Maybe a long walk and fresh air would work in clearing my head after all.

I hadn't lied to Matthias when I'd left; I *was* on my way to church. I simply hadn't disclosed the reason for it.

I'd started singing in a band in high school, mostly for fun. Gabrielle and I would go one night per week to Benjamin's place to practice in his basement. We'd all been part of our high school's jazz band and had decided to work on some covers just the three of us.

Then, two years ago, Gabrielle's cousin had gotten engaged, and she'd asked us to play at her wedding. We'd accepted, thinking it'd be a one-time thing, but after that, we'd received a few more contracts and never really stopped.

Now, I continued doing it because it gave me extra cash to pay the bills at the end of the month. It wasn't much, but it was still better than nothing. I also did it because singing was one of my favorite things in the world. So, even if I might've been better off doing stuff at home, I took this time for myself. This three-hour session every month or so was the one time I could think about nothing and just sing. During rough times, it was my beacon.

Except today, it had done nothing to calm my agitated mind. And, the worst part was, my mind had no reason to be so all over the place.

Matthias hadn't said anything improper when he'd alluded to wanting to get to know me better. His words hadn't even been hinting at something more. Still, my mind had clung to them and analyzed every single one of their possible meanings, leaving me utterly confused.

Because even if I hadn't thought about it before, the way I'd felt in his kitchen made me think I might have wanted there to be meaning behind his words. I wanted him to *truly* want to get to know me. There was no denying the rise of my pulse or the chills running down my arms when I'd been under his gaze, listening to those words. Even if I wanted to lie to myself, my body didn't work that way.

Everything I'd said to Stella was true. He wasn't so bad. Far from it. The deep love he had for his mother, which had made him seem like an asshole at first, was actually endearing when I saw them together, and he always made me laugh when our paths crossed at the end of my shifts.

But he was my boss, which meant these thoughts had no right to exist. Stella had dated a boss of hers a few years back, and when she'd wanted to break up with him, he'd dangled her job over her head to try to keep her. No way was I going to try to get close to a man who was responsible for my family's financial stability.

So why in the world hadn't my conflicting thoughts disappeared as soon as I'd left his house?

As I walked further, I unzipped my coat. I felt way too hot for a mid-April day.

Trying to distract myself, I put my earplugs in and put on some music. I tried, really tried, to focus on something else, but five minutes later, my thoughts were back to Matthias. More precisely, on why I couldn't be thinking that way about him.

Not only was he my boss, but he also kept a big part of himself guarded, and I wasn't sure what to think of it. He could tell me he wanted to make efforts to get to know me, but he was a lot more closed off than I was. He was witty and funny when we talked, but every time Helen or I asked questions that were somehow personal, he gave some bland answer and left. He knew a lot about my life, yet the only information I had of him, I'd gotten from Helen.

He might have been a shy man with no particular information to disclose, but somehow, I doubted it. No one without any history of heartbreak would be sealed so tight.

He was a puzzle, and it wasn't my place to learn how to assemble it.

Once I got back home and picked Louis up later that night, I made dinner, then played with him up until he had to go to bed. The more occupied I kept my mind, the better I'd fare.

As promised, in these letters, I'd like to give you some advice. Obviously, I would have preferred to be there in person to counsel you and help you make your decisions, but this is the best I can do. I hope when you need my help and wish I were there, you can read these words again and find what you're looking for. So here goes the first Helen Advice: Always say what's on your mind.

I might have collected a few regrets in my sixty-four years of life, but being honest has never been one of them. Keeping things hidden, though, has been.

Show your emotions. Cry when you're sad, laugh when you're happy, scream when you're mad, and kiss when you're in love. You have every right to feel whatever it is you're feeling, and expressing it can only help to show who you are as a person.

It can be nothing but helpful to the ones around you to know how you feel—how you really feel. And if they don't appreciate it, then Helen Advice number 1.5: kick them out of your life. They're not worth it. You deserve to be with people who want to know your truth and to see your heart above all else.

Love,
Helen

8

ADELAIDE

"*M*atthias, we have a problem."

"What? What's wrong?"

Holding the phone to my ear, I looked behind me at Louis, sitting cross-legged on the floor of our apartment and making loud siren sounds while driving his fire truck on the beige carpet. "I don't have anyone to watch my brother today." It was a Saturday morning, and Mrs. Zhu had called a minute ago to say Josh had a fever and they had to go to the clinic. "I've called Dora, but she already had things planned for the day."

He took a moment to answer, and in the silence, I could feel the tension radiating from him, even through the phone.

"Um… Can't your father watch him?" he said simply.

My eyes made the way from Louis to my dad sprawled on the couch, empty-eyed and more disheveled than ever. But Matthias didn't know that. At least not all of it. He'd probably gotten that I was Louis' main guardian at the moment, but he hadn't asked why, and I hadn't elaborated more than was necessary.

"No, he can't," I answered in a stern voice.

He stayed silent for a while, making me wince in expectation. I knew he had to work today, and springing this on him an hour before he had to leave was a bad idea, but it wasn't like I had a choice. My entourage in Portland was practically non-existent, and Louis needed someone. *I* was that someone, no matter what was going on.

"I'm really sorry, Matthias. I didn't know this was going to happen and I've been looking for a solution for an hour now, but I can't find anything and I—"

"Addy," he interrupted me, "just bring him with you then."

"What?" I still sounded breathless from my earlier rambling.

"Did I break up? I said bring him. It's fine. Helen loves kids."

I chewed on my bottom lip. "Uh... Are you sure? I wouldn't want to impose."

He huffed. "Addy, you could never impose even if you wanted to. Just bring him, and I'll try to make the place kid-friendly until you get here. See you later," he said before hanging up, leaving me open-mouthed.

I needed to go over the whole conversation in my head three times to make sense of it. Had he just said he'd adapt his house to make it more suited for Louis? And had he really trusted that nothing would happen to his mother while I had my brother to look after, without even needing me to reassure him about it?

I thought I might have been dreaming.

I packed Louis' favorite toys in a hurry and we rushed out to catch the bus to Cape Neddick. Forty-five minutes later, I was unlocking Helen's house, my little brother in tow.

"Hey!" Matthias yelled from the kitchen before heading our way, a travel coffee mug in hand. I had to suppress a smile when I caught his slightly disheveled and winded appearance. It wasn't that obvious, but compared to his usual perfectly neat image, it was noticeable.

He placed his mug on the floor while putting on his leather

loafers. "I went and grabbed some of my old stuff in the attic so that Louis could have things to play with. They're in the living room with Helen. She's watching a movie."

This time, I wasn't able to keep my smile away. I hid the fire truck I was holding behind my back. "Thank you, that was nice of you."

When Matthias stood straight again, Louis' hand squeezed mine tighter as he inhaled sharply. "Whoaaaaa, are you a pilot?"

Matthias glanced his way with a grin. "Yes, I am."

This was possibly the worst thing to say to a seven-year-old obsessed with vehicles. "I have a huuuuge plane at home! I wish I'd brought it to show you!"

Matthias' look softened even more before he crouched in front of my brother. "Well, you'll just have to bring it next time you come here, 'kay buddy?"

"Okay." Louis' voice was soft and low, like it so rarely was. He was star struck.

Someone needed to tell my chest to stop tightening right this moment.

"Okay, Lou, we'll let Matthias go to work now." I pushed him forward inside the house, and looked behind my shoulder, where Matthias was standing straight, eyes fixed on me. I smiled and mouthed, "Thank you."

He gave me a tight nod before heading out.

MATTHIAS

"So, what are you doing for the next hour and a half?" my copilot, Rosalie, asked. I turned my head to look at her. Her copper-red hair was tied in a knot at the base of her neck, her blue-green eyes lined with black, and her plump lips sparkly. I'd found her pretty from the first time we'd met. Beautiful, really.

Checking the panel in front of me to make sure everything was in order before leaving the plane, I said, "Probably just going to go wait inside the airport. Grab a coffee, maybe."

I pulled my phone out of my pocket to see if I had any missed calls, and that's when I felt her lips on my neck. She kissed me before letting her mouth linger on my skin. "Are you sure you wouldn't want to spend your time doing something else?"

She'd gotten divorced a few months ago, and we'd sort of been seeing each other ever since. It wasn't anything serious on either part, purely physical. We were both using each other, and I was more than fine with it.

I closed my eyes and lifted my chin, giving her easier access to my neck. Her lips trailed down from my ear to my Adam's apple, and I released a pent-up exhale when they reached my collarbone.

Her hands lifted to my neck, starting to unbutton my shirt. Then, her touch slowly moved down, nails scratching my chest before one of her hands palmed my dick through my pants. I groaned while tangling my fingers in her hair. As she kissed my chest, I rubbed her strands between my fingers, the texture feeling off.

And that's when it hit me.

I was expecting to feel hair that was curly and dark, not smooth and red.

Eyes bulging out, I jerked back, heaving under my half-open shirt. Rosalie looked up, an eyebrow arched and a frown overtaking her swollen lips.

"Uh... I'm sorry, I'm not feeling it today. Might have caught a bug or something," I lied. "Maybe another time."

She glared at me for a while like I was the stupidest man on earth—which I might have been—before getting up. "What's going on with you?"

I swallowed roughly. "I just told you, I think I—"

"I don't believe you." She crossed her arms and leaned on a hip. "I know you, Matthias. There's something on your mind."

I looked down and buttoned my shirt. "No, there isn't."

She huffed as if she didn't believe a word I was saying, but still shrugged. "Fine. See you later then." She left the cockpit, but I didn't follow her out right away.

Dragging a hand through my hair, I tried to understand the meaning of what had just happened without coming to any conclusion. Yes, I'd always found Addy attractive—okay, really fucking hot—but I hadn't realized I'd started to want her in *this* way.

Anyway, it didn't matter. Even if I did want her, which I wasn't sure I did, it could never happen. Not unless I wanted to risk a repeat of the disaster that had happened with my past girlfriend. Addy was off-limits.

Now the only thing I had to do was make sure my mind understood it.

ADELAIDE

*L*ouis smashed his hand on the Play-Doh ball, adding purple to his already-stained hand. "My snowman was too easy for you to guess. I'll make a harder one now."

I glanced sideways at Helen, finding her watching my brother with a smile matching my own. She lifted her eyebrows. "Try to make us guess your favorite summer activity," she said.

Louis placed a finger on his chin, looking up for a few moments. "I got it!" He grinned before starting to split the Play-Doh into three equal parts.

"Hey, I'm back!"

I turned around and felt the same squeezing sensation as I

caught Matthias making his way through the door. When he got to us, he looked around the room to the million games and toys sprawled on the floor. "Looks like you're having fun."

"Yeah, we are," I said with a smile, but he didn't even look my way as I spoke. It might have been my imagination, but he even seemed to look away from me.

Planting his hands in his perfectly-ironed trousers, he nodded, keeping his eyes on the floor.

Helen alternated her gaze between the two of us before she turned her chair in my brother's direction. "Hey, Louis, your sister told me you're the best at doing cartwheels. Would you like to show me how good you are? Let the grown-ups speak while we young-of-hearts have some fun?"

"Yeah!" It didn't take a second before Louis was running toward the patio door and leaping in the verdant lawn.

Helen winked at me before wheeling herself in the direction he left in. "Hey, wait up! These aren't race car wheels!"

When they were out of sight, I sat down on the couch. "Helen the matchmaker strikes again." I smirked at him, but he didn't laugh at my joke. He swallowed roughly before taking a seat opposite to me, avoiding my eyes the whole time.

"So, how did the day go?" he asked. Once he'd changed the subject, he finally allowed his eyes to meet mine, and I found them to be troubled.

"It was fine. How about yours? Is everything okay?"

"Yeah, yeah, everything's fine." A corner of his lips tilted up, but he didn't look sincere. One of my eyebrows quirked up as my gaze pierced his, and he released a breathy laugh. "I swear. Just had a rough day."

"All right." I didn't believe him, but I wasn't comfortable enough to probe into his personal matters. Our friendship, if I could call it that, was already fragile enough as it was.

I stood to pick up some toys scattered on the ground and regrouped them into a corner of the room. "Well, if I ever wondered how Helen was as a mom with you, I now know.

She was amazing today. Helped me keep Lou busy while I cooked and did some laundry."

Matthias laughed. "Yeah, she was a pretty cool mom."

I went down on all fours to pick some of the Play-Doh that had gotten stuck to the hardwood floors, scrubbing it with my chewed-up nails.

"Hey, um, can I ask you a question?" Matthias blurted.

"Sure," I answered, not bothering to look behind me.

"Why can't your father look after Louis?"

I closed my eyes and exhaled, letting my head drop for a while.

"I'm not asking because it bothered me that you brought him here today, not at all," he said. "I was just curious, but you don't have to answer that." He cleared his throat. "Actually, it's not my place to ask. I'm sorry."

I lifted myself from the floor and looked into his regretful eyes. "No, it's okay, I just wasn't expecting that question." Taking a seat at his side again, I glanced out the window at Louis doing cartwheel after cartwheel while Helen watched him, cheering. Behind them was nothing but the deepest blue of the ocean, not a cloud obstructing the sunshine. The view from the living room took my breath away every time I saw it, even after weeks of working here.

"Let's say my father isn't the same anymore," I said.

His eyes narrowed. "What do you mean?"

I pursed my lips and peered at my lap. "My mom. They, uh, they had dreams before she got sick. He lost everything when she died."

Matthias adjusted his seat. "Lost everything?"

I faced him once again, a sad smile on my lips. "Everything." I swallowed against the lump in my throat. "My mom and dad were the picture perfect couple. They met in high school, stuck together through college, got married after graduating, had me soon after." My brother waved at me from outside, and I shook my hand back with a smile. "Louis was a little surprise, though. I was sixteen when he was born."

Turning to face Matthias' attentive face, I continued, "They were each other's everything, you know. All their plans revolved around the other. Their one big, lifelong dream was to one day buy a motel by the coast of Maine, which they did when I was fifteen. We moved here, and everything was perfect. Then, my mom got sick and everything crumbled around them. Around us." I coughed, my throat very dry all of a sudden.

"Can you… I'm sorry, tell me if I'm overstepping, but will you tell me more?" His voice was low and surprisingly soothing, like a caress to my soul.

Exhaling shakily, I closed my eyes to regain control of my emotions. I didn't talk about it often, so it never got easier to tell this story. I loved to share good memories I had with her, but this wasn't one of them.

I could've told him I didn't want to talk about it. I could've found a thousand excuses, but when I opened my eyes again, Matthias was waiting for me, a fierce expression on his face. I wasn't sure if it was pain or interest or fear. Whatever it was, it reminded me he was going through something similar at the moment and might like to listen to someone else's story. So, for him, I continued.

"My mom's medical bills kept piling up, and eventually they had to sell the motel to be able to pay for it all. But I think my dad didn't even care about that. The pain I'd see in his eyes every time I caught him watching the woman he loved on her sickbed, it was…" I wiped a tear I didn't know had fallen on my cheek with the palm of my hand. "If there's one thing I could magically erase from my head, it's that."

I realized then that Matthias' eyes were as watery as mine. In a second, his hand was in mine, and I squeezed it tightly in return. I knew I should pull away, but for an instant, I let myself bask in the feeling of truly sharing a moment, a *feeling*, with someone. It should have felt wrong, to hold my boss' hand, but it couldn't; not when we were sharing something only the two of us could understand.

The spell broke when Louis released a yelp outside and I spun toward the window. My heart rate picked up, but I exhaled in relief once I saw the huge grin splitting his face as he ran, Helen chasing after him with her chair. When I returned to Matthias, he seemed more in control of his emotions than he previously had been. I was too.

I cleared my throat. "So, back to my father. When my mom died, a part of him died with her, if not all of him. It's been two years now, and he still hasn't come out of his slumber." I pulled at the skin around my thumbnail. "And, it's not that he doesn't love Louis, I know he does. He's just not in the right state of mind to take care of a kid. So, I do it for him."

Matthias hummed, scratching his cheek. "Have you thought about bringing him to see someone that could help him? A doctor or something?"

I shook my head. "I tried to. I think he might be depressed, but he doesn't want to go see anyone. And, honestly, we don't have the funds to pay for therapy."

He chewed the inside of his cheek. "I'm really sorry, Addy." And, in his eyes, I could see he was. He wasn't saying it to make me feel better. In some way, it was as if he shared my pain in this instant. And I'd rarely felt anything so beautiful.

"Thank you," I said with a weak smile before getting up and joining Louis and Helen outside. Staying here with Matthias was a bad idea.

A real bad idea.

I love kids.

I knew I did as soon as I was old enough to own a baby doll, which I dressed and brought with me everywhere. Her name was Gretchen, and you couldn't have separated me from her for anything in the world.

Motherhood was never an option for me; it was a certainty. There was no possibility of a world where I wouldn't be a mother. I might have come into the game late, but I did still.

It was incredible.

All through my adult life, I often felt like a little kid, wanting to run into the ocean and dive as if I were a dolphin, or make sandcastles, only for them to be washed away by the tide and start again the next day. Now, for a thirty-year-old lady to do that, it might have seemed weird.

But for a mother, it didn't.

People often talk about parenthood as if it only comes with sacrifices and troubles. And I won't lie, it does come with all of that. But, much, much more importantly, it comes with immeasurable joy, every day for the rest of your life. There's no better gift.

One of the greatest pains I feel comes from the knowledge that I'll never see your children. But, I rest assured in knowing that, no matter what they look like or who they become, they'll have the best parent watching over them.

Love,
Helen

9

MATTHIAS

$\mathcal{T}$he light coming through my hotel room was slowly fading, leaving me in a collection of shadows. With a yawn, I switched the channel for the tenth time in the last hour, not able to find anything good to watch that wasn't in Czech. Deciding on a nap instead, I turned off the television and laid down on the bed, just as my phone vibrated beside me.

Adelaide: House all decorated for Easter!

The text was accompanied by a picture of Helen, her wheelchair wrapped in violet and yellow ribbons. Behind her was our newly-decorated living room, filled with banners and ribbons showcasing Easter colors. I smiled at the sight of the happy expression my mother wore.

Me: Looks like you're having fun.

Adelaide: Helen was tired, so she's napping right now, but I'm sure I'm still having more fun than you are! Let me guess, laying on a hotel room bed, watching TV?

Damn, she was good. And she was right, I wasn't having so much fun. Before I had the chance to overthink what it meant that I wanted to talk to her "in person," I pressed the *FaceTime* button.

She answered on the first ring, her face makeup-free and her hair in a messy bun. It struck me as soon as she answered just how magnificent she looked, from the subtle freckles dotting her skin to her wide eyes and long lashes. I'd noticed before—more times than I could count, really— how pretty she was, but this was the first time I'd felt it so vividly. Well, except for the time I was with Rosalie. And I didn't like it. At all.

Interrupting my confused thoughts, she smiled before saying, "Calling me to prove I guessed right?"

I smirked. "Something like that, yeah."

The image on my phone became blurry for a few seconds, and when it came back, Addy was sitting on the back porch's three-seater swing. "Do you even like discovering new places? At least a tiny bit?" Her voice told me she was joking, even if her question struck a chord in me.

"Not that much, actually, no."

Her smile disappeared, a crease forming between her brows. "Wait, you're kidding, right?" When I kept a neutral face, she huffed. "You're a pilot. You *have* to like traveling."

I grinned. "I'm the living proof that you can become a pilot and actually not like to travel."

Her frown deepened even more. "Then why did you choose this job, if it wasn't for the chance to discover the world?"

I leaned back further into the pillows of the bed. I'd never put the reasons for my choice into words out loud before, not even to my mom, yet I somehow wanted to tell them to Addy. I didn't know what it meant, but I'd focus on that later.

I cleared my throat. "I like the feeling of control that flying gives me. I... When I was younger, I was always so different from the other kids. I had my growth spurt before everyone. I didn't have a dad. I wasn't born here. I liked quirky things like books and classical music instead of cars and sports like every other guy my age." Her traits softened on the screen. "Basically, I was different from anyone at every possible level, and the other kids reminded me of it every chance they got. And the worst part was, I had no control over the majority of those things, and I always hated it."

"So you became a pilot to make sure you'd have a job where you were fully in control," she said, finishing my thoughts with a stern face.

I nodded.

She scratched her cheek, looking to her left while sighing. "Is it weird that I feel like kicking some little shits' asses even if they're no longer kids?"

I burst out in laughter, leaning my head on the headboard of the queen-size bed.

"I'm serious, Matt. If I learned Louis was acting like that with other kids, I *would* kick his ass."

I laughed again, this time because I had no doubt she would.

She licked her lips. "Well, if it helps, those kids are probably bald and wrinkled right now, and they wish they could have your tall build and golden skin and charcoal hair."

My laughter got stuck in my throat at the sound of her words, making me break out in a coughing fit. Had she just complimented the way I looked? Or was she simply stating facts, no attraction involved? And why did I wish her words meant she found me good-looking?

I realized I'd been staring at her silently through the phone for a while when she cleared her throat and said, "Anyway, I have to go prepare the vegetables for dinner. I'll see you tomorrow. Bye!" Her camera cut off, bringing my phone back to its home screen. I closed it and dropped it on the bed with a sigh.

The more time passed, and the more I felt the temptation to break my only rule, consequences be damned. I couldn't get her out of my head. There was no denying it anymore. Every time we interacted, she occupied a bigger part of my mind, and I feared she would continue to do so until she'd invaded all of it. But, in this situation, the stakes were too high for the consequences to be damned.

I got up, deciding a cold shower was exactly what I needed. That, and more distance. I couldn't continue texting and calling her and expect my infatuation to go away. I'd have to find some self-control and keep her at bay; if I didn't, I might not be the only one to pay the price.

ADELAIDE

"Okay, do we have everything in place?"

Helen grinned. "Yeah, I-I think we're r-ready."

Her speech had become more slurred in the past week. Her voice had changed too, sounding hoarser than before, but we never talked about it. I could see traces of disappointment on her face when she had difficulty getting a word out, or when I didn't understand what she said the first time around. She struggled even more when she was tired, so she always made sure she got enough rest. But, other than that, her disease didn't affect our relationship. She was in a good mood pretty much all the time, which rubbed off on me. For the first time since I'd quit school, I wasn't coming back from work exhausted and down. If possible, I felt energized when I came back to Louis and my father. I might have been her employee, but Helen was as good to me as I was to her.

As I looked outside, an airplane flew above the water.

What was *he* thinking about right now? Was he as confused as I was?

Ever since our phone conversation yesterday, I couldn't get him out of my head. I didn't know if it was the way he'd looked, all laid-back and wearing casual clothes in his hotel room, or if it was how he'd opened up to me, but ever since, he'd invaded my brain every time I let my mind wander.

This morning, Helen had been listening to yet another romance audiobook, and my thoughts had me going crazy, so I decided to busy ourselves all the while lightening the atmosphere for the three of us.

Four hours later, and here we were. With everything ready, Helen and I just had to find a hiding place with a good view of the front door and wait for Matthias to come home.

After five minutes, we heard the door unlocking, which made Helen giggle. I pressed my index finger to my own smiling mouth, and she rolled her lips behind her teeth. Then, the door opened large and wide, as if Matthias had pushed it with a bit too much fervor, and it was show time.

"Hey, I'm—"

His sentence was interrupted by a large pot of lime-green slime that emptied all over his head and body. He gasped when the cold goo reached his head, and that was all Helen and I needed to burst out laughing. We couldn't control the tears running down our faces as we looked at the usually chic and tidy man who was covered in green, shock evident on his face.

Wide-eyed and immobile, he gaped at us for what felt like an eternity. When he finally moved, he lifted his hands ever-so-slowly to wipe the slime from his face and shook them once before meeting our eyes.

"You. Are. So. Dead."

Faster than I thought possible, he bolted for us and wrapped me in his arms before I could escape, wiping his sticky arms on my hair and back. I squealed, which got a deep belly laugh out of him. "Less fun when we're the victim, huh?" I could see in his eyes he was trying to keep a straight face. He twirled me around while drenching my clothes in slime, and he eventually cracked up again, joining us in our laughter.

This prank could've gone one of two ways, and I was filled

with relief and giddiness that he'd reacted like I'd hoped he would.

Helen was watching the two of us, still laughing so hard she had a hard time catching her breath. "Oh, you think this is funny, lady?" Matthias uttered. "That you can somehow get away with it and be spared? Oh, I don't think so." Then, he lowered me to the ground before scooping some of the goo that had fallen on the floor and dropping it all over Helen.

She shrieked like I had before, but still didn't stop laughing. There was slime in her hair, on her crisp white blouse, on her chair, but none of us cared. While he gave a big, disgusting hug to Helen, I imitated him and picked some of the leftover slime before I pulled back the collar of his shirt and dropped it on his skin. His back arched, and he turned my way with a look of fierceness in his eyes.

He straightened himself, looking at me sternly. A second passed where both of us breathed hard, and then he was lunging at me. Out of instinct, I ran away, feeling like a rabbit escaping a lion. I succeeded in reaching the kitchen, but before I got the chance to take another step, I got scooped away. I shrieked, kicking at my assailant, to no avail. An instant later, Matthias lowered me to the ground and followed me there. He laid me down in a puddle of cold goo that had surprisingly reached the kitchen, making me scream in laughter, but he didn't stop. Instead, he gathered more slime and dropped some on my face. I tried to fight him off in vain. He jokingly pushed me back down, spreading green on my forehead and cheeks.

I was panting under him, and we kept laughing until his fingers reached my lips. Then, our eyes met, and our smiles slowly died. We could still hear Helen cackling behind us in the foyer, but the only sounds coming from us were shallow breaths. His eyes lowered to my mouth as his index finger traced my bottom lip.

Panting, I let my lips part. I had no idea how we'd gotten in this position, but Matthias was now lying on top of me, his rock-hard body pressed against mine, and I was pretty sure I could feel how being on top of me made him feel. I swallowed, a deep want building in my belly.

He must have noticed how his body had reacted because his eyes averted mine, and he swallowed hard before getting up, leaving me on the floor in a puddle of pleasure, both figuratively and literally.

My Dear,

Ready for your second Helen Advice? This one is probably my favorite.

Never forget to have fun.

Life can get in the way of your happiness so easily, you don't notice it has happened until you can't remember the last time you had a good laugh. And I can't stress enough how important it is to laugh.

Without fun, you'll never find true happiness. You might have all the money in the world, a nice family, and a bunch of cars in the driveway, but you won't have this spark of joy in your heart.

I've had my fair share of gleeful moments in my life, where I laughed until I couldn't breathe and almost peed my pants. Those are the moments I remember now that I know the end is near.

When you are reflecting on your life, you don't remember the times you argued with your loved ones or the time you spent at work. You don't see images of neatly vacuumed floors and perfectly ironed clothes.

You remember the times you couldn't stop cracking up in the back of a classroom. You remember going for a swim in the Atlantic Ocean in May, even though the water is fifty degrees and the bite of the cold on your skin makes you shriek. You remember the time you and your friend dumped a bucket of slime on your son.

Those are the things you remember.

Love,

Helen

10

ADELAIDE

*H*elen was listening out loud to a podcast about the different types of parasites that could lead to bowel obstruction, and I'd tear my ears off if I had to listen to a single second more.

"Hey, I'm going to do some laundry," I said. "Just holler if you need anything."

She nodded once, keeping her eyes closed, her eyebrows slightly kinked, the way they always were when she was focused on something. Turning around, I headed toward the laundry room while selecting an R&B playlist.

Belting out the lyrics to my favorite Beyoncé tune, I started folding clothes and stopped in my tracks when I found an item that definitely didn't belong in Helen's laundry. Chuckling, I snapped a picture and texted it to Matthias.

Me: If I'd had to guess, I wouldn't have pegged you for the pink-boxers-with-yellow-and-green-toucans type of guy. ;)

It didn't take a minute for him to answer.

Matt: I know it's easy to get obsessed with me, but you

didn't need to scavenge for my boxers. I would've given you a pair if you'd asked.

I blushed at his answer. It had been a week since our slimy moment on the floor, and our conversations had been pretty stiff since then. Neither one of us had talked about it again, but it was clear we hadn't forgotten about it either. This was the first time he joked with me again, and my shoulders sagged in relief.

Me: What an inappropriate thing for an employer to say. I won't tolerate this.

I snickered as I pressed send. Coming back to my folding, I rapped with poor skills along with Jay-Z in his verse. The ring of my phone interrupted me before I could finish the song.

"Helloooo?" I answered with a smile after seeing who was calling.

"Are you still home? Have you left? Please tell me you're still there." Matthias' breathing came in pants through the phone, his panic obvious.

"Wait, slow down, what's wrong? What do you mean, have I left?"

"Well, you just… you…" I heard him swallow. "I thought maybe you were mad at me."

"Wha… Oh, Matt, I was joking. I'm sorry, I thought it was obvious." A message blared behind him in a language I didn't recognize. I could imagine him sitting in the coffee shop of an airport in God-knows-where, raking one of his hands through his hair as he held the phone with the other. His silence, coupled with the rhythm of his breathing, meant more than anything he could have said.

"And, even if I was mad, you know I wouldn't just leave, right?" I added.

He sighed and stayed silent for a while, concluding the call with, "Right, okay, thank you." The call disconnected before I had a chance to say anything.

Bringing my phone slowly from my ear to the dryer, I looked at it for a few minutes, not understanding what had just happened. The music continued to surround me, but I wasn't in the mood for it anymore.

As I made my way to the living room, I kept replaying Matthias' reaction in my head. It wasn't the first time we'd joked around together, far from it, but he'd never reacted that way before. The alarm in his voice had reminded me of the first time he'd returned home, when I was alone with Helen after Dora had left. As if all the time we'd spent together—where he'd seen what kind of person I was—meant nothing.

When I pressed pause on Helen's podcast, she opened her eyes and looked at me quizzically.

"Helen, can I ask you a question?" I sat on the couch facing her chair, clasping my hands between my thighs.

"Of course." She moved her chair forward so that we stood eye-to-eye. Her face displayed the same type of worried expression my mom wore when I'd come back from school, heartbroken from a breakup.

"Is there a reason why Matthias is so protective of you?"

She blinked fast.

"I mean," I continued, "not that it isn't a good thing, but I've noticed that he's extremely worried that I won't take good care of you, and I was wondering if there was a reason behind that."

All the blood drained from Helen's face at my words. Her worried expression was gone, replaced by pure distress. She coughed, and swallowed once, twice, thrice, before speaking again. "I don't... I... I think it would be better if you asked M- Matthias about it directly."

A lump took form in my throat. I'd suspected something had happened from Matthias' previous reaction, but Helen's response made me fear things might've been far worse than I'd imagined. I'd never seen Helen look this way, like someone was holding a gun to her temple. It made my skin drench in cold sweat.

I caught her eyes misting before she looked away. Jumping up to hug her, I said, "I'm so sorry for asking. Don't worry, I won't bring it up with you again." She couldn't hug me back, but from the way she nodded her head against my throat and breathed hard on my chest, I figured she would've wanted to.

And it broke my fucking heart.

MATTHIAS

*T*he sun was setting as I parked my Audi in the driveway, creating an aura of pink and marigold above the water behind the cliff. Sunsets had always brought a sense of peace to me. They were constant and repetitive, yet always somehow unique, ending each and every day on a high note. I got out of my car and leaned against the driver's door, looking at the sky and listening to seagulls cawing, until movement coming from the house caught my eye.

Adelaide was standing on the front porch, closing the door behind her. Her hair was loose today, forming a halo of dark curls around her round face. There was no ignoring her curves, even in leggings and an oversized hoodie, which brought my mind back to the time I'd felt her underneath me, all soft skin and shy looks.

Her expression was indiscernible from where I was standing, so I headed her way. As I got closer, the thousand-and-one freckles covering her face came into view. She was glowing in the end-of-day light.

"Hey," I said, a corner of my mouth twitching up.

"Hey. Um, do you mind if we talk here for a second?" She gave me the fakest smile I'd ever seen—which meant something, considering she'd given me millions of those when we'd first met—before sitting down in the highest step of the front porch. I nodded and took a seat facing her, our knees brushing over the cement. I had an idea about what she wanted to talk about, even though I would've preferred to avoid this conversation altogether.

"Look, about earlier, I—"

"What happened?" Her words interrupted mine, and my eyebrows drew together at her question.

"Care to clarify?" I said.

"What happened with Helen that has made you so protective of her?"

Passing a hand through my gelled hair, I sighed. I knew this question would be brought up someday, but I'd hoped it would be brushed off indefinitely. No such luck. Especially with Addy, direct as she was.

"Do you want the short or the long version?" I let out a humorless laugh, but she didn't reciprocate it.

"I want the real version." Her hazel eyes pierced mine.

I couldn't stand it, not sharing the truth. Not when she looked at me like that.

I cleared my throat. "Okay, here goes. So, a year ago, we desperately needed someone to care for Helen for a month or two. One of my, um, lady friends offered to do it, and I accepted." Heat crept up my neck. Talking about my old friend-with-benefits with Addy wasn't something I wanted to be doing, but it was necessary.

Her eyes showed no judgment, only focus and interest.

"Anyway, after she took the job, I didn't want to keep our intimate relationship going—I didn't think it was professional —and I was overseas when I told her." Lifting my hands in front of me, I assured, "I know, I know, it was a dick move. I've changed since then." A side of her lips lifted, but she didn't say anything.

"I was flying back and forth to Japan, with a day in

between the two flights, so I was gone for three days, more or less." Looking at my feet on the lowest step, I continued, "When I came back…" Suddenly, there wasn't enough air around me. I took a big breath, then exhaled through pursed lips. It didn't help. "When I came back, Helen was alone in the house, sitting in a pool of her own urine."

Hearing a gasp, I lifted my gaze to Addy, who was looking at me with eyes wide as saucers, both hands over her mouth.

"She, um, she could barely speak when I found her, her voice so hoarse from crying for help for almost two whole days," I finished before hissing through my teeth. I wasn't a resentful person, but I'd never, ever forget what had happened on that day. The feeling of pure helplessness in her eyes, the tears dried on her cheeks, the guilt that tore through me, and the anger. So much fucking anger.

Addy didn't move, her hands still covering her mouth, but a single tear fell from her eye, and I had to restrain myself not to wipe it with my thumb.

"I tried to take her to court, but we hadn't signed a real contract, so I had no proof that she was supposed to be looking after Helen. We had nothing against her, so we had to drop the charges."

Her mouth opened. "But… But… How…"

My lips thinned. "Yeah, I know."

We stayed silent for a while, until Addy found her voice again. "What's her name?"

"Why?"

"Because I'm going to find and then kill the bitch."

I laughed, even if there was nothing funny about the situation.

"I'm serious! I can't believe someone so disgusting could even exist! I want to strangle her with my bare hands."

Settling my hand on her knee, I gave it a squeeze. "I know you're serious, but it wouldn't be helping anyone to have you in jail."

She groaned, but didn't respond to my comment. Her head turned in the direction of the house, eyes roaming over the bay windows. She seemed lost in her thoughts, which was understandable. This story still sounded like a Stephen King novel to my ears, even after reliving it in my head every day for the past year.

Right as I pushed my hands on the stairs to get up, she jerked in my direction. "Wait, so, if I understand this right, you've been on my back this whole time because...what, because you think I could somehow do the same thing?"

I swallowed. Did I? Maybe?

Not sure of my answer, I kept my mouth shut.

Silence engulfed us for a long moment. Addy kept her eyes on the cement, breathing calmly and nodding. Then, slowly, she stood, fiddling with her hands. When her eyes met mine, they felt like daggers to my soul.

"You may not have meant it that way, but your actions are speaking much louder than your words, and they're telling me you meant it that way in your heart." She took a step away from me.

I stood up. "Wait, Addy, that's not what this is. I just... I..."

"It's okay, Matthias. You can feel whatever you want, and it makes sense that you're still suspicious. It just..." She wiped another tear with the palm of her hand. "It just hurts a little to think that this is the way you see me." She avoided my pleading eyes before swallowing. "I have to go."

I grabbed her forearm. "Please, stay."

Her eyes went from my hand on her arm to my face. "I really have to go."

"Where?" I didn't believe her for a second.

"Church."

I still didn't think she was telling the truth, but when she shrugged out of my grip, I didn't stop her.

You've always taken such good care of me.

I know there have been moments when you've doubted it, but I never did. Not even once.

And do you know why I didn't?

Because I knew you, and I knew your intentions.

Sometimes, the best way to care for someone is to try your best and show them your love and support. The little mistakes don't matter when your intentions are pure. That's one of the things I hope you'll keep in mind when you read this letter again. I never could've faulted you for the tiny things that might have or have gone wrong, not with the way I knew you always wanted the best for me.

This applies not only to giving physical care for someone — which I hope with all my heart you won't have to do again in your life — but to everything in life. If you give it your all and try your best, the people you love won't remember the mistake, but the effort you made to prevent it or to right your wrongs.

I guess that makes Helen Advice number three? Try your best, admit your mistakes when you make them, and focus on all the good you do rather than on the tiny faults you commit along the way.

Love,

Helen

11

ADELAIDE

"*H*ey Dad, I found something you might find interesting."

Turning his head in my direction at a snail's pace, his empty eyes met mine before he gave me an equally empty smile. "What's that, honey?"

I sat beside him, opening the ad I'd just seen on my Facebook feed. "Look, they're looking for a cook at the Seaside Inn. Wouldn't you like to apply for it?"

When I'd read the ad, I'd been filled with a newfound faith. Memories of the old version of my dad had flooded my head, making me think this was exactly what he needed to get back to himself.

As I entered the motel's kitchen, aromas of maple syrup and pancakes, of eggs mixed with everything bagel spices — my father's secret recipe — and of freshly pressed oranges filled my nostrils, making me hum in pleasure.

I navigated between the industrial ovens, dishwashers, and cooks to find my father hunched over a counter, whisking a weird-looking brown batter, his eyes focused on the task at hand. So focused, in fact, that he didn't notice me until I snuck behind him and poked him in the flank. He yelped and dropped his whisk in the metal bowl in front of me, a hand clutching his chest. "Jesus, Addy, you scared the living daylights out of me!"

I leaned forward and kissed his cheek. "Nice to see you too, Dad."

He chuckled before returning to his whisking. "You got here just in time, honey. I've been trying to hone this zucchini bread recipe for a while now and I think I've just mastered it."

I made a face, but before I had time to utter my disgust, he shoved a spoon in my mouth.

I tasted the batter reluctantly, but my eyes widened when I took in the sweetness and delicate spices of it. This didn't taste like zucchini at all.

"Oh my God, Dad, this is amazing!"

He smirked with a wink. "I know. That's why your mom always calls me her favorite chef."

I looked at him with an expectant smile, thinking this was the moment. With this job, my dad would be my dad again.

But all my hope died when his own face fell as I spoke.

In a monotone voice, he said, "Uh, yeah, maybe. I might look into it." Breaking our eye contact, he let himself fall down to his side so he'd be looking at the television lying on the couch.

I exhaled loudly, but didn't say anything else. It wouldn't lead anywhere. Allowing myself to watch him for a second, I rubbed his back. He might've been a remnant of the man he used to be, but he was still my father, and there were few things I wanted more than for him to get back on his feet and look happy again.

As I got up to put some music on in the kitchen, three knocks sounded from the front door. I wasn't expecting anyone, but it might've been Mrs. Zhu asking me to watch Josh. I opened the door with a grin, which dropped slightly when I realized Matthias was the one standing in front of me. Wearing a powder blue polo shirt and beige corduroy pants, he looked more handsome than ever. My heart rate sped up as I took him in, which was a bad sign. I was *not* supposed to be feeling these belly flutters when looking at my boss. Especially after I'd learned about his still-present trust issues with me. It wasn't like I didn't understand where his reluctance came from, but it still stung a lot to know he didn't see now how much I loved Helen and this job.

And anyway, what was he doing here? Had I somehow messed up my schedule and missed work?

"Hi." His smile was breathtaking. That was the only way to describe how it looked and how it made me feel.

"Hey. Is something wrong?"

He winced, his happy expression disappearing before he forced it back on. "No, not at all. Actually, I—"

"Wait, who's with Helen?" I asked.

"Dora. I called her this morning."

"So—"

We both glanced behind me when we heard Louis rushing in our direction. "Matthias!"

Matthias' smile was real this time as he crouched in front of Louis and me to give him a high-five. "Hey, buddy, how's it going?"

"So good! I was preparing a circuit for Marie Antoinette and Thomas Jefferson's competition. Wanna come see?" Louis grabbed his hand, but Matthias didn't budge, laughing instead.

"Actually, I had other plans in mind for the both of us." He poked my brother in the arm. "How would you feel about going to see a *real* plane?" He lifted his head to look at me. "If your sister agrees, of course."

Louis gasped and started jumping around. "Yes! Yes! Please, Addy, please, please, please."

I wanted to say something, but I was speechless. He'd come all the way here to take my little brother to a plane during what I assumed was his day off?

I didn't think this man could still surprise me, yet he kept doing so.

I usually wouldn't let Louis go anywhere with anyone other

than me or Mrs. Zhu, but I'd seen how well Matthias took care of his mother. Louis couldn't be in better hands.

After a moment, I realized both boys were looking at me expectantly. "Um, sure. Sure! Here, Louis, grab your coat. It's still cold outside." Focusing on Louis, I put his bright yellow windbreaker on his shoulders. "You be nice with Matthias, okay?" I kissed his cheek as he nodded.

"Don't worry. I'll take good care of him." Matthias' voice felt like honey, so thick and sweet.

Louis turned to me and gave me a confused look. "But why aren't you coming too?"

I took a step back. "Oh no, I have things to do here."

Of course, Louis wasn't having it. "No, please come with us," he begged, using his best weapon: the sad puppy eyes.

Matthias shrugged, smothering a grin. "You can't say no to that face." He winked at Louis, who shook his head.

I knew what the two of them were doing, and damn me, it was working.

"All right," I conceded before putting on my shoes. Beside me, two hands clapped together.

Once I got back up, I finally met Matthias' gaze, and my breath caught in my throat as I saw the expression on his face. It was full of tenderness.

Looking back down at my shoes, I said, "Okay, well, let's go!"

My heart had no right twisting like it did when I watched Matthias put his arm around my brother's shoulders, leading him outside.

*L*ouis was having the time of his life.

I settled in the co-pilot seat while my brother sat where the pilot would, making gun sounds as he fake-steered the yoke. He might have been confusing airplanes and spaceships, but I wasn't about to ruin his fun.

Matthias had spent thirty minutes showing Louis how all the buttons and machines worked before leaving to do something in the back of the plane. We were now alone in the cockpit, and I had to admit, Louis wasn't the only one impressed.

At the speed of light, my brother brought one of his chubby hands to the buttons in front of him, which I luckily stopped in its tracks. Matthias was a fool if he believed Louis would stay seated without touching anything in the cockpit.

"When I grow up," Louis started, hands back on the yoke, "I want to be a pilot just like Matthias."

"Yeah?" I couldn't help the smile splitting my face.

"Yes. This way, I can play in Galileo all the time."

"Galileo?"

"The plane," Matthias said from behind us, making me jump. I turned around to find him leaning against the doorway to the cockpit as if he'd been spying on us for minutes. He was unable to hide his grin. I returned it to him before looking at my excited little brother.

"I'm so glad you're having fun," I stated. Getting up, I hugged my brother and took a big inhale of his citrus soap and unique Louis smell. He tolerated it for only a second before pushing me away.

"Let me go, I have a mission to finish here!"

I'd never get this kid. "Okay, you rude boy, go ahead and continue. I'll be right behind you with Matthias." Before turning, I added, "Don't touch anything!"

He nodded and looked ahead of him, resuming his pistol sounds.

I walked to the back and joined the man who confused me to no end. Matthias was still leaning against the door, arms crossed in front of him, making his biceps bulge. I'd never given it much attention before, but his body was sculpted to a

T, with broad shoulders and a lean chest. It was much more obvious in his polo shirt than in his loose-fitting work shirts.

I stepped forward to be closer to him, speaking low to keep our conversation privy from a little boy's ears. "Thank you for bringing us. I… I really appreciate you taking the time to do this for him."

One side of his lips went up. "It's a pleasure." He then took a step to reduce the distance between us even more. "And, I owed you." His right hand went up and softly touched mine. "My words got mixed up yesterday, and I'm sorry if they hurt you. It wasn't my intention. I do trust you, Addy."

I released a shuddered breath as his thumb stroked the back of my hand. A simple caress that was enough to make my whole body erupt in goosebumps.

"Thank you. That means a lot to me." I looked at our feet, mine in used sneakers, his in freshly polished leather loafers. "And I guess I overreacted anyway. You had every right to be wary."

"Well, I'm not anymore."

I lifted my eyes back to his, finding that they were not black after all. From up close, it was actually possible to discern the deep chocolate of his irises from the ebony of his pupils. His lashes were impossibly long, and I found myself wondering for a second how they would feel against my skin.

He leaned forward, and I caught my breath, my heart coming to a halt in my chest. But instead of leaning toward my mouth, he pressed his lips to my cheek before taking a step back and leaving to join Louis.

The whole thing had lasted less than a second, but I'd felt it *everywhere*.

*L*ifting the covers to his chin, I finished singing Louis' favorite Ed Sheeran ballad. His eyes were closed, and I thought the song had done the job, but as soon as I lifted myself from his mattress, his brown gaze caught mine. "Addy?"

"Yes, Lou?" I sat back down next to him on his twin bed and brushed brown strands of hair away from his forehead. He crossed his arms over his bedspread, which made me realize his Spider-Man pajamas were becoming tight for him. My little brother was getting older, no matter how much I wished he'd stay this young forever.

Louis' head tilted to the side. "When are you getting married?"

I lifted both eyebrows. "What do you mean?"

He rolled his eyes like this was the most stupid question he'd ever heard. "You and Matt, when are you getting married?"

I choked on my own saliva, coughing and laughing inside my elbow at the same time. "Never? We're not even together! Why would you ask that?"

He yawned and closed his eyes before turning his back to me. I thought this was it, but as I got up again, he floored me with his answer.

"Because he looks at you the way Daddy used to look at Mommy."

I opened my mouth and closed it repeatedly, unable to find the right words. Matthias didn't look at me like that. I would've noticed if he did.

But, as I walked toward the bedroom door, there was still something about Louis' words that sparked a feeling in my chest. I didn't know if it was hope, or lust, or want, but it was there.

Turning off the light, I said, "Goodnight, Lou."

When I was a little girl, my daddy used to say, "You'll never get any fish if you don't put your hook in the water." I don't know if he heard it from somewhere, or if the quote came from his own mind. He was a fisherman to his core, after all.

You've never had the chance to meet him—he died when I was seventeen—but I'm sure you would've loved him. He was one of the best men I've ever known. He was also the smartest and wisest person I've met in my life. I've learned in all the years I've lived that all he ever said to me was true. He taught me everything I know, and so I hope you learn from him too, even if only through me.

You'll never get what you want if you don't work for it. Nothing in this world comes for free, and the best thing you can do for yourself is work your butt off for what you believe in. Fight, tooth and nail, for the people you love.

That makes Helen Advice number four, although it's mostly Gerald Advice number one. And remember: Gerald was always right.

Love,

Helen

12

MATTHIAS

"*H*ey, what are you doing for the rest of the night?"
Rosalie lifted her brows in expectation as we
headed out of the plane into the Frankfurt airport. The click of
her heels resonated all through the passage around us,
reminding me of a metronome.

"Um…" I cleared my throat, not sure what words were the
right ones to use.

She smiled and nudged me with her shoulder. "Hey, I
didn't mean it in that way. I was talking about drinks at the
airport bar."

I exhaled in relief and let out a small laugh. Tonight was the
first time I was alone with Rosalie for a long period of time—
except while flying—since I'd turned her down a month ago.
I'd been afraid things would be awkward between the two of
us, but she was cool enough not to make it so. We'd both been
aware this thing between us wasn't serious, so there was no
reason for her to be mad at me. Still, I was glad she was so
casual about it.

"Yeah, okay, sure," I said.

We made our way to the bar closest to the airport hotel and
grabbed metal stools at the modern granite counter. Blue and

red lights shone through the room, as if trying to create a nightclub ambiance. I'd never been one to visit those kinds of places, but even I knew the attempt was a fail.

I lifted two fingers at the barman. "Two whiskeys on ice, please." The middle-aged man nodded before turning around to prepare the drinks. Rosalie liked her drinks straight like I did. Once they were set before us, she and I clinked them in cheers.

After taking a sip, she asked, "So, who's the lucky girl?"

I choked on my drink. "What? What do you mean?"

"Come on, Matt," she said, rolling her blue-green eyes before she gave me a dazzling smile. "We've known each other for so long. You can tell me. I've never heard you refuse sex before, so I assume there's a girl behind this."

She wasn't angry, I could see it in her eyes. And she was right, we'd been friends for a long time. More than eight years, to be exact; ever since we'd met at the same flight school. She knew about the few girls I'd dated through the years and I knew all about her divorce. You get a lot of opportunities to talk when you share an enclosed space with someone for so many hours... Well, she chatted. I mostly listened.

I sighed before downing my drink, wincing at the burn of the alcohol coating my throat. I lifted my hand to the barman, asking for two more. "I don't even know if there *is* something happening. There might be a girl, but I'm not sure what I feel for her, or if she feels something for me. And, anyway, it could never happen."

Rosalie tossed her red curls behind her shoulder. "And why is that?"

"Because she's my mother's caregiver."

She leaned back, nodding. "Ah, so you're afraid what happened with Krystal will happen again if you date her and decide to go your separate ways."

I shook my head. "No... No, that's not even it. She's so

different from Krystal, they can't even be compared. She's compassionate, and kind, and funny, and—"

"So what's stopping you, if you don't think anything bad could happen?"

I unbuttoned the top of my shirt, tugging at the neck of my undershirt. Was it just me, or was it really fucking hot in here?

"I didn't say nothing bad could happen, I said she wouldn't do what Krystal did," I replied, voice low. "But, things could still get messy if we had something going on. She's my employee, and bosses should not date their employees. It's a known fact." I took a sip of my freshly-served drink. "Anyway, as I said, I don't even know if there *is* something going on between us."

She laughed in her glass. "The fact that you're even wondering about it tells me there's definitely something going on."

I groaned, passing a hand through my hair.

"But," she continued, "you do well taking your time to figure things out before rushing into something you're not prepared for. Wouldn't want to end up like me, thirty years old and divorced."

I nudged her with my elbow. "Oh, come on. We both know as soon as you put yourself out there again, there'll be a line of men and women waiting to take you out."

She huffed before finishing what was left of her first whiskey. "Speaking of dating, are you coming to Alejandro's wedding in three weeks? I could sure use a wingman."

"You got it." I smirked at her before clinking my glass with hers again. She took a big gulp before her phone started blaring a funky tune. She looked at it and rolled her eyes. "Sorry, I gotta take this." I nodded and watched her walk away to a quieter corner of the bar.

She really was a beautiful woman. She had curves for days, a great sense of style, and a killer smile. But, whereas before, I wanted her, *craved* the touch of her milky skin on my fingers, now, I felt nothing but friendship when looking at her. And if I was being honest with myself, it was pretty fucking scary.

ADELAIDE

*H*elen and I were both humming the notes of an old Céline Dion song as I curled the ends of her silky blond hair. It reminded me of a time when I used to do the same thing, except the hair was espresso-colored then. When my mom's illness had progressed and she had become bedridden, she said there was nothing she could do about her sickness, but she still had control over other things, her image being one of them.

"I-I love how you d-d-do it. It looks good," Helen said.

"Yeah, it does." I forced a smile on my face, hoping my eyes didn't betray me. She was struggling a lot today, even more than most days. Her legs had been stiffer than usual when I'd stretched them, and she had difficulty getting the words out. But that didn't stop her from trying again and smiling through the hardship.

The song on the bathroom speaker changed to Taylor Swift's "Soon You'll Get Better," and a lump formed in my throat when I listened to the lyrics. Curling one of the last straight strands around the iron, I chewed on my cheek.

"Helen, can I ask you a question?"

Her eyes lit up. "Always."

I'd been wondering about this for a while now, but failed to ask about it every time I had the opportunity. This was it, though. As my mom used to say, 'there's no moment like the present.'

"How does it feel to be sick as a doctor?"

She smiled, her eyes crinkling as they looked at me in the

mirror. "That's a hard one to answer because knowing exactly w-what is happening to me is b-both a blessing and a c-curse."

I nodded, continuing to curl her hair so she didn't feel like I was staring at her.

"Because of my knowledge, I d-don't have to live in the dark like some patients do. But, a-at the same time, I know the e-exact sequence of the functions I have lost, and the f-f-functions I have yet to lose. I know how this ends, and I know everything th-that will happen to me until then." She sighed, her eyes clouding. "When I think about it too much, I can practically see the p-pathology slides showing my f-failing neurons. I can see the edema forming in my l-legs and imagine the sores f-forming on my skin."

She looked at me and smiled sadly, making me realize I had stopped curling her hair and was now focused entirely on her, my mouth slightly open.

"I'd like to have the b-b-blissful ignorance some patients have. When I was p-practicing, I would tell some patients that their t-treatments were only palliative, and sometimes they w-w-would convince themselves that the treatments would actually c-cure them, that they were the one-in-a-million. At times, I'm jealous of their h-hope."

Helen turned her wheelchair around, facing me. I put the curling iron down on the counter and sat on the edge of the claw foot bathtub. "I know my d-disease is progressing, and it's progressing fast. I'm a-aware the end isn't too far away."

The lump in my throat tripled in size at her words. "No, Helen, please don't say things like that." The thought of losing her was almost unbearable.

Her eyes were both comforting and sad. "It's true, Addy. I know it, and y-you know it. It's inevitable, and at the rate the d-disease is advancing, I can tell you my time isn't counted in y-years anymore."

I choked on a sob and leaned forward, grabbing both of Helen's hands in mine. She gave me a reassuring smile, which was ironic, considering she was the one who was sick. "There's nothing we can do about it e-except prepare for when it happens. And, I'm r-really happy you brought this up today because I actually have a f-favor to ask you."

I nodded vigorously. "Anything."

I know you haven't always understood my choices. Sometimes, you wished I would have made different decisions, but still somehow supported me, and I thank you for it.

You'll realize as you grow old that the choices you have to make keep piling up, just as they get harder and harder to make. Maybe when you're my age, you'll understand more of the decisions I've made.

Sometimes, there are no right and wrong choices. You have to choose the lesser of two evils, knowing that whatever you decide, hearts will break.

Know that through all the time we spent together, it has never been my intention to hurt you with my choices. And, if it ever happened in the process, I deeply apologize. Loving you sometimes made it harder to come to a resolution.

Love,
Helen

13

ADELAIDE

*H*elen had been staring at the chessboard for the past five minutes, eyes narrowed and roaming from piece to piece. With a yawn, I leaned backward on my chair and crossed my hands behind my head.

After an eternity, she lifted her eyes at me and smirked. "Move my queen forward three spaces."

I followed the movement her piece would make with my eyes and sighed. "Ah, crap." As I moved her queen in the direction she told me to, my phone vibrated on the dining table, its screen brightening the dimly-lit room. Spring had started giving its place to summer, but today's gloomy temperature reminded me of early April days in Maine.

Matt: Picking up Helen's favorite clam chowder for dinner. Want some?

Gagging internally, I picked up the phone.

Me: Would've loved to stay with you two, but I hate seafood with every fiber of my being.

I stared at the screen, waiting for his answer, but after three minutes, I figured he wouldn't text back. Dropping the phone on my thighs, I returned my focus to the pieces in front of me. I sucked at chess, and I had even less of a chance of beating Helen if I wasn't fully concentrated on the game.

After twenty minutes of headache-inducing focus, Helen said the word that brought me to my demise. "Checkmate."

I let my head drop on the table, cursing myself for my poor last move. When I looked back at her, she was grinning like crazy. "Good game, Chess Master," I said.

"What can I say, we can't all have my incredible talent."

"Yeah, right," I answered with a wink.

The sound of the front door opening and closing made us both look in the direction of the entryway to the kitchen where Matthias appeared a few seconds later, raindrops covering his beige trench coat and dark hair.

"Hey you," I said, but my greeting went unanswered. Instead, Matthias stormed in my direction, carrying two white plastic bags in his hands. After putting them down in front of me with a bang, he leaned over the table and drilled through me with his eyes. I lifted both eyebrows, waiting to hear what all of this was about.

"How can you call yourself a New Englander and not like seafood? What kind of blasphemy is this?"

Helen and I both burst out laughing. "That's why you're acting all caveman-like? Because I don't eat seafood?" I grinned again, and a corner of his lips went up, even if he looked like he was trying hard to smother his smile.

"As I said, you can't be born in Maine and not like seafood. It's just not possible."

I huffed. "Well, smartass, if you have to know, I moved to Maine when I was fourteen. I wasn't even born in the U.S., if that helps you make more sense of this culinary taste situation."

His eyebrows drew together as he took a step back.

"What? Where are you from then?" Helen's face was bearing the same confusion.

"I was born in Montreal, Canada. We moved to the States when my parents decided to make their dream come true and open their motel." I chuckled. "Why are you looking at me like that? I told you about this."

"Yeah, you told me you moved, but not from another country! I thought you were from New Hampshire or something like that."

"I can't believe we've been together most days for the last two-and-a-half months and I didn't know about this," Helen said.

I shrugged. "Never came up, I guess."

She closed an eye and looked up, thinking. "Wait, so if you're from Montreal, does that mean you speak French?"

"Bien sûr que oui, je parle français. Quoique je suis un peu rouillée." *Of course, I speak French. Although, I'm a bit rusty.*

Matthias' lips parted as he gazed at me in a way that made me blush. I looked away as fast as I'd met his eyes.

"My mom was the francophone in the family," I said. "My dad mostly spoke English, so I haven't practiced my French since she died." The few times I'd spoken *Frenglish* with Stella didn't count.

Helen moved her chair closer to me. "Maybe you could try to do it with your father. He might enjoy it." She gave me a smile, which I tried to return as genuinely as possible.

"I'm not sure he'd like the memory. He always shuts me down when I talk about her."

"Well, if you ever want to talk about her with someone, I'm all ears," Helen said.

Matthias grazed my back with his hand. "Same for me." A shiver ran down my spine, and I had no idea if it was because of his words or his brief touch.

"Thanks, guys." It had started to smell like clams in the

room, and I again repressed a gag. "I'll leave you two to it. I have a little guy who's probably famished at home."

I turned around to leave when Matthias called, "Wait."

He stepped beside me, extending one of the two plastic bags he was carrying when he came in. "It's minestrone. There's enough for Louis and your dad too."

How could my stomach twist like that with such mundane words? I stared at him for a second. This was so...nice. There was no other way to put it.

Helen interrupted my thoughts by wheeling her chair toward the dining room and saying, "Tell your family I said hi!"

Matthias gazed at me for a moment longer before he said, "Me too." He followed Helen.

"Sure will," I muttered once alone in the kitchen.

*T*he next day, I arrived at work a bit early, and the moment I opened the front door, the sound of a piano melody wrapped me up like a hand-knitted blanket on a cold autumn morning. Stepping inside the house and quietly removing my Chucks, I followed the music through the house. It led me to what I'd assumed was Matthias' study.

Taking soft steps, I approached the thankfully-opened door. Once I could see inside, I leaned against the hallway wall and let myself take in what I was seeing and hearing.

Matthias was playing on a glossy black grand piano, dressed in a charcoal V-neck t-shirt and sweatpants. His hair was mussed, strands pointing in every direction, a slight curl in them. He was so rarely dressed casually, it did things to me every time. My belly clenched as I looked at him swaying to the music, eyes closed, completely entranced by the melody.

I might've been entranced by the music too.

He was mesmerizing. He'd never told me he played the piano, but at that moment, he was doing more than playing. He was *feeling* the music, pure and simple. The ballad he was executing was slow and melancholic, and the way he moved his head to the rhythm told me this song spoke to him on a personal level.

"Hey Addy, I didn't know you were here already!" Helen said from behind me.

The harsh squeak of a surprised pianist caused me to jump, just as Matt's head whipped around. I tried to escape his scrutiny, but it was too late. I'd been caught. Still, I took a step back, but my movements were too fast, too rushed. My socks slid on the freshly-waxed floor, and before I could react, I was looking at the built-in lights of the ceiling.

"Oh God, Addy!" Helen yelled behind me as I realized I was draped on the hardwood floor. And as soon as I wrapped my head around what had just happened, I burst out laughing, not able to stop thinking about how ridiculous I must have looked, secretly listening to someone playing, then getting caught and falling on my ass while trying to escape.

Once my laughter died down and I opened my eyes again, I saw Matthias leaning above me, unable to keep his grin away. This was the second time I was on my back on the floor of his house in too brief an amount of time for it to be considered normal. He held out his hand, which I took. Helping me get back on my feet, he teased, "Enjoying the show, were we?"

He knew I was embarrassed, and he was making the most of it. Jerk. Still, I couldn't stop myself from smiling when I looked at him. He might have been a jerk, but he was a cute jerk.

"How could I not? You were so good." He might have been joking earlier, but I was fully serious now. He was amazing.

"Thank you. Mendelssohn is my favorite to play when I have the time."

"You're one to talk about secret talents. I might be able to speak French, but this?" I pointed to the piano inside the room. "This is on a whole other level."

He smirked. "I'm full of secrets." With a wink, he added, "Who knows, maybe one day you'll learn a few."

I inhaled sharply as my lungs tightened. I wasn't sure about it before, but now I knew. I *wanted* to learn all those secrets. I wanted to know him like I knew myself. I wanted to be close to him, to *feel* close to him.

What I was feeling might have been more than a simple crush after all.

I've always been so proud of your talents.

    Maybe I was biased, considering I loved you more than I did the rest of the population, but I always thought you had something special, something extra that others simply didn't. I still do, you know. Today has been a rough day, I won't lie. But, thinking about all the times you've taken my breath away with your prowess has helped me get through it.

    Even when I try long and hard to think about it, I can count on my hand the number of people who impress me like you do. It's like whatever you try, you excel at it. And, even when you don't, you make the best of the situation and still impress me through your humbleness.

    Basically, all of this is to say that I'm your biggest fan.

    Now, don't let all of this get to your head. I wouldn't want to be responsible for your too big of an ego.

    Love,
    Helen

14

MATTHIAS

"*Y*ou look amazing, honey."

I tightened the black satin bow tie around my neck as my mom looked at me in the mirror. Dipping my head in thanks, I turned around and leaned on the bathroom counter to face her.

"So, do y-you have a date for the night?" Helen gave me a smile, but there was no denying she appeared tired. Her eyes were underlined by dark bags, even though she was napping more than ever.

I shook my head, pushing the negative thoughts away. There was no use in focusing on this. She was okay. She was good.

"No, I'm going solo. Meeting colleagues there."

"And is there a reason why you didn't invite Addy?"

I rolled my eyes. "Why would I have invited her?"

"Oh, please Matthias, I might be old, but I'm not stupid."

I raised my eyebrows at her in questioning.

"You think I h-h-haven't noticed how you act around her? How I've seen you smile more in the past three months than in the last five years?"

I swallowed roughly and turned around to comb my hair

for the fifth time. She had a point, but there was no use in acknowledging it. We couldn't afford to lose an aide—not one this good. Even if I did possibly have feelings for Addy, I wouldn't act upon them and risk everything, so what was the use in saying it out loud?

"You know, Matt, I wouldn't be mad if you w-wanted to be with her. On the contrary, I'd be happy t-to know you'd have someone there for you once I'm gone."

I spun on my heels. "Oh, come on, Helen. Don't say things like that when you're not going anywhere."

She moved her chair forward, getting closer to where I was standing. "Matt, please, you know that—"

"I have to go. Dora will stay with you until I come back." I'd asked Addy, but she'd said she was busy tonight. I gave my mom a kiss on the cheek before heading out.

"You need to wrap your head around it, Matt," she shouted behind me.

I was already too far gone to answer that I never would.

ADELAIDE

*C*hewing the skin on the side of my thumb, I looked up and repeated in my head the order of the songs we were going to perform.

I wasn't usually like that before singing, but we'd had to change the whole set list twelve hours ago—thanks to the bride's last-minute change of heart—and we'd barely had an hour to practice the new songs together. Needless to say, I was a jittery mess.

"You're gonna be fine," Benjamin said as he laid a hand on my shoulder. I nodded and forced a smile, which probably looked fake. He returned to his place beside Gabrielle, smiling, and he whispered something in her ear. She giggled.

Looking down, I smoothed my three-quarter length burgundy dress, the feeling of the tulle skirt under my fingers soothing the urge to touch my hair again. My curls had a mind of their own today, and even though I'd tried hard to tame them, nothing had worked.

Benjamin looked down at his wristwatch before saying, "It's almost five. We should get set, the bride's coming in soon."

I nodded again, and we moved from the small underground room where we'd been practicing to the front of the beautiful church, Benjamin with his cello, Gabrielle with her violin. The walls and ceiling were covered in paintings, golds and blues intertwining, creating the most beautiful of backdrops for the ceremony.

As soon as we took our place, I looked down at my black heels, focusing on my breathing. Singing was usually the one thing that could calm me down, but today, it was the opposite.

From the corner of my eyes, I followed the priest as he made his way to the front of the church. Once he was set in position, he said in his microphone, "All rise for the bride."

Beside me, Benjamin whispered, "Five, six, seven, eight," before they started playing, the music acting like a balm on my nervous heart. The bride had asked to walk down the aisle to "Can't Help Falling in Love" playing in the background.

The doors to the church opened at the same time as I started singing, lifting my head to see the audience and the bride come in. I glanced through the guests, my attention never staying anywhere for longer than a second.

And then, ink eyes.

My own gaze flicked back. Had I imagined it?

But no. There, in the audience, was Matthias, his gaze focused on mine. He was sitting in the third row, right in front of me, dressed in a white shirt and classic black tuxedo, looking even more heavenly than usual.

I could see the bride walking down the aisle in a magnificent satin gown, but I couldn't bring my focus to her, no matter how hard I tried. Matthias wouldn't look away, and I wouldn't either. While the two-hundred-something pairs of eyes in the room were set on the glowing bride, his was on me.

There was surprise in his expression, but also so much reverence. I knew I was a good singer; I'd been ever since my mom had made me sing along to kids' songs with her. But, with the way he was looking at me, I didn't just feel good. I felt *prodigious*.

And so, for the next minute and a half, I sang to him about the impossibility of not falling in love with someone.

I'd never sang anything truer.

*T*released a quiet moan as I took a bite of the piece of red velvet cake sitting on my gold-rimmed plate. I'd been singing almost non-stop for the past four hours, and I didn't think I could've spent another five minutes standing in these heels.

As I leaned forward for another divine bite, two hands landed on my bare shoulders, making me squeal in surprise as warm breath tickled my ear. "Hey you."

I turned around with a grin, and there he was. He'd removed his tuxedo jacket during the evening and had rolled the sleeves of his white dress shirt, exposing corded forearms that made every part of my body tingle.

He pulled on the back of the chair next to mine and sat. "So, that's what you meant when you said you were going to church."

I smirked and brought the fork to my lips to hide the red rising to my cheeks. Putting a hand in front of my full mouth, I answered, "Was I not in a church earlier today?"

Chuckling, he slipped his hands into his pockets. "I suppose you got me there."

I winked. "I'm a woman of many talents."

"That, you are." He grinned at me, and I found myself getting lost in the darkness of his eyes, just like he seemed to be in the green of mine. We'd been stealing glances all night, but this was the first time we were this close, and it made my blood run hotter than it ever had.

I cleared my throat. "I assume you're friends with the groom? It took me a whole hour to make the connection."

"Yeah, he's a colleague of mine." He scratched his neck. "You were absolutely fabulous out there. I can't believe you've never told me you sing."

"Just like you forgot to mention you play the piano like Mozart?"

He rolled his eyes.

Since our set had ended, the music had started coming from the DJ's booth at the front of the large conference-space-turned-ballroom. He was currently playing soft ballads and a few couples had joined the new husband and wife on the dance floor to slow dance.

I brought my eyes to my cake, taking a third delicious bite, and when I looked up, I found myself under Matthias' scrutiny again. It was like his eyes were an inferno, and I was a moth drawn to the flames.

I swallowed roughly and took a sip of water. Before I'd even had the time to put the glass back down on the table, Matthias' chair was scraping against the beige tiled floor. He was suddenly standing, looking down at me with an extended hand. "Dance with me?"

MATTHIAS

*T*had no idea why I'd just done that.

Actually, that wasn't true. I knew exactly what had forced the words out of my mouth. She was so adorable, taking the most ginormous bites of cake for such a small person. And simply put, I hadn't been able to keep my eyes off her ever since she'd appeared on the side stage at the front of the church earlier today.

The way that dress looked on her, hugging her chest in all the right places and showcasing her never-ending legs... I'd never known I had a thing for legs until I'd seen her standing there. Her eyelids were subtly lined with black, and her hair was loose and curly and wild. I loved it.

So when I got the chance to get close to her for a few minutes, even if it was in the context of a dance, I took it.

She looked at me with wide eyes before letting out a chuckle. "This might be hard to believe, but I'm a horrible dancer."

"Oh, really? From what I recall, you seemed *extremely* steady on your feet a few days ago when I caught you sneaking up on me."

"Prick," she said as she took my hand, grinning.

I led her to the black-and-white checkered dance floor. Once I let go of her hand, my heart started racing. How would she want us to dance? Was she the 'hands on shoulders' type of person?

She didn't let me question this for too long, right away wrapping her hands around my neck and bringing her chest and hips flush to mine. I exhaled through pursed lips as I softly laid my hands on her hips. With her heels on, her head reached my shoulders, her mouth at the level of my neck. Behind her, I caught Rosalie giving me two thumbs-ups before she reached the dance floor with a woman I'd never seen before.

Addy and I had joined in the middle of a song, so once the closing chords melted away, we didn't let each other go. In the brief moment of silence between songs, she leaned her head on my shoulder, her stomach inching even closer to mine, and I had to focus not to let my body react to hers being so close. It had been embarrassing enough for me to get a boner during the slime incident. No need for a repeat.

As the next song started, she tensed beneath my fingers, gasping close to my ear. She stopped dancing for an instant, then went back to swaying her hips to the rhythm, as if nothing had happened. I pulled back a bit to look at her face.

"What's wrong?"

She shook her head too vigorously for it to be natural. "Nothing."

I dipped my chin down, gazing at her with a raised eyebrow. "Addy, tell me."

She sighed, then continued dancing for a few moments before answering. "It's just... This was a special song for my parents."

I looked up, focusing on what was playing. Recognizing Ben E. King's "Stand by Me," I asked, "Wanna tell me about it?"

She dipped her head for a while, as if fixated on her shoes. The song continued to play around us, and for maybe the first time in my life, I focused on the lyrics. When Addy brought her gaze back to mine, it was troubled.

"My mother... She loved music. I know that's something everyone says, but for her, it was different. It was part of her being. She needed it to function like she needed air to breathe." Her voice was soft, almost airy. "And, there were a few songs that had extra special meaning to her. She had this one Cyndi Lauper song that made her laugh every single time she heard it. She never told me what was funny about it though. When I'd ask, she'd just shrug and snicker by herself."

I chuckled when I remembered the one time I'd come inside the house and seen Addy snapping her fingers to the rhythm of a pop song. She probably had no idea just how similar she was to her mother. How special she was too.

"And, this one," she continued as she pointed to the ceiling, "was another one of those special songs. It was the first song she and my father danced to at a high school dance. And so, they had this kind of unwritten rule that whenever it started to play, they had to drop whatever it was they were doing and dance to it together." She beamed at me. "It didn't matter if they were working in the garden, or shopping at the mall, or cooking dinner. They'd just stop and dance for a while."

"Your parents seemed like a great couple," I said.

The grin she gave me was bittersweet. "The greatest."

She took in a big breath, the smile disappearing from her face. "But, now that she's gone, my father doesn't get up to dance anymore. He doesn't even react to the song, like it never meant anything to him."

She leaned her head back down on my shoulder, and I brought my hands from her hips to her back, giving it soft strokes. I closed my eyes and we continued to dance, listening to the ending of the song.

As I held her between my arms, it dawned on me: I wanted that type of love for her. I had no idea if she'd had boyfriends before, or if she'd ever been in love, but I wanted her to feel it. I wanted her to have it all.

"I don't think it could ever mean nothing to him," I whispered on the top of her head. "Maybe that's just the only way he's found to make the pain lessen."

As we finished dancing, she pulled back from me and climbed on her tiptoes. My breath hitched in my throat when she seemed to hesitate, her lips so damn close to mine. I exhaled—in relief or in fury, I wasn't sure—when they landed on my jaw before she headed back to her table.

I'd join her later, but I needed a minute to cool down. Making my way to the bar, I ordered a whiskey on ice.

As I downed my drink, I found myself thinking I could understand her father. This moment we'd just shared would forever be embedded in my mind. And if I knew I'd never see Addy again, there would be no listening to that song without feeling my stomach twist in pain.

I don't think I've ever told you about the one and only time I've been in love.

It was brief, but it meant everything to me. My heart had never felt fuller than in the months we were together.

You probably remember the stories I told you about the two years I spent working in India. What you don't know, though, is the story of how I met the one person who stole my heart. Prisha.

She was beautiful, her ebony hair shining in the sun like a black diamond and her eyes a warm brown, like the purest of dark chocolate. And she made me laugh. Oh, did she make me laugh. We met in the clinic I worked in during my first year with Doctors Without Borders and spent almost all our time together. She was my best friend. She was also the person who made me realize what I felt for men was nowhere close to what I felt for her.

I'm sorry to tell you this story doesn't have a happy ending. At the time, I was too afraid to admit what it was I was feeling, both to her and to myself. So, in the end, I left the country without ever telling her how I felt. I never heard from her again.

I don't have a lot of regrets in my life, but that is the biggest one of them all. I'll die without having been able to tell her I loved her or to ask if she loved me back. Though, at least in this ignorance, I can leave imagining that she did.

Don't repeat my mistakes. I ask you—beg you—to tell the people you love that you do. Don't keep this to yourself. I know it can be scary, to live in the risk, but I can assure you that it can't be worse than not knowing what might have happened if you'd had the courage to act on your feelings.

Love,

Helen

15

ADELAIDE

"*H*ey, vacation boy!" I shouted as Matthias entered through the front door.

"Fucking finally." He hung his trench coat on the foyer rack.

"Language, Matthias," Helen corrected from beside me.

He made his way to where we were in the kitchen, going straight for the refrigerator. The *pschit* of his beer opening filled the room before he took a heavy gulp and exhaled, which almost sounded like a growl.

"So, what are your plans for the week?" I asked, wiping my hands on my jeans.

"I don't have any. Just to sleep in every day and do nothing."

"Oh, come on, that's so boring," I said.

"What can I say, I'm a boring guy." He gave me a smirk, which told me he knew all too well I didn't believe a word he was saying. I took a sip from my glass of water, an eyebrow raised at him.

"I remember when I was your age," Helen said, "my favorite thing to do when summer started was going to the Lobster Festival."

I choked on my water. "Lobster Festival?"

Helen turned her head in my direction, her eyes gleaming in excitement. "Yes! It's this two-week l-l-long festival happening at Old Orchard Beach. I used to go with my friends every year before I left f-for India with DWB. There were food trucks, and games, and cute little kiosks. There were hot people sometimes too."

It was obvious from the grin she gave me that the 'hot people' were the highlight of the festival for her at the time.

"And does it still take place?" I asked in a nonchalant tone.

Matthias blurted out a "No" at the same moment Helen asserted, "Of course!"

I grinned at him as I said, "Well, I, for one, would love to go to this Lobster Festival." It didn't matter that I hated seafood. If it made Matthias squirm, then I was all in.

Helen gasped. "Really? You would?"

"Of course! Let's go this week. Matthias is on vacation, so he can take us!"

I bit the inside of my cheek as I saw his eyes widen. "No. No, no, no, I'm not going to the Lobster Festival."

"Hmm, I don't think you have a choice," I said.

Right as he opened his mouth to plead his case, my phone rang, *Stella My Favorite Person In The World* calling. "Saved by the bell," I said to Matthias before answering.

"Hey girl," I said.

"Hey," my best friend replied. "I've been dealing with babies crying all day, so I needed a distraction. How are things going with The Hottie?"

My eyes widened at her question, and I escaped through the patio door without meeting anyone's eyes. I looked at the phone's screen to make sure it wasn't on speakerphone, just in case. You can never be too careful.

As I made sure the door was closed behind me, I said, "Nothing new. And how do you know he's a hottie?"

"You know me, Professional Facebook Stalker Extraordinaire. Seriously though, you could've told me that your boss was hot when you got the job."

I rolled my eyes even though she couldn't see me while sitting on the wooden swing overlooking the ocean. I still couldn't believe this was someone's backyard. I didn't think I could ever get tired of this view. "Maybe I was too busy telling you how much of a jerk he was at first to mention his physique."

"Grave mistake. And, somehow, I don't believe nothing has happened since the last time we talked. I know you, Addy. I can hear it in your voice when you're lying."

Yes, she could. "Well, nothing *big* has happened. We've just been spending a lot of time together. And he's been really nice with Lou too. And he's kind of amazing."

"Damn, girl, sounds like you've got it bad." She took a large breath. "Just be careful, okay? I wouldn't want what happened with my old boss to happen to you."

I bit my lower lip. "Oh, Stella, I —"

"Shit, Addy, one of the babies on my watch is crashing. Gotta go, talk to you later!"

She hung up before I had the time to answer.

Walking back inside the house, I couldn't get Stella's words out of my head. I *did* have it bad. Ever since the wedding, I hadn't been able to stop thinking about Matthias. How he'd made me feel comfortable enough to talk to him. How he'd listened to me without saying useless things. How it had felt when he'd touched me, like his hands were searing through my skin, marking me forever. How I'd felt like he couldn't get close enough. How I'd woken up during the night after dreaming of his mouth worshipping my body, my pajamas drenched.

But the rest of her words hung in my head too. *Be careful.* I couldn't be falling for the person who paid my bills; I'd made this rule for myself. It didn't matter if it was getting harder and harder to respect.

I wished I had someone to talk to about it. I could tell Stella anything, but we were both always so busy, we didn't get the chance to talk nearly as much as I would've wanted to.

"Who was that? The best friend?" Matthias asked as he drizzled oil in a pan, pulling me out of my reverie. Helen was sitting beside him, examining me.

"Um, yeah."

"Why the sad smile?" he asked.

I hadn't realized I had a sad expression, although he always seemed to read my face like an open book, no matter what I was trying to hide.

"Nothing, I just... I miss her."

"Why don't you go see her?" he asked. "You could do that instead of going to the Lobster Festival!" He smirked as I swatted him with the back of my hand.

"You're not getting off the hook that easily," I said. "And anyway, it's a little harder than that to see her. She lives in Montreal."

His lips thinned. "Oh."

"Yeah. We've been friends since kindergarten, and we didn't lose touch when I moved here, but it's getting harder and harder for us to see each other as we're growing older. She has a crazy schedule with medical school, and I'm almost always busy, so I don't have the time to go see her." I leaned my head on my hand. "And, it's even harder for her to come visit now because there's no place for her to sleep in our apartment, so she has to pay for a hotel."

He hummed. "I see. Well, I hope you get the chance to see each other soon."

I gave him a half-smile. "Me too." I then turned to face Helen and clapped my hands together. "So, about this festival."

"*F*uck no, I'm not wearing that."

I pinched my lips together to tame my laughter down. "What, you think you'll feel less of a man with this on?"

He rolled his eyes and pointed to his chest. "I've already agreed to wear the shirt. This was supposed to be it. You're not forcing me to put this on too."

"Oh, come on, Grumpy."

His eyes narrowed in on me. "I'm not grumpy."

"Yes, you are," Helen and I answered in unison.

He rolled his eyes again, but didn't say anything else this time. Pushing my lower lip out, I used the last weapon in my arsenal: tugging at his heartstrings. "Please. For me."

He stared at my sad puppy face—the one Louis had taught me to master—with an impassable expression for five seconds. Looking in his eyes, I knew the moment he decided to give in. "Fine."

Beaming at him, I stepped closer and put the headpiece in his hair. He looked at the sky the whole time I squeezed it around his head to make sure it would hold. Once my craft was done, I took a step back and automatically brought a hand to my mouth. Matthias now had two springs attached to his head, at the tip of which stood red lobster claws. The mix of his 'kill me now' eyes and 'I'm ready for the festival' outfit was to die for. But if I laughed at him, he'd never agree to come with us, so I acted as if I needed to cough while putting Helen's and my headpiece on too.

"You look so pretty," I said to Matthias with a wink. At the same moment, my phone started vibrating and shrilling in my jean shorts' back pocket.

"Hello?"

"Hi Addy, it's Julie." I had to scavenge my head to remember this was Mrs. Zhu's first name. "I've been called in to cover for someone at work. I'll be bringing Josh to my parents' place, and I was wondering if I could just drop Louis with your father?"

I closed my eyes and repressed a sigh. It wasn't Mrs. Zhu's fault Louis didn't have a large support system, but couldn't I have one day of fun, just for once?

"Um, yeah, for now it'll be okay," I answered. "I should get there in about an hour."

"Okay. Sorry about that."

"No problem. Thank you for calling me. Bye."

I hung up and glanced at Helen and Matthias—who looked so silly in their outfits it seemed like a joke—with a frown. "I have to go home to watch Louis. Guess I'll have to wait another year for my first Lobster Festival."

Before Helen could say anything, Matthias blurted out, "Why don't you bring him with us?"

"Oh no, I wouldn't want to impose my babysitter duties on you, especially not during your week off."

"When will you finally understand that you could *never* impose?" He walked toward the front door and opened it, motioning for us to follow him outside. "I love Louis, and I'm sure he'd love to come with us. I can even give him my headpiece so he'll feel included in our amazing costumed gang!"

Oh, Lord. Why did my legs feel weak at his words? I didn't think there could be anything sexier than Matthias taking the lead and asking me to dance with him at a wedding, but looking at him right now, in his stupid lobster shirt, saying that he loved my little brother topped it.

"Okay, thank you." I gave him a shy smile before taking a step forward and grabbing him by the shoulders. "But dream on if you think I'll ever let you take this headpiece off."

The day we went to the Lobster Festival together is one of the most beautiful I have ever experienced. I don't think I could ever explain to you how it made me feel to be there that day with you. It was like I was…free. For the first time since I'd received my diagnosis, I felt like I was living my life to the fullest.

Seeing you laugh, tasting the food that brought back so many memories for me, playing carnival games with you, seeing Louis' wide eyes when he experienced all of these things for the first time… My body might not have been functioning like it had in the past, but still, there was nothing holding me back. I was fully and wholeheartedly there with you on that day, and that's something I will cherish forever.

Love,
Helen

"*Y*ou should've seen your face," I shrieked as we got out of the car.

Matthias glared at me, but he wasn't able to hide his giant smile. "How was I supposed to keep a straight face when I learned exactly which part of the lobster I had in my mouth?"

I broke down in another bout of laughter. I hadn't been able to stop teasing him about it ever since we'd left the festival.

I caught my breath while Matthias made sure Helen was okay to wait for us in the car. Louis, Josh—who we'd decided to bring with us too—and I walked to the apartment building.

Well, I walked. They raced home. Oh, the joy of being a seven-year-old with endless energy stores.

"Thank you for bringing him with you," Mrs. Zhu said after Josh walked past her and she ruffled his black hair.

I put my hands on Louis' shoulders and smiled. "You look after Louis all the time. It's really no problem at all."

She dipped her chin, and we made our way to our own door. Once inside, Louis rushed to the bathroom, claiming he'd been needing to go "for forever." Matthias, who'd followed us inside, went to check on him.

Dropping my purse and water bottle on the kitchen table, I jumped when I caught my father sitting straight on the couch.

"Hey Dad, I didn't know you were up." When Matthias and I had come to pick Louis up, he'd been on his way to bed, saying he had a headache.

He didn't turn his head in my direction when he answered, "Yeah, wasn't able to sleep."

Humming, I trudged closer to him and stood in front of the television so he'd look at me. "So, have you thought about the job I showed you?" I'd given him enough time to rummage over this.

"What job offer?" His voice didn't contain any tonality, any liveliness. It was like all of it had been sucked out of him years ago.

"The one at the motel? To work in the kitchen?" I crossed my arms in front of my chest.

His eyes didn't widen in forgetfulness, and his eyebrows didn't shoot up in recognition either. "Oh, yeah, I don't think it's going to work for me."

I balled my hands into fists, not bothering to ask him why. I knew all too well he didn't have a reason other than not wanting to get out of the house and get back to his previous life. He'd given me the same answer with all the other job postings I'd shown him before.

His eyes fell to the hands in his lap, his mouth remaining shut. Not wanting to get mad at him, I headed out of the living room, but turned around when I remembered something I'd told myself earlier today I had to ask him.

"Oh, and speaking of your job, you remember you're going to Dad Day at Louis' school tomorrow to talk about your job?"

This time, confusion twisted his face. "What? No, I never said I was going anywhere."

"Yes, you did."

"Well, I...I can't. Not tomorrow."

"But you—" I ground my teeth together, not trusting what I was going to say next. Especially with Louis who could come into the living room at any moment. Without finishing my sentence, I stormed out of the room and left the apartment, needing some peace for a second.

Pacing over the beige carpet of the hallway, I closed my eyes and put my hand to my forehead. *Think, Addy. Think.* I couldn't go instead of him; it was specified that the presentation needed to be done by fathers or important men in the kids' lives. Both our grandfathers were dead, and we didn't have any uncles. I could try to force my dad to go, but would this really make Louis proud? Having an unprepared and unwilling father talking in front of his whole class?

Louis *could* say he hadn't found anyone to come, but how would that make him feel? It was so easy to imagine him breaking down in front of his friends because he didn't have anyone there for him.

I came to a sudden halt in my pacing when Matthias' warm hand dropped on my shoulder. "I couldn't help but hear what's going on, and I might have a solution."

I held my breath as I waited for a miracle.

"I could do it," he continued, his sentence sounding more like a question than an affirmation. "I mean, if that's all right with you."

"You would do that?"

He nodded. "I would do anything for—" His Adam's apple bobbed. "For Louis."

I released the biggest of breaths and grabbed one of his hands with both of mine. "Oh my God, you're a lifesaver. Thank you, thank you, thank you. I'll spend the day with Helen, of course, and I'll owe you one."

He smirked. "Repay me by coming to the beach with Helen and me on Friday." He'd asked me earlier, but I hadn't given him an answer yet.

Letting go of his hand, I nodded and smiled. "Will do."

*L*ouis came out of his room the next day, his huge backpack on his shoulders, and sat down at the kitchen table to put his shoes on. While I finished making his ham sandwich, I asked, "Do you have everything? Red binder? A coat in case it rains? Marie Antoinette?"

When I didn't hear an answer, I stopped packing his lunchbox and glanced in his direction. My heartbeat skyrocketed once I saw Louis' crumpled face, tears sliding down his cheeks. I rushed to him and kneeled next to the chair he was sitting on. "Loulou, what's going on?"

The question only intensified his crying, making it impossible for him to utter a word. My eyes widened and my face twisted in anxiety as I examined him, looking for something that might have hurt him. He was wearing his red t-shirt with a large train on it, navy Bermuda shorts, and his favorite sneakers—the ones that lit up when you walked on them. I hugged him, feeling on the verge of crying myself from seeing him like this and not knowing what to do to help.

"Please, Lou, tell me what's wrong."

He hiccupped before taking in a big breath. "Who's going to take care of me once you're gone?"

His words were a freight train against my chest. For a second, I lost the ability to breathe. I squeezed my arms tighter around his tiny body, hiding my own tears behind him. "Oh, baby, why would you say that? You know we'll always be there to take care of you!"

He pulled himself out of my grip, and I quickly wiped my eyes. He looked so young, sitting on the tall chair, his feet not even touching the floor, yet the look in his eyes was one of someone much older. "Daddy doesn't even want to come to Dad Day at school with me. And you'll leave at some point, when you go to school or get married and have kids of your own."

A sob threatened to erupt from my throat, but I pushed it down. Louis needed me to be strong, so I would be. For him.

Grabbing him by the cheeks, I forced him to face me. "Louis, I need you to listen to me very closely. Daddy loves you more than he could ever tell you, but he's still really, really sad about Mommy's death, and it makes him...um, not well. But it's not that he doesn't want to go with you. As for me, I'm not going anywhere."

His eyes drifted down to my neck. "Look at me, Lou." His chocolate gaze met mine again. "I will always, *always* be there for you. As long as you need me, I'll be by your side. Maybe even when you don't need me anymore. I love you so, so, so much. Do you understand me?"

His little head bobbed in agreement, and I kissed his forehead before wiping his cheeks with my thumbs. "Now, go get ready to spend an amazing day with Matthias. I'm sure no one will have brought a pilot with them like you." With that, he shook his head and gave me a tiny smile that was enough to mend some of the pieces of my broken heart.

At the same time I got up, someone knocked on the front door. Louis rushed to open it, and as soon as Matthias walked in, Louis hugged him, his head barely reaching Matthias' belly button.

"Hey, bud." Matthias hugged him back and raised his eyes to mine with a wide grin, but his face dropped once he looked at me. He always did see right through me, even if I gave him a fake smile. "What's going on?" he mouthed over Louis' head.

"I'll tell you later," I replied, equally as silent.

He eyed me warily, but ended up nodding. Once Louis had let go of him, he crouched in front of my brother. "Ready to impress all of your friends?" The smile he offered with his words, coupled with the way he looked at Louis, made me feel more grateful for him than I ever had.

MATTHIAS

*L*ouis hit his shoes together repeatedly, creating flashes of green, purple, and blue beside me. Before that, he'd moved his seat back and forth with the mechanical buttons at his side. It was like he needed to be doing *something*, no matter what it was.

"Those are really cool shoes you have there, buddy," I said once I'd stopped the car at a red light and had gotten a good look at him.

Louis' eyes wandered to his shoes, which he tapped together twice in a row. "I know." His voice was still high-pitched, making the little boy irresistible. "Everyone in school had them, and I was sad I didn't, but Addy got them for me for my birthday."

I smiled as the light turned green. She really was amazing. No word could've been more appropriate to describe her. I guessed those shoes were expensive, and I would've bet my car that she'd thought of all the ways she could save money so she could buy them and make Louis happy.

Keeping my eyes on the road, I said, "You know, you lucked out with your sister, huh?"

He turned his head in my direction and gave me a tiny smile in the rearview mirror, his chubby cheeks lifting. "I know. My friends at school tell me it's not normal that my sister acts like my mommy, but Addy has always taken good care of me. She lets me eat cookies at night when I finish my plate, and she helps me with my homework all the time. Even if they say it's weird, I wouldn't want anyone to replace her."

I hissed through my teeth. "Fu... Screw those kids. Your sister is wonderful and it doesn't matter how she's related to you. The only thing that matters is that she loves you." Putting my blinker on, I looked behind my shoulder and changed lanes. "You know, I used to have a weird family too. I had a mom, but I didn't have a dad, and all the kids in class teased me because of it. But I knew in my heart that it didn't matter if I didn't have a dad because my mom was great enough by herself. I think Addy's great enough too."

He hummed and nodded, but didn't say anything in response. Starting to tap his shoes together again, he looked out the window. From where we were, we could see the ocean if we squinted.

After five minutes of silence, Louis spoke, his words making my heart stop. "Addy talks about you all the time. She always says she thinks you're so great, just like you said she was."

I turned my head in his direction, but didn't know how to answer that. She'd said that about me?

Before I got the chance to say something, he asked, "When are you going to marry my sister?"

My eyes popped out of their sockets for a moment. What kind of conversations were going on at Addy's house? "I, uh, what? What makes you ask that?"

He looked at me like I was the seven-year-old and he was the adult. "Well, I asked her and she said you weren't going to get married and I didn't understand why. Because you both come from special families." Turning his head back toward the window, he continued, "I thought maybe one day, we could form a special family together. You, just your mom, me, Addy, and my daddy. It would be awesome."

I swallowed, my throat feeling dry all of a sudden. We finished the drive in silence, and even after we'd gotten out of the car and entered Louis' school, I couldn't shake away the picture he'd described. Awesome indeed.

ADELAIDE

I paced through the kitchen, biting my nails as I looked at the time on the oven. Louis' school ended at three, so they should be getting back soon.

I couldn't have been more thankful for Dora's offer to take my shift today because I hadn't been able to relax all day. Not after what Louis had said. The sight of his crying face, the warmth of his tears dripping down my neck, the sound of his sniffling, it was all seared in my mind. And I hadn't even had the time to make sure he was okay before watching him leave with Matthias. I knew Louis liked him, but what if he hadn't been ready to go to school after talking about his feelings like that? What if he needed to stay here with me? I could've scratched his back and played with his hair, like our mom used to do when we were sick.

I'd felt the urge to talk to my dad when he'd passed by me to go from his bedroom to the living room, but what was I supposed to say? I had no idea how to make things right, even though I wanted to, more than I'd ever wanted anything else.

Right as I looked at the oven's clock again, the front door opened, Louis bursting inside, followed by a laughing Matthias. His eyes were on Louis, but once they lifted and met mine, it felt like a punch to my stomach. He was so utterly *beautiful*, with his shiny white smile and tanned skin, I could erupt in flames right there on my kitchen floor.

"Addy, it was a-ma-zing!" Louis ran around the kitchen counter like he had too much energy to spend all of a sudden. "Matt showed them pictures of Galileo and his presentation was *so* much better than all the other dads. Now everyone in my class wants to become a pilot!"

I beamed at him. "I'm so glad everything went well."

His eyes made a back-and-forth trail between me and his room. "I'd love to tell you all about it, but I have this new friend in class who gave me his number so that I could call him tonight to talk about cars and planes. Can I borrow your phone and go talk to him for, like, an hour?"

"Yeah, sure." As soon as my phone was in his hands, he bolted, slamming the door of his room behind him.

"He's something, huh?"

Matthias' laugh was deep and airy in my ears. "That, he is."

"So, how did it go?" I glanced in his direction and noticed for the first time how soft his lips looked. It was like every time I saw him, I discovered something new about him that made him more handsome, more perfect.

"Good," he said. "I was a little nervous when I got there because every kid was with their father, from what I understood, but once I started speaking, I won them all over." He smirked, and I had no problem believing him.

Still, I flinched when he said Lou was the only one whose father hadn't come. I didn't have to burden Matthias with this any longer though. "Thank you so, so much for today," I said. "You have no idea how much this means to me."

Before I could overthink it, I stepped forward and wrapped my arms around his shoulders, giving his neck a peck. His arms barely had the time to wrap around my body before I'd taken a step back.

When he spoke again, his eyes were wide, and his cheeks red. "Um… Yeah, no problem." He turned as if to head out, but looked at me again when he seemed to remember something. "Oh, and Louis asked me when we're going to get married." His lips twitched.

If I'd been holding a glass, it would've shattered on the floor. "What? He did it again?"

He grinned like the devil. "If it's any consolation, if I had a kid, I'd want one just like him."

I snickered at the thought of Matthias' face when Louis spurted that on him. "Thank…Thank you for today. Really," I said.

"Like I said, I'd do anything for Louis," he stated before he turned around and disappeared down the stairs.

After closing the door behind him, I made my way back to the kitchen and started pacing again, but for another reason this time. Louis' father was the only one in the class who hadn't gone. If Matthias hadn't been there, Louis would've been all alone.

It wasn't enough that he'd lost his mother before being old enough to get to know her; he also had to lose his dad, even if he was still very much alive.

It wasn't normal that the only person other than me who'd do anything for Louis was my boss.

Suddenly, it became very clear what I had to tell my dad.

With a newfound fire burning inside, I made my way to the living room where my father was lying on his side, watching another unimportant soap.

"Dad, I need to talk to you."

He hummed in answer, but didn't take his eyes off the television.

Okay, that was it.

Grabbing the remote, I turned the show off before hurling it to the floor. "I said, I need to talk to you," I gritted through my teeth. My patience had run out.

He turned to me, his hair and beard still in desperate need of a trim I didn't have the time for. "What is it?" He was looking in my direction, but his brown eyes felt dull on mine.

I took him in, and at that moment, I didn't recognize the man sitting in front of me. His eyes didn't hold the twinkle they used to when, as a little girl, I'd ask him to tell me the story of how my mother and him had met for the thousandth time. His shoulders were hanging low, the total opposite of the proud man who used to welcome his motel's clients with a straight back and a blinding smile. Even his arms looked different; they were too small to be the ones that used to throw me in the ocean during my summer break. The simple sight of him made me deflate.

I took a seat by his side and released a shaky breath. By the wary look he threw me, I could tell he knew something was about to go down. Things would be said, and there would be no coming back from them. I knew that too, but maybe that was exactly what we needed. To move forward.

"Things are not working anymore," I said.

He didn't even react to my words, his face remaining blank. "What do you mean?"

"I mean we can't keep going like we are right now."

His eyes finally showed recognition, like he understood exactly what I was talking about. "You're sick, Dad, and you need help."

"Addy, please, I—"

I held a hand in front of him. "No, I need you to let me finish." His jaw tightened, but he gave me a tight nod, urging me to go on.

"You'll never hear me complain about all I had to do to keep this family afloat for the past two years. I can stand pretty much everything, but Louis is my limit. I won't stay put if your behavior hurts him. That's where I draw the line. I would've understood if he had been alone for Mother's Day at school, but he had to bring my friend for *Dad* Day, for Christ's sake! Louis still has a father! And this father needs to step the hell up!"

I'd gotten up while speaking. His eyes were on mine, more aware and present and alive than I'd seen them in the last two years. "I know you took Mom's death hard, I get it, but this has to end at some point. You might've lost a wife, but we lost a mother." A tear left my right eye, and I swiped it right away with the back of my hand. "I sacrificed my time to grieve so you could have more, but now, it's enough." I cleared the knot in my throat. "I'll get you all the help you need, but you need to decide to help yourself first."

My last words were the ones that broke him. His face crumpled in front of my eyes, and he dropped his head in his hands as he erupted into sobs. I finally sat back down and wrapped my arms around his back, trying to soothe him with my embrace.

"I'm... I'm so sorry, Addy." His voice was muffled from speaking through his hands, and his back shook under my hands. "I just... I don't know how to live anymore. I don't know who I am without her." He hiccupped. "I didn't just lose my wife, I lost my purpose. I can't see a future without her."

I closed my eyes, unable to hold the tears in. I'd known he was suffering, but hearing it was a different thing. I wished so much that he'd told me all of this before.

Lifting his head from his hands, he gave me a look that cracked a hole in my heart for the hundredth time in the same day. I leaned forward, grabbing his hands and squeezing them tightly between mine. "It's okay, Dad. We'll get you the help you need. And we'll figure out who you are now."

He closed his eyes, more tears streaming out of them. He'd never reminded me more of my little brother than in this moment of vulnerability.

"Yes, we will," I continued. "We'll figure it out together. You're not alone in this."

The look of gratefulness he gave me then made me want to curse myself for not bringing this up sooner. But there was no use in rehashing the past, in regretting what we had or hadn't done. The only way to look was forward. So, I did.

Your loving and generous heart is one of the things I've always loved the most about you.

I know you've never been able to stand other people suffering, no matter what they'd done to you in the past. I also know you've hated that part of you from time to time, when you couldn't hold grudges against people that had wronged you. Well, not that you've never held grudges, but I'm talking about smaller wrongs here, not the kind that do deserve animosity.

However, I hope you know now that your big heart has never been and will never be a weakness. It is one of your greatest strengths, no matter how badly you might want to stop caring sometimes. I don't know that many people who have a heart as big as yours, which our society definitely needs.

I think that leads us to our Helen Advice number five: never let the world ruin your heart of gold. No matter how much pain you go through, no matter what is thrown your way, no matter how people treat you, just don't lose it. You might want to give it up for some bad people, but they're not worth it.

With love and empathy, you can never lose.

Love,

Helen

17

ADELAIDE

*S*waying to the voice of a crooner coming out of the speakers in the kitchen, I opened the refrigerator door. "What do you feel like eating for lunch?"

I turned to look behind me. Helen was sitting by the dining room's bay windows, offering one of the best views in the house. It felt like there was nothing between us and the ocean, like we were on a boat floating above it. Sun rays pierced the glass, illuminating Helen, making her hair look more white than blond. Even the moon-shaped golden ring she never took off her right middle finger gleamed in the light.

"We can just reheat yesterday's soup," she said. "I'm not that hungry today."

In two strides, I was by her side. "Are you okay? Is something wrong?" I pressed the back of my hand to her forehead, then to her neck.

"Yes, I'm all right, don't you worry." She laughed and smiled, but something was...off. I couldn't pinpoint what it was, but something wasn't right. If she didn't want to talk about it, though, there was nothing I could do.

I stole a glance to my left before bringing my gaze back to hers, but she didn't fail to notice. "He's not coming back home before noon, you know. No need to look at the door every five seconds."

I gaped at her, mouth opening, then closing, while she gave me a smug grin and winked.

"I... Uh, I..."

She rolled her eyes at me. "What, did you think I was b-blind?"

Striding back to the refrigerator, I answered, "I don't know what you're talking about." It felt easier to lie when I had my back to her.

"Oh, I don't believe that for a second." I heard the sound of her wheels rolling on the shimmery-white ceramic floor before her chair was next to me. "You should see yourself whenever he walks in the room. It's like there's a light that g-g-gets turned on inside of you. You literally glow. There are h-hearts in your eyes and everything."

Did I really look like that? I didn't think I was this obvious, but then, I did feel that way when he was around. Like everything was easier, prettier, *better*.

Taking the pot of carrot-ginger soup out of the fridge and putting it on the stove, I cleared my throat. "I don't know what to say."

When I faced Helen again, her eyes were lit with what I could only describe as joy. "There's nothing to be embarrassed about, Addy. I really d-do think you're a great fit, and I'm not just saying that because I'm his m-mother." Her lips twitched up. "That man has his flaws and c-comes with baggage, but there's literally n-nothing he wouldn't do for those he loves."

I bit my lower lip. I didn't doubt what she was saying for a second. I'd seen it myself, how good and kind he was.

"You have no idea how happy it makes me, knowing that once I'm gone, he'll have you."

I stepped forward and swatted her lightly with the back of my hand. "Don't say things like that! I don't see you going anywhere anytime soon."

She grinned, ignoring my comment. "My son might be great, but if he was with you, let me tell you, he would be equally as lucky."

Before I could answer, the sound of the front door opening resonated around us. I turned around to see Matthias coming in with a reusable grocery bag in each hand.

"Well, look at that," Helen started, "you're home early." She lowered her voice just a little bit when she said, "You don't have to watch the door anymore, Addy."

I choked on my air and broke into a coughing fit. Beside me, Helen giggled like a schoolgirl.

I had no idea whether Matthias had heard what she'd said when he looked at us with drawn eyebrows and an amused expression. "What did I miss?"

Helen and I turned to each other, exchanging a knowing glance. She grinned right before opening her mouth, but I didn't trust what would be coming out of her mouth, so I uttered the first thing that came to mind. "Uh, who wants soup?"

With a faint shake of her head, she made her way out of the kitchen to the dining room. I heard her snickering all the way there.

*C*lothes in hand, I left the bathroom. Once I reached the kitchen, I said in a singsongy voice, "Who's ready for some beach time?"

Both Helen and Matthias were still dressed in their everyday clothes. Matthias was telling her some kind of joke, I assumed, considering she was laughing, but their heads turned in my direction once I walked in. His eyes widened as they landed on me, and I felt like covering myself with my hands all of a sudden. I was wearing a short yellow sundress over my bikini, which was far from provocative, but it was true I'd never been this underdressed with them before.

I caught Matthias' eyes raking down the length of my body, from my bare shoulders to my legs. Once they came back to my face, his cheeks were flushed.

He jumped up. "I'll go get changed!" Practically running down the hallway, he left and came back less than a minute later in striped navy-and-white swim trunks and a white V-neck.

Oh, crap.

My next breath was heavy. How could this man look this good in everything he put on?

I clapped my hands together while turning to Helen. "Let's get you ready."

She cringed. "You know what? I'm feeling a bit under the weather today, so I think I'm just going to stay here for the afternoon and watch a movie or something."

Matthias bolted forward, patting her face with the back of his hand, the way I'd done less than an hour before. "What's wrong? Are you sick? Do you need to go see a doctor?" His voice had climbed a tone.

She rolled her eyes at him the way she had at me. "No, silly, I'm not sick. I'm just tired."

"Okay, well we'll just stay here with you then," he said.

I nodded, but Helen shook her head.

"I don't need you to watch me get some rest. You're going to the beach."

Matthias' mouth opened. "But—"

"No but. The beach is right down the street. I have my phone here with me if I need something, which I won't. You're going to the beach, end of discussion."

Both of them turned their heads at me, like I was the one who had the final say. I didn't feel good leaving Helen alone, even if it wasn't for long, but I could see in her eyes that she needed this. Some kind of independence.

I bit my lip as my eyes alternated between both their faces. Finally, I said, "The beach really is less than two hundred feet away."

Helen beamed at me, and Matthias sighed in resignation. "Fine, but know that I don't like this." He leaned forward to give her cheek a kiss. "If you need anything, whatever it is, you call, okay?"

She nodded. "Yes, sir."

Winking at her, I made my way outside. Matthias followed me, and we grabbed folded chairs from the garage before walking to the beach down the street. Once we got there, I sat down in the sand, not even bothering to open my chair. I closed my eyes and inhaled deeply. There was, in my mind, no better scent than that of the ocean. Salty, a bit tangy, common, yet still unique. I could smell it when I was at Helen's place, but it wasn't exactly the same as the one here.

With the sun on my face, the wind in my hair, the sand under my legs, the seagulls in my ears, and the ocean air in my nose, it felt like summer, real and true.

I started speaking without really realizing I wasn't talking to myself anymore. "I used to come here every summer with my family. Well, not here, here, but in Southern Maine." Matthias didn't say anything, but it was clear he was listening. "We would rent this tiny cottage right by the beach, and the first thing I'd do when I got out of the car after a long ride was run to the beach and lay down. I even did a snow angel once… Well, a sand angel, I guess."

Matthias snickered, and I realized he was closer than I'd thought when his warm breath reached my shoulder. I opened my eyes and found him sitting in the sand right next to me, his espresso eyes burning through me. After a second, I gazed in front of me at the never-ending water. "Even though I was only ever here two weeks a year, this place has always felt like happiness to me. Pure, untainted happiness."

"Yeah, I really get that," he said.

We stared into each other's eyes for a second too long. Suddenly, I was really hot. Getting up, I removed my dress and scavenged my tote bag to find my sunscreen tube. Once I grabbed it, I turned around. "Do you mind putting some on my back?" I extended the tube to him, but it was like he didn't even see it. His eyes were on my body. It lasted less than a second, but I noticed. How could I not, when his stare felt like fire licking my skin?

I was wearing my black bikini, not particularly revealing or daring, but with the way he was looking at me, I felt...*sexy*. More than I ever had before, even with past boyfriends.

"Um, sure," he said after what felt like forever. He grabbed the tube, and I turned around, holding my hair up. A squirting sound interrupted our silence before cold cream touched my shoulders. Reflexively, I arched my back, and he laughed, his mouth again so close to my skin. "Sorry, sorry."

Then, his hands were on my neck, on my shoulders, on my back, and it wasn't cold anymore; I was ablaze. His thumbs massaged my muscles as he spread the cream, doing a thorough job at making sure I was covered.

God, this was a bad idea. I'd never be able to fall asleep tonight without dreaming of his warm, strong hands all over me.

Once the cream had penetrated my skin, his hands stopped their movements, and one of his fingers grazed the skin of my right shoulder. "What happened here?"

It took me a moment to figure out he was talking about my scar. I forgot it was there most of the time since I couldn't see it unless I looked for it. "Oh, it's nothing, I just had some skin removed when I was younger."

"What do you mean?" His answer came right away, the feel of his breath on my neck making goosebumps erupt on my skin.

"I had this sort of...skin infection. I felt some kind of itch mixed with a burning pain over my shoulder, but my mom was really sick then. She'd just come back from a trip to the hospital, and she needed me. I didn't want to talk about it, so I waited until the next day, when the pain had become so unbearable I had to tell someone about it. Turns out, I had this nasty infection, and they needed to remove some of the bad tissue. That's it."

I turned around and let my hair fall back over my shoulders, not wanting him to examine my scar any longer. I looked up at him and smiled, but he didn't return it. He was so much taller than me, he shielded me from the sun from where he stood.

His hand moved forward, almost like he didn't mean it to. His fingers barely grazed mine, but I still felt it all through my body. "You were caring for everyone, but who was taking care of you?"

I shook my head. "I didn't need anyone taking care of me."

"But you did, though." This time, when his hand moved forward, his little finger hooked around mine, and I knew it wasn't accidental. My heart was racing in my chest as I stared into the abyss of his eyes. His breath was shaky as he exhaled. "When will you let someone else return the favor?"

I swallowed. I didn't like asking for help from anyone. Never had, never would. But, as I let his words sink in, I found myself thinking I wouldn't mind letting him help me. I wouldn't mind asking him for back rubs when I was sick, or having him run upstairs to grab my purse when I forgot it.

It was then, standing on the Cape Neddick beach, looking at him, looking *through* him, that it dawned on me: I didn't just like Matthias. I was in love with him.

But I couldn't. This was bigger than the two of us, and even if I wanted him, I couldn't make it known. Not when it was Helen who was hanging in the balance. As long as I worked for them, I'd keep this feeling safely tucked into a corner of my mind and heart.

A shiver ran down my spine as I pulled my hand away.

Gazing at the ocean, I smirked. "Want to make a run for it?" I asked, tipping my head in the direction of the water as I tried to take my mind elsewhere.

"You know it's cold as shit, right?" His breathing was still fast, but I didn't dwell on that.

Instead, I answered, "Is big, bad, grumpy Matt scared of some cold water?"

He huffed, shaking his head slowly, and in an instant, he was lunging at me. Luckily, I was faster. I raced toward the water, shrieking when I felt him getting closer to me. I didn't stop running when I reached the ocean. With water this cold, you couldn't go in slowly. It was either all at once or not at all.

Matthias cursed as he followed me in. I laughed out loud, a deep belly laugh.

When it felt deep enough, I dove into the water. Matthias did too. As I emerged back up, I let myself float on my back, and Matthias imitated me. Two big star-shaped forms drifting above the water.

With a sigh, I closed my eyes. "This is still my happy place."

I know I have talked to you a lot about love already, but I still have some things to say, believe it or not. Even if I didn't have the chance to live a great love story, I've still gotten a lot of insight on love throughout my life, all coming from different places. Some from the novels I've read, some from the patients I've treated in the ER, some from the villagers where I worked in India or in Congo. Through all these experiences, I had the chance to learn that love doesn't have any language. Love gets expressed in all types of ways, sometimes a lot different than what you'd expect.

Love might not have a language, but different people have different languages to express and receive their love. I'm not sure whether you've heard about that already, but if you haven't, this is your chance to learn.

Your love can be expressed in thousands of ways, none better than the other. The important thing is to find the one that works for the person you're with.

Some people might feel loved by being told so. Others might feel another's love by being given gifts, or by being touched, or by being cared for. Some might feel like they're in love when they can speak freely, without any fear of being judged, while others might love by doing house chores for their significant other.

It doesn't matter what it is. It only matters that you know what it is.

Speak their language. And if you don't know what their language is, then find out. Observe them, or ask the people who know them best, and do everything you can to understand them and be understood in return. That makes Helen Advice number six: Love your significant other in the right way.

Love,
Helen

18

MATTHIAS

$\mathcal{I}$ hung up the phone and walked into the kitchen, a smug smile on my face. I'd been mulling about this plan ever since Addy had talked about *her* a few weeks ago, but now that everything was coming into place, I couldn't keep my excitement in.

"W-What are you smiling about?" Helen moved by my side, eyebrows raised, one slightly higher than the other. The circles under her eyes were darker than usual, and the muscles of her face struggled to accomplish their function. Still, it was my mother's smile. The one I'd seen every step of the way growing up, from my first piano recital to my graduation from flight school.

"I just called her," I said. "She's in."

Her eyes widened as she gasped. "Oh my God, she's going to be so happy! I can't wait!"

I tried to tame my excitement a little, not wanting her to imagine things. Yes, I was doing this for Addy, but that didn't change the fact that she was still my mom's caregiver. No matter what feelings I might've had for her, she was out of reach. That didn't mean I couldn't do something I knew would make her happy though. I simply had to keep my heart from thinking this meant we could be something *more*.

Opening my phone again, I searched for Addy's name in my contacts. I couldn't find it at first, but grinned from ear to ear when I found the new name she had in my phone. She must have changed it while I wasn't looking, probably after we'd argued for the umpteenth time about the legitimacy of pop music.

Me: Doing a little something for the 4th of July, nothing big. Wanna come?

She answered less than a minute later.

Addy The REAL Music Connoisseur: I've been a Canadian much longer than an American. My family and I don't really celebrate it. ;)

Me: Just consider it a random social gathering with fireworks then.

Addy The REAL Music Connoisseur: I wish I could, but I wouldn't want to ask Mrs. Zhu to look after my brother on a holiday... :(

Me: I wasn't just inviting you, dummy. Your dad and Louis are more than welcome to come with you and stay for the night.

The three black dots appeared, then disappeared, again and again for two minutes. I had no idea the simple sight of these could make my chest tighten this easily until today. After an eternity, the dots disappeared, replaced by her answer.

Addy The REAL Music Connoisseur: Count us in. :)

I released a sigh and turned in Helen's direction. I could tell she was holding her breath, face anxious for my answer.

"She's in."

Helen squealed, and this time, I wasn't able to control my smile.

ADELAIDE

"*C*ome on, Lou, we're gonna be late!"

I wiped my sweaty hands down the limited length of my jean shorts. If I'd thought June had been hot, it was nothing compared to what July felt like, especially in our cramped four-and-a-half.

"Coming!" Louis yelled from his room, which, in Louis language, meant coming in five minutes.

Sitting back down, I looked to my right, where my father was seated at the kitchen table. I'd finally cut his hair a few days ago, and he'd shaved and showered, which made him look at least ten years younger. He was dressed in a short-sleeved light pink shirt—what used to be my mom's favorite—and beige Bermuda shorts. It was the first time I saw him actually dressed up since my mother's funeral, and I couldn't help the tingle of hope brewing in my chest.

Grabbing his hand sitting on the tabletop, I said, "Thank you for coming with us. It means a lot to Louis and me."

He turned his face in my direction and gave me a wobbly smile. His body trembled under my hand, but he didn't say anything about not coming. I knew he didn't feel like going to a stranger's house tonight—far from it—but the simple fact that he was trying meant the world to me. It felt like a step in the right direction.

I grinned and wrinkled my nose at him just as Louis came running from his room and said, "Okay, I'm ready!"

He was also dressed in a pink shirt and beige Bermuda shorts. I'd bought him this outfit a year ago when he'd said he wanted to get dressed like Dad. At the time, I thought it might've been his strategy to grab our father's attention, but I still proceeded to buy it for him, and now that I was looking at them both, I couldn't regret my choice. My dad and Louis already looked alike, with their brown hair, chocolate eyes, and pointy noses, but today, they were literal twins.

"You look good, Lou," my dad said with a half-smile.

My brother's face lit up, and it was enough to make my heart burst with happiness. Before I could forget, I grabbed my phone and snapped a picture of my two men in their matching clothes.

I knew my dad's morale wouldn't always be like it was today, but whatever would happen in the future, I'd always have the memories of this day with me.

We left right after, taking the bus to Cape Neddick. I couldn't remember the last time the three of us had done something together. Louis was laughing at something my dad had said, snorting by accident. I couldn't wipe the smile off my face the whole ride to the Philips' place.

When we got to the house, I led Louis and my father to the backyard. I had a feeling this would be where the party would take place, especially considering Matt had told me we would be eating barbeque.

Once we reached the back of the house, I spotted Matt right away, standing at least two inches taller than anyone present. There was Helen too, speaking to some man beside her. I recognized the couple from the wedding Matt and I had attended, as well as a gorgeous red-haired woman whom I'd also seen at the wedding.

Behind them, the sun was slowly setting above the Atlantic, spreading a burnt orange tint over the surface of the water. A bonfire was crackling in the middle of the yard, surrounded by white Adirondack chairs. The charcoal scent of the barbeque filled my nostrils, and my father and Louis probably smelled the same thing because we all sighed in unison.

Walking toward the small crowd of people, I realized Matt wasn't alone. He was speaking to a woman who had her back to me. Her long, light brown hair floated in the wind, and I had this intense punch-like feeling to the gut. Who was she?

But, with the way she was talking, her hands moving as she explained something and made him laugh, I felt this wave of familiarity. And her hair...

Suddenly, she turned around as Matt spotted me and pointed in my direction, and all the air whooshed out of my lungs. Before I'd fully realized what was happening, my feet were slapping the ground, running faster than they ever had before.

"Stella!" I screamed as I jumped in her arms and wrapped her in a bear hug, making her fall backward in the freshly-cut grass, my body sprawled on top of hers.

"Jesus, Addy, you wanna kill us both?" She chuckled, and I released an incredulous laugh too. I couldn't believe it. She was here. Really here. I grabbed her shoulders, looking at her with wide eyes, my heart thump-thump-thumping against my chest.

"What are you doing here? I can't believe you're here!" My cheeks were wet; I guessed I'd started crying at some point. I hadn't seen her in person in more than a year.

"Your...um, friend invited me to stay at his place for the weekend," my best friend said.

She nudged her chin to something behind me. I twisted my neck to find Matthias standing there, dressed in gray chinos and a white shirt, hands in his pockets, beaming at me.

As rapidly as I'd ran toward her, I got up from Stella and raced toward Matthias, jumping in his arms. His arms came up right away, circling my body tightly before he spun me around, laughing loudly against my neck.

169

"Thank you. Thank you, thank you, thank you," I whispered in his neck. "God, I could kiss you right now."

I realized what I'd said too late. Damn verbal diarrhea. His throat bobbed beside my head and his body stiffened beneath me. As he cleared his throat, I released his neck from my arms. He let go of my back shortly after, and I didn't look at him again. Instead, I turned back toward Stella. I swore I heard him mutter something under his breath, but I didn't try to figure out what it was. My focus needed to be on my best friend tonight. We had so much to catch up on.

MATTHIAS

I didn't think I'd ever seen her this happy. Addy was always smiling, always giggling in her day-to-day life, but today, it was different. It was like she had this aura to her, this glow, screaming how joyful she was. It was a sight for sore eyes.

Taking a swig of my beer, I continued to watch her. She and Stella were sitting on adjacent Adirondacks, and they'd been talking non-stop for the past hour, speaking on top of the other and at a rate no one else would have been able to follow, as if they had too much to say and they didn't want to forget any of it.

Looking at her laughing and gesticulating while talking was a much-needed distraction to keep my mind off what had happened before. *I could kiss you right now.* She'd said it so casually, like it was the first thing that had popped into her head. But for me, there was nothing casual about it. I'd been tempted to say fuck it and kiss her, right then and there, in front of all our families and friends. I wanted to. I really fucking wanted to. She was so beautiful in those cut off shorts that showed her infinite legs and black t-shirt, her famous Chucks at her feet. It was a simple outfit, but it was so *her*. I loved it.

But just as the words had left her mouth, she'd stiffened, like she'd said something inappropriate, something she didn't actually believe. And then, she'd turned around and avoided my eyes for the next hour. So, in the end, I was lucky I hadn't listened to my instinct and kissed the hell out of her. Would've been awkward to get rejected in front of everyone by my mother's caregiver. I had to remind myself that was what she was. That was all she could be.

From the corner of my eye, I caught a flash of red hair. Rosalie threw me a grin as she took a seat beside me.

"So, you gonna ask her out yet?"

My eyebrows shot up. "What are you talking about?"

She rolled her eyes and smirked. "Come on, Loverboy. It's written all over your face. I think I even caught you drooling a bit during the whole hour you've been staring at her like a stalker."

Had I really been that easy to read? I shook my head. "It doesn't matter, it can't happen. And I wasn't fucking drooling," I growled.

"Sure you weren't." She winked before looking off toward the ocean for a while. When she came back to me, she had this naughty grin on her face. "You know what would help?" She turned toward everyone seated in the circle surrounding the fire pit and yelled, "Shots!"

I didn't need to think about it for more than a second to know this was a bad idea. "No. Oh, hell no."

But, Rosalie's proposition made Stella's head turn in our direction, and she had the same wicked facial expression. "I think shots are a *fantastic* idea."

Addy looked behind her, her eyes roaming over the yard. She bit her plump lower lip, as if she wasn't sure this was the best of ideas either. Stella nudged her with her elbow. "They're staying here to sleep, Addy. Nothing will happen to Louis, even if you get drunk a little."

I gazed in the direction Addy had before. Her father and brother were seated around a Connect 4 game, and while they didn't seem to be having the time of their lives, they appeared to be faring quite well.

Addy's jaw moved back and forth for a minute, the mitigated look in her eyes never leaving, then said, "All right, let's do this."

Pushing my hands against my knees, I got up. "Well, I'm gonna leave you to it."

She shot to her feet. "Oh, no. If I'm doing this, you're doing this too."

I had to admit, I hadn't gotten drunk in a while, and the prospect of keeping my head away from all the inappropriate thoughts I had about Addy right now would be welcome. Feeling too many things for someone I could never have seemed like a pretty good reason to get wasted. But, there was also Helen to think about.

Addy probably saw the hesitation in my face because she said, "Dora's inside, if Helen needs something. She doesn't need us to be her caregivers for the night, just her friend and son."

It was as if she'd read my thoughts. Then, she raised an eyebrow and gave me this daring grin. "Come on, Grumpy."

That was it. It was a done deal. I couldn't resist her, no matter how hard I tried.

"Fine." I pointed an index finger at her. "But we're going shot for shot. If we're doing this, we're doing it together."

Rosalie and Stella both jumped up, clapping their hands in glee, while Addy smirked wickedly, burning my skin with her stare. It was then I realized this was a dumb fucking idea.

ADELAIDE

*M*atthias was wasted.

I mean, as wasted as someone like him could be. I'd never witnessed him abandon his usual self-control like he had tonight. I didn't even think he had it in him to get drunk like this. When he'd accepted to drink with us, I'd expected him to take a shot or two, but that wasn't how it'd went down. He'd gone all-in. And now, he was swaying in the middle of the yard, giggling like a little kid, holding onto Helen's arms and making himself twirl underneath them. It was the funniest thing I'd ever seen.

I had to admit, I wasn't exactly sober myself. I didn't drink often, but when I was with Stella, it was inevitable. On my eighteenth birthday, I'd driven back to Montreal to go club-bing with her, and she'd made me drink so much, it'd taken me a whole week to recover from it. Ever since that night, she tried to repeat the experience whenever we saw each other. Thank God I could handle my alcohol better now.

My father and Louis had gone inside to sleep an hour or so ago, but other than that, the majority of the guests hadn't left yet. We were something like fifteen people around the bonfire and in the yard, some playing board games, others still doing shots, the majority chatting.

Beside me, a man I didn't recognize—early thirties, curly blond hair, cute smile—sat with an acoustic guitar in his hands. Propping the instrument on his knees, he started strumming one of my favorite songs, Coldplay's "Fix You." The moon was casting a silvery glow over the water, but beside it, there was nothing but darkness. I loved the view we had here during the day, but at night, it was just as peaceful, if not more.

The music resonated around me, *through* me, and I did the only thing I could do when I felt this way. I closed my eyes, let myself get transported by the music, and sang.

Stella let out a *whoop* beside me as I finished the first verse.

I opened my eyes and winked at her. Aside from my mother, she'd always been my biggest fan. Some people hate it when their friends receive all the attention, but my best friend wasn't like that. She put the spotlight on me anytime she could.

I realized after singing for one or two minutes that Matt had stopped dancing around his mother. He was now seated cross-legged in the grass like a child, eyes wide and mouth curled into a smile. And, just like that day at the church, I couldn't keep my eyes off him, like I was singing to him. He was the best audience I could've asked for, with his attentive eyes and awe-filled face.

Once the song ended, a couple of people applauded around me, while Stella wrapped her hands around her mouth like a megaphone and yelled wildly inappropriate things, which made me crack up. Matt and I weren't the only ones who had downed tequila a few hours ago.

Suddenly, a loud pop resonated around us, followed by a burst of red and green in the sky. Stella and I both shrieked in surprise, and then everyone got up to head closer to the cliff, where we could see the fireworks coming from the beach to our left even better.

Gasps and exclamations were released as light kept popping in front of us, illuminating the sky in golds and pinks and blues. The breathtaking view, mixed with the warmth in my belly from the alcohol, the salty breeze whipping around my head, and the heat from Matthias' gaze on my profile made me dizzy with excitement.

Matt and I had exchanged glances all through the night after my stupid comment from earlier. I wasn't sure what exactly those stolen looks meant, but when I turned my head to the left, beaming, the expression in his eyes reminded me of lust. And it made something in my belly clench, leading to an ache building between my legs.

Fireworks continued to pop in front of us, but our eyes were locked together, entranced in something unrelated to the party taking place, but just as festive. The end of the show was near, considering the increase of explosions surrounding us and the *ooh*'s and *aah*'s exclaimed by the guests around us. Still, Matt's eyes didn't falter away from mine. Blood was thumping in my ears, almost as loud as the fireworks.

Once the last firework burst in the sky, Matt made a beeline at me, making my heart stop. He walked with overconfidence through the crowd, long strides and stiff jaw that made liquid heat course through my veins. However, this overconfidence also cost him his balance. Before he could reach me, he tripped on someone's foot and wasn't able to stay upright.

I giggled as I made my way to his sprawled body and crouched in front of him. "Are you...are you okay?" I had trouble getting the whole sentence out, laughing too much. There weren't a lot of things I found funnier than seeing people fall, but add to that the fact that I was pretty tipsy, and it was Matt—always in control, always confident Matt—who had fallen, and there was the recipe to make me laugh for the next hour.

He answered with a groan, which made me laugh even harder. Grass covered the front of his shirt as he pushed himself up into a sitting position. Once he was seated, his eyes widened before he screwed them shut.

"I think you've had enough for tonight, Grumpy. Let's get you to bed." I offered him my hand and helped him stand. Once he was up, I offered him my shoulder to lean on, but he groaned again. "I can stay upright, I'm no drunker than you are."

I hid a grin. "Right." Lightweight.

He waved at some of the guests as we made our way to the house, stopping by the drinks table on the way for two glasses of water, which I forced him to gulp down. When he was done, we finished the small trek home. He might not have wanted my help, but I preferred to see him safe in bed for myself.

Inside, I walked in the direction of his room, diagonal from

Helen's, and opened the door. I'd never gone inside, and found it to be just as I'd imagined it. White walls, a simple and modern wooden bed frame, and a light gray bedspread. There weren't a lot of personal items, which shouldn't have surprised me, but still did. Matt had told me a while ago he'd moved back in with his mother three years ago—when she'd gotten sick—yet his room still looked almost uninhabited.

Matt had decided to drape an arm over my shoulders after all, and when we reached his bed, he dropped his body on it, pulling me down with him. I giggled—which seemed to be doing non-stop tonight—as I tried to push myself off him, but this just made his grip tighten on my back.

"Okay, Matt, time to sleep now," I said, a big smile on my lips.

His eyes were pleading. "But just stay with me for a while."

I sighed as he squeezed me again, his warmth spreading through my skin. I never would've let myself enjoy this, not with my boss, but it felt as if I'd lost all my good reason in the last three shots I'd taken. At that moment, I didn't see how any harm could come from enjoying his touch for a minute more. I leaned my head on the bed, facing him.

This was dangerous territory, yet I couldn't find it in me to move.

His nose nudged my neck before he inhaled deeply. "You smell so good. Like a…like a rose."

Laughing, I said, "Not the best at thinking of good similes when you're drunk, huh?"

"I'm not that drunk. Just a little tipsy."

I looked at him once more, and he seemed to be telling the truth. His eyes weren't as glossy as before. The moonlight traced his profile, his jaw appearing even sharper, his lips plumper. Less than three inches separated our faces, his rapid exhales tickling my chin. Shifting my butt, I moved a bit closer to him, and he swallowed before dropping his gaze to my lips. It didn't stay there for a long time, but it was long enough for me to notice it. An alarm bell rang through my head, but I ignored it. My breath hitched as his face inched closer to mine, until our noses were brushing. His musky scent was a drug to me, and my eyelids fluttered as I took another hit.

Slowly, he lifted a hand and tucked a strand of hair behind my ear, the tips of his fingers caressing my cheek before resting on it.

God, I'd never stood a chance.

Before I could register who had moved first, his lips were on mine, so soft but also demanding. He kissed me through closed lips. I gasped, feeling a thousand conflicting emotions at once. Need. Wariness. Love.

When his tongue licked my lips, something took over me and I opened them, giving him full access to me. All of me. And he took it. Climbing over me, he plunged his tongue into my mouth. I let out a moan. God, this felt good. Heavenly good.

Groaning, he gripped my ass, shifting us so he was on his back and I was straddling him. His breathing came in pants against my skin as I fisted his hair, already feeling heat building between my legs. His lips moved to my neck, kissing and sucking until they made their way to my collarbone. I heaved as he took my shirt off, and when his teeth bit softly in the flesh of my breasts, I moaned and rubbed my pelvis against his growing hardness.

"Fuck, Addy, don't do that if you don't want me to come before this has even started."

His voice brought some sense into me, and as fast as I'd climbed on top of him, I jumped to my feet on the floor. "We can't do this. Not right now." As much as I craved his body, it wasn't right.

He sat up. His chest rose and fell rapidly, hair sticking in every direction. "Why not?"

"Because you're drunk, and I don't want you to feel like I'm...taking advantage of you."

One of his eyebrows shot up. "Take advantage of *me*?" He

got on his feet, meeting me in the middle of his room. I looked down, but his index finger tilted my chin up. "First, I'm really not drunk anymore. And second, Addy, you have *no idea* how much I want you. Now, and yesterday, and every second of every fucking day."

I swallowed against my suddenly dry throat. "But you're… you're still my boss."

Matt's eyes closed for a fraction of a second before he leaned forward, his face now dangerously close to mine. "Forget about it." His lips brushed the skin in front of my ear, where he whispered, "Let's pretend we're just two people who really, really like each other." His mouth trailed down, leaving a feather-light kiss on my cheek. "Just for tonight." The next brush of his lips was on my chin. "Let's pretend."

It wasn't a good idea. I knew it wasn't. But with the throbbing between my legs and Matthias' index finger brushing the skin over my collarbone, I couldn't think clearly. And, when his finger dipped in my bra and caressed my nipple, I couldn't think of a single reason why we shouldn't do this anymore. Not when it felt this right.

Throwing my head back, I gave him access as his mouth pressed gentle kisses from my jaw to my neck. My hands reached his neck, nails biting in his skin when his tongue slipped out of his mouth and traced a wet path over my shoulder.

A whimper escaped my mouth as his hand moved away from my breast, then a yelp when he turned me around in one swift move, pressing my backside against his hard length. Gasps replaced my breaths as his hand met my body again, but this time, lower. His long digits spanned my belly, descending in a sweet torture until they reached the button of my shorts. Then, they slipped inside, ever so slowly, always giving me the time to back out.

Goosebumps rose on my arms as his breath hit my ear. "I could make you feel *so* good." His voice was low and slow, thick as honey. My body was in sensory overload, and when his middle finger brushed against my throbbing bundle of nerves, I knew there was no way I could turn him down, not when I wanted him this much. I'd think about the consequences tomorrow. Tonight, I needed him.

The material of my jean shorts was rough against my sensitive skin as I pushed them down my legs, panties going too. After stepping out of them, I turned around and faced Matthias' wide eyes. They got even larger when my hands reached for the collar of his shirt and unbuttoned it, my fingers brushing against his chest in a way I knew would drive him crazy. Two could play this teasing game.

When his shirt was off, his gaze seared through my skin, moving from my heaving chest to my taut stomach, and ending in between my legs.

Then, in one quick motion, my back was against the wall, Matthias' hands framing my head, and he was kissing me. His tongue brushed against mine with confidence and need, and I answered each of his gentle assaults with one of my own.

As he was dipping his tongue deeper, kissing me like I'd never been kissed before, his hands reached behind my bra and unclasped it with ease, freeing my breasts. I threw it away and arched my back when I felt his hands on my sensitive skin, soft yet relentless with each of their teases.

Matt lowered his lips from my mouth to my breasts, earning a moan out of me when his tongue flicked against one of my nipples while his fingers pinched the other. "You're so perfect," he murmured against my skin. Wetness accumulated between my legs with every movement of his tongue. My breathing accelerated even more, coming out in little gasps.

Matt groaned as I pulled on his hair after getting a nipple bitten, feeling like I could burst at any moment. I'd never felt like this before, as if my whole body was made of dynamite and Matthias was a lighter.

"Matt," I whispered, his name a prayer on my lips. Abandoning my breasts, he kneeled in front of me, his beard tickling the inside of my thighs, and I shivered right as he stuck his tongue out and licked my dripping seam from bottom to top, his movement painfully slow. I cried out in pleasure, closing my eyes and leaning my head back. He repeated the movement, again and again, keeping an unhurried pace until my legs felt like Jell-O. I'd never felt anything so good, so carnal and raw and incredible. My stomach was already tightening in anticipation for what was coming next.

As my legs wobbled, he gripped one of them and put it on his shoulders, allowing his tongue to go even farther and deeper. And, when his tongue dipped inside me, I thought I might die from pleasure. Though if I had to die, this was the way I wanted to go.

He pressed a slow, tongue-filled kiss to my middle. "You taste so fucking good." The pads of his fingers stroked my thighs. "I could do this non-stop, forever." His voice had lowered down a tone, and this, mixed with the sounds of his licking and sucking, was the sexiest thing I'd ever heard.

"Please," I moaned as my eyes rolled back in my head, though I didn't even know what I was asking for. I couldn't imagine feeling anything better than what I was experiencing right now.

That was, until he made me realize I had no idea about the extent of how good he was.

Shifting his mouth, he started sucking on my clit, all the while adding a finger inside me. I moaned even louder as his digit stretched me open. Matt took his finger out and repeated the pumping motion, again and again until all that was left of me was a puddle of want.

My nails dug in his scalp as he lifted my other leg on his shoulder and hoisted me up so I was leaning against the wall, his face perfectly settled between my legs. Slowly, he added a second finger, continuing to pump at a steady rhythm while his tongue and lips never stopped teasing my clit. I could feel my nerves getting ready to fire up, and when I opened my eyes and caught him watching me, ebony eyes full of lust and want, I let myself go. My muscles pulsed around his fingers as I cried out, the pleasure more intense than anything I'd ever felt before. I didn't know how Matt had done it, but I was high and never wanted to come down. I came and came and came until I was a panting mess on his shoulders.

When my breathing had slowed down, Matt lowered me to the floor, keeping me steady when my legs felt like failing me. My fingers were still tangled in his hair, and I pulled him toward me to show him how I felt with my mouth. I kissed him with everything I had, tasting myself on his tongue.

When I unlocked our lips, we were both gasping for air. "Bed. Now," I grumbled.

He didn't wait a second before pulling me behind him by the arm. I let myself get dragged through the room, still stuck in my post-orgasmic daze.

When we reached his bed, though, I had come to all my senses, and I didn't need him to tell me what to do. In three quick motions, his pants were on the floor, and his erection was freed, impressive and so, so ready.

"Condom?" I asked.

Matt leaned back, grabbing a foil packet in his bedside drawer. As soon as he passed it to me, I opened it and lowered the condom down his erection. He groaned, jaw tight, as if a simple touch was too much for him. Once I was done, I straddled his lap, but I didn't have time to lower myself down on his erection before I was flipped to my side, facing him as we both laid.

"You sure about this?" His face painted both concern and extreme desire.

"Yes. Please." Two words that lit a fire in his eyes.

Just as the plea escaped my mouth, he lowered a hand to where our bodies connected and pushed his length inside me. I gasped at the sheer thickness of him. It'd been a while since I'd been with anyone, and I gritted my teeth as he pushed himself deeper and deeper with a grunt. When he had entered my body fully, he stilled. "You okay?"

I nodded instead of answering, taking a minute to breathe through the stretch until it didn't feel painful, only good. When I started moving against him, Matt brought his lips to mine and sucked on my mouth and on my tongue, making me breathless all over again. Pulling himself out, he pushed inside me for a second time, and I gasped, this time from pure pleasure. He did it again, finding his rhythm based on the sounds I let out. He adjusted all his thrusts to the moans and sighs I made, creating a pattern that was steady and oh so amazing.

Sweat coated our bodies as we kissed and moved. With every plunge his erection made, I ground my pelvis against his, making him grunt each time. And, when I contracted my inner muscles, squeezing him inside me, he cursed under his breath. "If you do that again, I won't be able to hold off."

To this, I answered with another contraction. His eyes closed and his breathing became more frantic. The stretch of him felt divine, bringing me close to the edge all over again. I leaned my head back, allowing his mouth to roam over my neck. He took the opportunity to lick my skin, all the while bringing one of his hands between our bodies, rubbing soft circles around my clit.

This did it. Gasping, I came, muscles tightening again and again around his length. And so he joined me, sharing my ecstasy with curses and groans until we came down, breathing hard against each other.

Pulling my head against his chest, he sighed. "Goddammit Addy, I knew this would be good, but... Fuck."

I laughed, understanding exactly what he meant. I wasn't a virgin of any sort, but being with Matt, it felt like I hadn't yet understood what sex truly was. Like I'd never known how good it could get until today. And I imagined it had a lot to do with the way I felt about this man. "I know."

Getting up, I quickly went to the bathroom to clean up. When I came back to the room, Matt was facing away from me, naked from head to toe. I felt a sudden tug to the heart when I thought about what I should do next.

It might have been the alcohol, or the post-orgasmic bliss, or everything I felt for this man, but somehow, I didn't want to leave. Even though I knew I should, I couldn't. I hoped the deal we'd made could stay in place for the rest of the night and just this once, we could fall asleep together. An illusion of perfection.

But, did he want the same thing?

My fears were brushed aside when he turned around, lips tilted upward. With a dip of his head, he invited me to his bed. I didn't hesitate, jumping in with him and snuggling against his toned body.

In seconds, I was asleep.

I was too hot.

Everything around me was blazing, suffocating me. I moved my body, suddenly sensing something hard beneath my head.

What. The. Hell.

I stretched my legs a little, jumping when my skin rubbed against body hair.

That's when last night came back to me. The hug. The fireworks. The kisses. The sex.

Oh, God. I was in deep shit.

When I opened my eyes, I sighed in relief. Matthias' eyes were closed and his breathing was slow and steady. Maybe if I escaped his room before he woke up, I could hope he'd never remember any of it?

It wasn't that I regretted what had happened per se. I'd had sex—the most amazing sex—with the man I was in love with.

That would've all been fine and dandy if this man wasn't also my boss.

Slowly, I pulled myself away from his warm body. I gasped internally when Matthias moved, but he didn't wake. He scratched his beard before turning over to the side opposite to mine.

Bingo.

On my tiptoes, I got up and walked across his room, retrieving last night's clothes and putting them on. Taking a quick glance behind my shoulder, I exhaled. Matthias was still very fast asleep.

Blessed be the deities watching over me, the door opened without so much as a squeak. At least my walk of shame would be unnoticed.

But of course, that was only a fantasy. When I reached the kitchen, both Stella and Helen were seated at the table, facing me with the most infuriating smirks.

"So," my best friend started, "I gather you've had fun last night?" One of her eyebrows shot up. Heat automatically crept up my neck and cheeks. I'd kill the bitch.

"I don't..." I walked to the coffee pot. "I don't know what you're talking about."

"So y-you did not just come out of my s-s-son's room?"

Facing Stella was one thing, but Helen? Oh God, I was her caregiver and she very well knew I'd slept with her son. *Great job, Addy!*

Keeping my back to them, I shook my head, not having the force to say anything out loud. They snickered.

When I made my way to the table with them, I glared at their amused faces. "You two better stop talking about this, or I'm leaving."

"Fine, fine," Stella said, giving Helen a look.

"Stop talking about what?" a deep voice asked behind me.

This *really* wasn't my day.

I turned on my chair and held my breath as I took Matthias

in. His hair was in a disarray, like it'd been when I'd left his room. He wasn't dressed the same as yesterday like me, but instead had put on gray sweatpants and a black t-shirt, which hugged his chest in the most aggravating way. And when his eyes caught mine, the flutter in my chest told me I could never regret what had happened yesterday. At least not fully.

"Hey, Stella, how about we go chat outside?" Helen, Queen of Subtlety, uttered.

"What an amazing idea!" Stella got up and winked at me before heading out the patio door, Helen right behind her. When the door clicked shut, I headed toward Matthias.

Keeping my eyes on my feet, I cleared my throat. "What happened yesterday, it, um, it can't happen again."

He stayed silent for a while. I lifted my head, finding his eyes narrowed in on me.

"However great it was, you're still my boss," I continued. "It's not like we can ignore that part."

His nostrils flared. After a second, he nodded once. "Right. It was just...pretend, right?"

I gulped. "Right."

Just pretend, except for the fact that my heart wanted to burst every time he was around me. No big deal at all.

The last Fourth of July I celebrated was my favorite one to date.

There weren't too many people, only the ones who were really important to us. I got to meet Stella, who I liked right away. We talked about our respective careers and our favorite medical anecdotes. I laughed like I hadn't in a long time.

Louis was there too, running around the yard with a kite I'd asked Dora to get out for him. Right before he went to bed, I taught him how to make the best s'mores, and he gave me the cutest grin, chocolate-covered face and all. It made me feel like a kid all over again.

I knew it would probably be the last time I'd get to celebrate with all of you, so I made sure to enjoy the most out of it. And I did. It was a night I will never forget.

But, now that I think about it, I shouldn't have waited to become sick to start enjoying the most of our Fourth of July parties. Or of anything, for that matter. So, this leads us to Helen Advice number seven.

Don't wait until you're old or sick or dying to appreciate things. Live life to the fullest. Always. Starting now. Look at everything around you, be thankful for it, and enjoy the most of it. Time goes by so fast, blink and you'll miss it. So never wait for anything. Your moment is now.

Love,
Helen.

19

ADELAIDE

"*H*appy birthday, Addy!"

I opened my eyes to find Louis' face hovering over me, a toothy beam illuminating his face. His body was crushing mine on the futon, but I didn't complain. I couldn't think of a better way to wake up than this one.

"Thanks, Lou." Bringing my arms out from under the covers, I wrapped them around his body, which had grown remarkably in the last few months. Thinking that my little Louis was growing into a man made me squeeze him tighter.

Lifting his head from my chest, he got a folded paper from his pajama pants and gave it to me, his grin widening. As I pushed myself into a seating position, I grabbed the paper, which was a birthday card. Louis had drawn hearts and what might or might not have been my face on the cover.

I didn't wait to read what was inside before leaning forward and squeezing him tightly in my arms again. "Thank you, Loulou."

At the same time, my father walked into the living room and his eyes narrowed on the birthday card. His face became an unusual shade of red. "I'm… I'm sorry, I forgot, Addy."

His guilty expression broke my heart, and I got up to

squeeze him tight in my arms too. It wasn't like he had remembered my birthdays during the last two years either, but the
fact that he'd noticed today made me feel hopeful all over
again. "It's okay, Dad."

Rubbing my back, he said, "Happy birthday, honey."

He took a step back, holding me by the shoulders, and
smiled. "I remember the day you were born so clearly. It was
the happiest I'd ever been. Your mother too."

I didn't trust my voice, so I answered with a smile.

"How about we go on a walk to the park later, maybe grab
some ice cream?" he said. "To celebrate?"

Nodding way too hard, I stepped in for another hug. My
dad's shirt smelled like his cologne, which he hadn't worn in so
long. It reminded me of the hugs he used to give me when I
hurt myself as a kid and he gave me his special kinds of boo-
boo-healing kisses. It smelled like comfort, like love.

While he released my body, three loud knocks on the front
door startled us.

"Were you expecting someone for your birthday?" my dad
asked.

"No," I said. "At least I don't remember inviting anyone."

I looked down at my pajamas, which were actually a loose
pair of white cotton shorts and a red t-shirt I'd kept from my
days as a camp monitor. It would have to do.

I gasped as I opened the door, finding Matthias standing on
the front door mat, clad in forest green shorts, a black V-neck,
and aviator sunglasses, a breathtaking smile splitting his face.
"Happy birthday, Addy."

Nope, I did not get a sudden flash of what he looked like
without his clothes.

"What... How did you know?" I said. "I didn't even
mention it."

He smirked. "You told Helen a few weeks ago. Not the best
at keeping secrets."

Warmth spread through my body, either from the inappropriate images racing through my head or from the thought that he had taken the time to come here to wish me a happy birthday. He didn't have to do that. He was just my boss, after all. What had happened on the Fourth of July hadn't meant anything. At least that was what I kept reminding myself, over and over again.

"Thank you, I really appreciate it." I smiled, and when he didn't say anything else, my heart started beating faster in my chest. "So, what are you doing here?"

"Isn't it obvious?"

When I raised an eyebrow, he rolled his eyes and laughed. "I'm here to take you on a birthday activity." He leaned forward and whispered above my ear, "Just as friends, don't worry."

I swallowed hard. "And what is that special activity?" Why did my voice sound so strained all of a sudden?

"That's a surprise." He winked, and I felt it straight to my core. "Hurry, you have..." He looked down at his chrome wristwatch. "Five minutes to get ready."

"But... I..." Turning around, I made eye contact with my father and Louis. I couldn't leave them alone, especially after they'd offered to do something with me for my birthday this afternoon.

Dad shook his head. "It's okay, Addy. Louis was supposed to go play with Josh today. I'll drop him off at Mrs. Zhu's place later."

"Are you sure?"

A corner of his lips twitched up. "Yes, I'm sure. Go!"

I looked back and forth between Matthias and my dad before blurting out, "Okay then!" I giggled all the way to my closet, feeling excited like I rarely had.

MATTHIAS

*"W*hat is this thing?"

I chuckled at Addy's horrified look as we got out of the car at the airport.

"That's a plane, Addy."

She gave me a death glare before returning her eyes to the plane. "Yes, I know it's a plane, Matt. But it's so... tiny! Can this thing really fly?"

I chuckled again as I grabbed her hand, pulling her toward the Seminole. "Yes, it can fly. As a matter of fact, we're flying in it today."

She started pulling on my hand and backing up. "What? No!"

"Addy!" I laughed, meeting the fear and excitement in her eyes. She was reacting exactly the way I'd expected her to. "Do you trust me?"

She bit her lip. "Of course, I trust you."

My stomach dipped. Instead of showing what her words were doing to me, I grinned. "Then get in the damn plane with me."

She tapped her foot a few times, never dropping my gaze, and then must have fallen short of a witty remark. "Only with you."

That hit me right in the core again. I tugged her hand and she fell into step next to me. After ensuring everything was okay with the plane, I led Addy to the door and urged her inside, plugging her headset at her feet and putting it on her head. Once I made sure she was buckled, I threw her a wink, her expression of horror and excitement making me laugh. Looking at her, I had the strong urge to lean down and kiss the freckles on the tip of her nose. Instead, I circled the plane, took my seat to Addy's left, and put my headset on. As soon as I did, I heard her breathing hard.

"If we die today, I'll kill you in the afterlife."

I glanced in her direction, seeing her hands shaking in her

lap. "Deal. But, I promise we won't die. That would be a really terrible birthday gift."

She smacked my shoulder. "Don't be a smug prick. Focus on flying this thing instead."

Repressing a smile, I said, "Aye, aye, captain."

After turning on the engine, I drove us to the runway, all the while asking for the all-clear to take off. Beside me, I could tell Addy's eyes were squeezed shut, and her hands were turning white from holding onto the seat so tight.

Once the control tower told me we were okay to go, I asked Addy, "Ready?"

Keeping her eyes closed, she muttered in her headset, "Ready."

As soon as the words were out of her mouth, I pushed the plane to the high speed required, adrenaline shooting through my veins as if this wasn't the thousandth time I had done this. The sound of the engine overtook everything around us, and in seconds, I lifted the plane, the front wheels leaving the ground, followed by the back ones. We wobbled a little, making Addy shriek.

As the cars got tinier below us, I turned to her. "Open your eyes!"

Slowly, she peeled her eyes open. As a pilot, I had seen hundreds of pieces of the world, but the look on her face as she surveyed the land beneath us was more beautiful than all of them combined. It reminded me of how I'd felt the first time I'd flown, how fascinated I'd been to be in the air, how freeing it had felt. I'd known right away this was what I wanted—what I *needed*—to do when I was older.

Soon enough, we were soaring over the Atlantic, and I could hear Addy gasping and laughing as she leaned closer to the window.

"I've never seen anything so beautiful." Her voice was strained. I gazed at her, understanding exactly what she meant, even if she couldn't tell my eyes were only on her.

"I know."

We kept to ourselves for a while, the silence forcing most of my focus to the woman beside me. To her fruity perfume enveloping me. To the way her lips parted and her chest rose rapidly.

Blue surrounded us from everywhere. Only a few clouds adorned the sky—which made Addy scream when we passed through them—and the sun was shining bright, making the water underneath us sparkle like diamonds.

When the plane was stable enough, I glanced her way, smirking. "Now it's your turn."

Her eyes became round. "What? What do you mean?" The words came out fast.

"You steer the plane."

"NO!"

I laughed at the panic in her tone. "Relax, Addy, I'll be right beside you if anything happens. It's just to give you a sense of what it's like to control a plane."

She shook her head. "I really, really don't think this is a good idea."

"I thought we were trusting me today?" I smiled, but her lips didn't even twitch. I nudged her with my elbow. "Come on, place your hands on the yoke. In ten seconds, I'm letting go and it's up to you to steer us."

She squealed but did as I said.

"Good. Now, just try to keep us on a straight trajectory."

Her throat bobbed as she nodded. When she looked ready, I told her it was time for her to do it. Her face took on this determined look as she squared her shoulders, more concentrated than ever on the task at hand. She looked so adorable at that moment, I had to bite my cheek not to smile.

After a few seconds, she said, "I'm doing this. I'm really doing this. I'm flying a plane." Her tone was soft, like she had to say it aloud to truly believe it.

"You are."

Her lips turned upward then, and she gave me the most gorgeous smile I'd ever seen. I realized then that she reminded me of the ocean. So much deeper than anyone could imagine. Scary, yet soothing. Tempestuous at times, serene at others. And always the most beautiful thing I could ever lay my eyes on.

When she'd been steering for a few minutes, I took back control of the plane. "You can let go now."

Her hands moved from the wheel to her chest, where she clasped them together. Her face was a mix of awe and happiness. I thought she might say something, but she didn't. Instead, she stayed silent as I made a slow turn and headed back to the airport.

After I got the okay to land, I did, smoothly. There was almost no wind today, making the landing so easy I could've done it with my eyes closed. The plane slowed and finally came to a halt.

Turning off the engine, I twisted my head in her direction. She was still staring straight ahead, her hands unmoved from their position on her chest.

"Are you okay? I asked.

It took her a whole minute to answer, and my heart was in my throat the whole time I waited for her to do so. When she did, all of my body relaxed.

Gazing at me with those gorgeous dark green eyes of hers, she said, "This was the most amazing thing I ever did. The feeling of being in control..." Her head shook from left to right. "I get what you meant when you said it was the one thing that made you want to do this." She inhaled a big breath. "Thank you so much for bringing me here."

I answered with a grin, and something happened then. Her eyes dropped to my lips before making their way back up, filled with something I'd been dreaming of seeing in them again, ever since she'd left my bed days ago: lust. It was clear in the way her gaze darkened, her chest pushed out, and her breath hitched. I exhaled shakily, torn between thinking I had no right doing this and thinking nothing would feel more right than being with her again. I'd thought once I was with her, maybe my desire would lessen, but the opposite had happened. She was a drug, and I needed more.

But this would be her decision. I knew how she felt about our previous time together, and I didn't want to be another cause of regret for her. I wouldn't act on my instinct, even though every cell in my body told me I should kiss her right fucking now.

But if she made the first move, I'd never be able to resist her.

When her eyes returned to my lips, they didn't hold any question. Only answers.

In a split second, she moved from her seat beside me to my lap, and before I could take a breath, her lips crashed onto mine. I released a sigh I'd been holding in for days. Wrapping my arms around her back, I squeezed her tighter to me as her hands roamed from my arms to my shoulders, finishing their course in my hair. Her fingers gripped strands as her mouth opened, allowing my tongue in.

She moaned when our tongues collided, twisting and lapping, all warm and wet. At that moment, I found myself thinking this was it. I'd felt it on the Fourth of July, and it was confirmed all over again: this was what it was supposed to feel like. I didn't think I could ever come back from this.

Suddenly, she pulled her lips away from mine. My breathing was harsh as I looked at her, and her chest mirrored mine. In a breathy voice, she said, "Just one more time pretending."

My breath caught in my throat. Did I want this? To pretend? Yes, I'd be with Addy again, but at what price?

"No." The answer was out of my mouth before I fully realized I meant it. "We're not pretending anymore."

She scooted back, my chest cold without hers against it.

My hands tightened against her hips. "Come on, Addy. We're both feeling this." Her breath hitched. "I *know* we are. So let's stop pretending."

I felt like my ribcage was crushing my lungs as I waited for her answer. Her eyes were fixed on mine, as if searching for something in them. She inhaled deeply, and in a flash, her lips were on mine again. I sighed, returning her embrace. She moaned in my mouth, the most beautiful sound to ever be made.

My mouth trailed kisses from her lips to her chin, and when it reached her neck, she arched back to give me easy access. I kissed and sucked and licked her skin, and it tasted like pure heaven. Feeling my cock getting hard, too hard, I adjusted myself underneath her, and I could tell from the gasp she released that she'd felt it.

Then, ever so slowly, she rocked her pelvis on mine, and I was a gone man. This was how I was going to die.

Once my mouth reached her collarbone, I pulled on the neck of her black t-shirt so I could access her shoulder. Doing so, I gazed up to find her looking down at me with a newfound glint.

"This okay?" I asked.

"Yes, yes, it is." Her voice was soft and airy and I couldn't get enough. "Don't you dare stop, Grumpy."

Laughing, I grabbed the hem of her shirt, lifting and removing it in less than a second. I didn't give a fuck if we were in the middle of an airport tarmac, or if someone could walk in on us at any time. The only thing that mattered was her.

I groaned as I revealed her deep red bra. Fuck. The one from the lingerie store.

I didn't think I could ever tire of seeing her like this.

Keeping my eyes on her face, I leaned forward and pressed slow, light kisses from her neck to her chest, resting my mouth between the cups of her breasts. She released soft breaths, head leaned back and eyes closed. When I lifted my hand and slowly dragged her bra down, she gasped. I took a break then, making sure this was still okay with her. I was moving slower than last time because this wasn't pretending anymore, and I needed to make sure she was still with me every second of the way. But when a second passed, she opened her eyes and glared at me. "I. Said. Don't. Stop."

I chuckled before taking her nipple in my mouth, gently biting on it, then sucking. She arched her back even more and moaned. "Fuck, Matt, this feels so good."

It really did. I had no idea why we'd fought so hard against it when it so clearly felt *right*. Cock throbbing against her ass, I moved my mouth to her other breast, feasting on it. This was heaven. There was no getting better than this. Well, unless we were getting undressed completely.

After releasing another moan, Addy grabbed my jaw and brought my mouth up to hers again. She kissed me with a passion I didn't know existed, ravaging me with her tongue while she grinded against my groin, creating the most delicious friction. I grabbed ahold of the silky strands of her hair and pulled on them slightly, making her breasts push against my chest.

The only sounds inside the plane were our moans and groans until suddenly my phone rang in my front pocket. We both jumped, our mouths separating for a second, but just as rapidly, I leaned forward to reconnect my lips to hers. She was a banquet, and I was a starving man. I let the phone ring, bringing Addy's pelvis even closer to mine as I gripped her ass.

But when my phone rang for a second time in less than a minute, I interrupted our kiss. Closing my eyes, I sighed as I leaned my forehead on hers. "Fuck, I don't wanna stop, but I have to take this. Might be important."

She nodded, swallowing. "Sure, okay."

Her chest rose and fell rapidly over mine as I grabbed my phone. My heart was beating erratically, but it stopped altogether when I saw Dora's name on my screen. Dora never called me.

"Hello?" I cleared my throat when I heard how rough it sounded.

"Matthias, you need to come back. It's your mother."

My heartbeat went from fast to downright erratic. "What happened?"

Addy's brows drew together as she gazed at my face, which must have been ten thousand shades of panicked.

"She's having difficulty breathing. I called her doctor. He should be here soon."

"I'm on my way."

I've always wondered how I was going to die.

I'm not saying this to creep you out, or to make you relive my death all over again. It's simply a fact that's followed me all through my life.

When I was a little girl, I thought we chose how we wanted to go. And so, I told myself I would want to die in a giant palace of sweets and chocolates, where I could go with a full belly, surrounded by the things I loved the most in the world.

As I grew up, I learned that my childhood dream was a bit naïve. I became more realistic. I knew there was no controlling when or where or how I would go. I could die in a minute or in eighty years. The ways in which I could die seemed endless, even if I never could've imagined what would really take me six decades later.

Now, I realize I'm a combination of both those younger versions of me. When I think of it, it wasn't so naïve, after all, to want to die surrounded by all the things I loved in the world. My dying wish hasn't changed that much. The only differences are that I'd prefer the palace to be my house overlooking the ocean, and the sweets to be replaced by the people I love. Still, I know I can't control how I die, at least not completely. My disease will do that for me.

I'm not afraid, though. I know when my time will come, I'll go in peace.

So when you read this, know that I left with a smile on my face and the memories I shared with you etched on my heart.

Love,
Helen

20

MATTHIAS

$\mathcal{I}$ couldn't have said how long the drive back home took if I tried. My thoughts were all over the place, and I couldn't focus on anything other than the fact that I needed the car in front of me to move faster.

Addy and I didn't speak a word. As soon as I'd hung up the phone, she put her shirt back on and we hurried to the Audi, not going over what had just happened. I didn't think I had it in me to discuss what our kiss meant for the both of us. The only thing I could focus on was Helen.

At one point while I was speeding on the highway, Addy put her hand on my thigh and gave it a squeeze. I let myself exhale deeply for the first time since I'd received Dora's call. I might've been in a panic, but at least I wasn't alone in this. Addy's hands trembled as much as mine did.

Just as I parked the car in the driveway, Addy and I got out and hurried inside. From my first step into the house, I knew something was wrong. It was like the air was thick with a darkness I'd rarely felt. This house used to be a safe place for me. It was where I'd first learned to play the piano and flown kites in the garden, the wind picking them up as my mother cheered me on. Now, it felt the opposite of safe. It was the unknown, and I loathed it to no end.

We made our way to my mother's room, where we found her in her mechanical twin bed, Dora and Dr. Swainson at her side. Helen made a sound I'd never forget; a whine that came with her breaths, like each one of them was a struggle.

How had she gotten to this point in mere hours?

Dr. Swainson leaned forward, his stethoscope placed over Helen's chest. I tried deciphering his expression, but it was impossible to tell whether it was worry or relief on his face. When he was done with his examination, he straightened his back and passed a hand through his scarce white hair. Dr. Swainson had been our family doctor ever since I could remember, and we'd seen a lot more of him ever since Helen had gotten sick.

When he looked at me, I knew I wouldn't be given good news.

"Helen has a fever and her lungs are full of fluid. We won't know for sure until we've done some more tests, but I think this might be pneumonia."

I looked down at Helen, who was watching us intently, expecting her to smile at me. She didn't.

Gazing back into Dr. Swainson's piercing blue eyes, I lifted my brows. "So you'll just give her antibiotics or whatever it is she needs and she'll get better, right?"

He sighed before putting his stethoscope around his neck and taking a step in my direction. "It's a bit more complicated than that, Matthias. You might want to sit down while we talk about this."

"I'm fine where I am," I stated.

He gave me an expression I hated, like I was some weak bird that needed protection. "Right. So the thing is, Helen's respiratory muscles are much weaker due to her disease, which means it's a lot harder for her to cough and clear her lungs. Yes, there's a possibility antibiotics could help, but it's also very much possible that her lungs might be too weak to get through this on their own."

I swallowed against the lump in my throat. "So what can we do then?"

"Well, there's always the possibility of intubation."

Addy took a step beside me and grabbed my arm. "Matt, do you think we could go sit somewhere else? There's something I need to talk to you about."

Shaking my head, I looked in her direction. "Now's not the time, Addy." Her eyes were troubled, getting cloudy with unshed tears. I didn't know why though. Helen would get through this. She'd gotten through other illnesses before. This was just another hurdle in our path. Nothing more.

Helen cleared her throat, bringing our three pairs of eyes on hers. "I w-won't be intubated, Matthias."

I kneeled beside her, grabbing her hand. "Well, of course, we'll hope it doesn't get to that, but if that's what you need, then we'll do it. It's all going to be okay."

A hand I assumed was Addy's landed on my shoulder. "Matt—"

"You d-don't understand," Helen continued, her voice weak. "I won't be i-intubated, even if it g-g-gets to that."

I looked back and forth between Helen and Addy's faces, both full of sorrow and regret.

"I don't... I don't understand," I said.

My mother gave me a sad smile. "I don't want extraordinary m-measures taken. If this is m-my time, then I want to go p-peacefully."

I got up, eyes narrowing and mouth opening and closing. This wasn't happening. My throat constricted while my heart hammered against my chest.

Turning around, I begged Dr. Swainson with my eyes. "She can't refuse this, right? She's clearly not in her right state of mind. If it comes to this, I can make this decision for her. I'm her legal caretaker after all."

Dr. Swainson cleared his throat. "Um…"

"Matt, can we just—"

Twisting my body, I looked at Addy's pained face. "No, we can't talk! I'm busy right now."

I was breathing hard, my chest feeling like it was constricted with a vice.

Helen exhaled through pursed lips, creating a sound like shoes on gravel, before lifting her eyes to mine. "You're not my legal caretaker anymore, Matt. Addy is."

My eyebrows drew together, and again, I looked back and forth between the two of them.

"What? I don't… I don't understand."

"You can't m-make this decision for me anymore. I don't w-want to be intubated if it comes to it, and Addy will make sure my w-w-wishes are respected."

"But, that's impossible." I turned toward Dr. Swainson, panic overtaking my body. "I'm her son. I'm legally responsible for her."

"Not if it has been notarized that someone else is responsible for me. W-Which it ha-ha-has been." Helen's eyes were filled with water. "I'm sorry, Matt."

Turning on my heels, I stared at Addy, whose cheeks were stained with tears. Pointing a finger at her, I said, "You knew about this?"

"Matt, I… I couldn't tell you. I promised I wouldn't." She dropped her face in her hands, her body shaking with her sobs. I took a step back, not able to take my eyes away from her, but at the same time unable to look at her for a single second more.

"Get out."

She lifted her head. "What?"

"Matthias." Helen spoke behind me, but I didn't care what she had to say.

I gritted out slowly, punctuating every word, "I said get the fuck out of my house." My voice was low and stiff. I barely recognized it.

"But, Matt —"

"GET OUT!"

She jumped at my scream, looking at me with eyes full of pain, but I didn't give a single shit. She'd betrayed me. She'd let me talk to her, kiss her, make love to her, all the while knowing that she'd let my mother die when the time came.

Chin quivering, she gazed at the three of us before running out of the room. Her sobs resonated through the hallway until she left the house.

Once she was gone, silence filled the room. And, even if I wanted to speak, my trembling lips wouldn't allow it. Helen cried behind me, but I didn't turn around to comfort her. I couldn't even look at her right now.

Gazing to my right at Dr. Swainson, I said, "Get her better."

Then, I left.

You were one of the two persons who cared for me the most.

Do you know how I know this?

Because I've never seen pain like the one written in your eyes when you learned I was probably going to die. And you have no idea what it did to me to see you in such distress.

I've hated being sick ever since I got my diagnosis for so many reasons. I couldn't give hugs anymore, even though one of the ways I showed people I loved them was by offering a touch. I couldn't work anymore, even though medicine had always been my one true passion. I couldn't do simple tasks like take a bath or go to the bathroom by myself anymore, even though I'd always put so much value in my freedom and independence.

But, on that fateful day, I learned that all these things weren't so terrible after all. Because nothing could compare to seeing you in so much pain. At that moment, when the situation fell over you like a tidal wave, I wished you didn't love me like you did. Because if you didn't, then learning I would die wouldn't have broken you that way, which broke me in return a thousand times more.

I know I have told you that love is the most wonderful thing in the world, but sometimes, it feels more like a curse than a blessing. I know it all too well.

Love,

Helen

21

ADELAIDE

*B*reathe in, breathe out. In, out. In, out.

This was the only thing I could do to stop myself from becoming a sobbing mess in the middle of the bus. To my left, a lady in her seventies, maybe eighties, looked at me and gave me a sad smile. I tried to return it, but my lips became wobbly, and I had to clench my teeth and look away to keep the tears at bay.

Helen would never get to look like that. She'd never get to become a grandmother, to sing Matthias' kids to sleep, to knit them wool sweaters, or pick them up at school when their tummies would hurt. Even if she got through this pneumonia, there would be other infections, other problems that would arise. It hit me now that she'd been preparing me for this ever since the day we met, but I'd decided to ignore it. If I didn't know, then it didn't hurt. But now, I knew, I really knew, and for a second I feared I would get sick from the pain in my stomach.

"Be strong," my mother had said on her hospital bed, cheeks hollow and legs swollen from a heart that had given up on her. And I'd been strong. I'd done what she'd asked. I'd recovered and worked and provided for Dad and Louis when they needed me. I'd cried when they'd lowered her in the ground, and then I'd moved forward, not because it was easy, but because it was what I had to do.

But, I couldn't do it again. Being strong for everyone else had been the hardest thing I'd ever had to do, and I didn't have it in me to be strong anymore. Every time I closed my eyes, I saw her—my mother—lying on the hospital bed, her skin tinted blue and her eyes half-closed. I saw the EMT's gloved hands on my shoulder and the sound of the zipper of the white bag closing, shielding my mother's body from me. I felt Louis' infant body wrapped around my calf and heard his plea for his mommy to come back.

Except, sometimes, it wasn't my mother's body I could see. It was Helen's. Helen's corpse being draped by a white sheet. Helen's skin that was pale and cold. And it wasn't Louis I was seeing, crying by my side. It was Matthias, kneeling by the bed, begging Helen to stay with him.

And it was still me, being left to pick up the pieces. I felt terrible having this thought, but I couldn't push it away. Yes, Matthias needed it more than me, but for once—*just this once*—I wished I could be the one getting taken care of for a change.

Because I would be grieving too.

The air in the bus was too thick. My thighs were sticky against the leather seats. A ringing in my ears drowned everything except for the loud pulse of my blood. I took a breath, but my lungs were stiff, like air was foreign to them. And I needed it. I was gasping for air, but there was none around me.

In an instant, I was up, running toward the front of the still-moving bus. I had no idea where I was, but I couldn't stay inside. It felt like my chest would cave in on itself if I stayed in a second longer. The lady behind the wheel looked at me with a raised eyebrow before stopping the bus and opening the door.

Rushing out, I closed my eyes and tried breathing in through my nose to tame my beating heart, but even outside, the air felt scarce. Still, I forced myself to calm down, to inhale and exhale slowly through pursed lips.

After what could have been minutes or hours, I could somehow breathe again. I opened my eyes, looking around me for the first time. I didn't know where I was, but there was a park not far from the sidewalk I was on, so I headed there and sat on a swing, the metal of the chains squeaking under my weight. I needed this moment to think before going home. My father and Louis didn't expect me anyway.

I looked at my phone. It wasn't even noon yet. Still my birthday, although it felt like the opposite of a special day. How was it possible that a few hours ago, I'd been flying in a plane for the first time with the man I loved? That we'd kissed without any restraint, that we'd shared a moment so special, only for it to be stolen from us, from me?

I shuddered as I recalled the hatred in his eyes when he'd told me to go. He was hurt, I knew that. I would probably have reacted the same way if the roles had been reversed. But I'd done what I'd been asked to do. I worked for Helen, whether he liked it or not, and her needs came first. I'd known ever since she'd asked me to go to the notary with her that this day would come, but I'd had no idea it would be this soon, nor that I'd feel this heartbroken when the time came.

He'd shut me out. And if I had to guess, he'd probably shut Helen out too. But if he kept everyone at bay, who would be there for him? Who would hold him and rub his back while he cried? Even after the way he'd told me to leave, I couldn't find it in me to resent him. I'd been in his shoes before. I knew what it was to be helpless in the face of sickness, to feel like time was ticking away like sand running through your fingers.

I wanted to be there for him, even if it meant I'd have to be strong again, but how could I be when I was the villain of his story? The disgust in his eyes as he'd understood what we'd done would be etched in my mind forever. It'd been like a knife stabbing my heart, leaving me bleeding and destroyed in front of him.

And not only did I know he needed me, but I needed him too. I needed his soothing words and his calming smiles. I needed the feel of his large palms on my back and the warmth of his body around mine.

I couldn't go to my father for reassuring words, not when he had so recently started on his path to recovery from my mother's death. I couldn't talk to Louis about it, not when he needed me to be tough for him, to be his pillar when things were rough. Stella was more than three hundred miles away and was too busy at the hospital to talk.

A sob erupted from my chest when all I could think was that I wanted my mother more than I ever had before.

MATTHIAS

Tilting my head back, I downed my third glass of whiskey and slammed it on my night table. The alcohol burned my throat as it descended, but it didn't make me feel better.

I'd told her to leave. I'd screamed at her.

She'd fucking lied to me.

I poured more whiskey. Drank it. Stared at the empty side of my bed.

Again, the alcohol didn't make me feel better.

Not yet.

I poured another one and downed it too.

Ever since I met you, I knew you felt each emotion much deeper than the average person. But then again, you've never been average.

Let me tell you a secret: I do too.

It has its downsides, I have to admit it. When I had to give bad news to my patients, I had a hard time keeping my heart away from it. More times than I can count, I cried with the families of patients I couldn't save in the emergency room. It might not have been the most professional thing to do, but I couldn't stop myself from feeling, even if I wanted to. I was a person before I was a doctor.

When I fell in love, I fell hard. I couldn't just like. It was always full-on love or nothing else for me. And when I didn't end up with the one my heart wanted, then I wasn't just sad. I was devastated.

But being highly connected to our emotions also has its upsides. When you're in love, you feel on top of the world, like nothing can stop you. When you receive good news or spend quality time with the people you care for, you're elated, jumping on the walls from happiness. At least, that's how it was for me. I know sometimes people may feel their emotions strongly inside but don't let it show on the outside. That's okay too.

The important thing is to let you feel. Whether it's good or bad, whether you prefer doing it alone or in public, it's important that you acknowledge your emotions so that they don't end up drowning you.

That makes Helen Advice number eight: feeling is never a bad thing, no matter how many inconveniences it can bring.

Love,

Helen

2 2

MATTHIAS

*L*ight was pouring in through the bay window, the sun not yet eclipsed by the dark clouds looming ahead as I knocked on Helen's door. I usually didn't do this, but after the way I'd barged out last night, it didn't feel right going in without her permission.

Her voice was strained and weak when she said, "Come in."

The door creaked as I pushed it open and made my way to her bed. Helen's room was all white, from the walls to the curtains to the duvet comforter. The only thing that seemed out of place in the whimsical room was her small mechanical bed.

When the sound of her labored breathing hit me, I turned around to grab a chair, hoping she hadn't caught the wince I'd made. I cleared my throat as I sat, keeping my eyes on her hands. These still looked the same. They were still my mother's hands.

"I'm hap-py you're here."

This simple sentence had seemed to drain her of energy. Her nose was now underlined by a transparent oxygen tube, and she inhaled hard after speaking. She still wasn't able to catch her breath.

"Just because I'm here doesn't mean I've forgiven you. I'm still fucking pissed." I grabbed her hand.

She laughed, at least as much as she could. "Language, Matt."

When I raised my eyes to look her over, I didn't recognize my mother. This wasn't the smile I loved, her cheeks too weak to hold it in place. This laugh, it wasn't the one I'd heard for twenty-seven years. Was it possible that she'd deteriorated this much in only a day?

When she spoke next, her voice was barely more than a whisper. "I didn't do it to h-hurt you."

Sighing, I closed my eyes. "I just... I don't understand this." My blood was boiling inside. I'd thought I was ready to speak with her about this, but clearly, I wasn't. Jumping to my feet, I tugged at the roots of my hair, turning my back to her. "I don't fucking understand why you'd do this without even telling me first. Why you'd ask the woman I... Why you'd ask *her* to lie to me and do this."

Silence answered me. After taking a deep breath, I turned around and sat back down. Helen was looking at me with a sad smile that made me feel like the seven-year-old I once was, the one who'd gotten laughed at in school because he didn't have a father to make a card for on Father's Day. When I'd come back home on that day, Helen had told me to celebrate her instead, considering she was better than all those fathers combined. I'd had to agree with her.

"I needed to do it, Matthias."

"I still don't understand," I muttered. "You thought I wouldn't take good care of you? Is it because of what happened with Krystal? Because I thought you knew how terrible I still feel about it."

Her eyes narrowed. "Of course not, Matthias. You always c-c-cared for me better than I could've wished—" She coughed weakly. "—wished for."

"Then why?" My trembling voice made the question sound more like a plea.

I leaned over the railing of her bed, needing to watch her up close. She would tell me the truth today.

Closing her eyes, she exhaled, which sounded like a whimper. Her lips wobbled, but she forced them into steadiness. Then, she took a wheezing breath and looked at me, a half-smile on her lips.

"Because I knew you would never let me go. And I need you to let me go."

ADELAIDE

Sweat pooled beneath my thighs, the leather chair against my skin feeling too hot on this end-of-July day. A bell rang as the front door opened, and a middle-aged woman walked in and sat in the chair beside mine even though the whole waiting room was empty. I gave her a tight-lipped smile before returning my eyes to my phone.

I'd been waiting for it to ring for more than a week, without any luck. Ever since Matthias had told me to leave his and Helen's house, he hadn't tried to reach me. I was still in contact with Helen's doctor, who updated me with important information regarding the state of her health, but that was it. I was dying to know how Helen was doing, *really* doing, day to day, but only Matthias could tell me that, and I didn't feel like it was my place to call him to receive news.

And I wouldn't lie; I wasn't dying for him to call *only* to know how Helen was doing. My chest had felt empty the whole week. I hadn't realized how used I'd become to having him in my life until he wasn't. I missed the way he'd wink at me when he said something he knew Helen wouldn't like, or when he'd text me to ask what was the newest addition to

Louis' famous car toy collection. He had this ability to make me feel seen, even when I didn't want him to see me.

I had no idea whether he'd forgive me one day for what I'd done. If only I'd had the chance to explain why I'd made the choice I had. It'd never been to hurt him. It'd all been for Helen. We might not have handled the situation well, but our intentions weren't bad. If I saw him again, I'd apologize for how things had happened, but I wouldn't apologize for doing it.

The door in front of me, which was covered with posters on suicide prevention, opened, and I stood on my feet as my father came out of the room. I looked for clues of how the appointment had gone, but the blank look on his face didn't give me anything.

After the talk we'd had a few weeks ago about him needing to get better, he'd accepted to go see a doctor, who'd diagnosed him with a severe depressive episode. He'd been prescribed medications, as well as psychotherapy, to which he had all complied.

The stiffness in his chest and the tremor in his hand on our way over told me he wasn't feeling comfortable seeing a therapist, but he hadn't complained. My dad might've been many things, but he wasn't a promise-breaker, and he'd sworn he'd get some help.

"How did it go?" I whispered to him as we headed outside the office.

"It was fine, I guess."

I begged him with my eyes to elaborate, but he didn't, and I knew I shouldn't press him. What he talked about with his therapist didn't concern me, and I had no right to ask, though easier said than done.

Avoiding mid-day pedestrians on the sidewalk, I said, "Are you at least going to go back for another appointment?"

That, I could ask.

My father looked at his white New Balance shoes that

probably dated from the eighties and walked in silence for a while. When he spoke again, his voice was uneven. "Do we even have the money to pay for this?" He swallowed, his Adam's apple bobbing. "I don't want to be another burden to you."

The truth was, we did and didn't have the money. For the time being, we were doing good. Matthias and Helen had paid me more than what was expected for my job, and I'd been able to save some of it. But considering the fact that I'd taken Matthias' 'get the fuck out of here' as a dismissal from my job, we would soon go through my savings if I didn't find a replacement fast. However, my dad's mental health was more important than all that.

"Sure, we can pay for this, Dad." Laying a hand on his shoulder, I said, "I just want you to get better." I'd find a way to make it work. I always did.

He gave me a half-smile. "All right, then."

Just as we turned the corner of the street on our way home, my phone vibrated in the back pocket of my shorts. My heart stopped beating as soon as I realized I was getting a call, and when I saw Matthias' name on the screen, I almost sobbed in relief.

"Hey!" I said. "I'm so glad you called!"

The only sound that greeted me was a throat-clearing. No "How are you" or "I'm happy to hear your voice."

"I'm calling because Helen wants to see you." His voice was stiff, careless, and his message was clear. *Helen wants to see you, not me.*

"Oh," was the only thing I found to say. "Is... Is everything all right?"

He sighed and cleared his throat again. "She doesn't seem to be getting better despite the antibiotics." I knew about that, to a certain extent, but my hand still went up to my mouth. "Unless she goes back on her...wishes not to receive extraordinary measures, she probably doesn't have long."

His words were like a knife to the gut. I'd been prepared for them; I'd even started expecting them in the past few days. But they still turned the blood in my veins cold. I couldn't imagine a world without Helen in it. I hadn't known her for long, but it still felt surreal to think that she might not make it through this.

"I'm so sorry, Matthias." *For everything*, I wanted to add. I didn't.

His only answer was silence.

"I'll come tonight," I said.

"Okay," he said before hanging up.

When I stopped walking to catch my breath, I remembered my dad was there. "Are you okay, Addy?" he asked.

I nodded, even though I was the farthest from okay I'd ever been. My heart was breaking from two different places. I might have to say goodbye to Helen, but I might also have to do the same to Matthias. And I had no idea how I would do it.

One thing was for sure: Matthias and Helen Philips had carved their names into my heart, each in their own way, and I didn't know if there was such a thing as getting over them.

A shiver ran down my spine as I climbed the front porch steps, even with humidity clinging to each of my pores. The sky above me was a gray-black, threatening to break and pour over us in a matter of minutes.

I was a cloud too, darkening and on the verge of collapsing.

Once I reached the door, I froze. Was I supposed to knock? I hadn't in a very long time, but then again that was when I was still employed here.

I pounded my fist on the wooden door with the same strength my heart used against my ribcage. Less than a second later, Matthias opened the door, not giving me time to think about what I was going to say. When my gaze caught his, I desperately wished he would have given me that time.

His jaw ticked as he took me in, from the bun that stood askew on my head, to my simple black sweater and gray shorts. When his eyes came back to mine, I recognized something in them—regret? Affection?—but it soon faded away, replaced by a hard stare before I could put my finger on what it was. The harsh look he was now giving me felt like a jab to the cheekbone, making me look down at my shoes.

"So, how is she doing?" I asked.

"Bad."

Straight-to-the-point Matthias giving me a simple word that meant so much.

"Bad how?"

He bit his lip and looked behind him before returning to me. "Really bad. This might be your last chance to see her, Adelaide."

My breath got stuck in my throat, both from the use of my full name—which he hadn't so much as pronounced in months—and from thinking this might be it. It wasn't hypothetical anymore.

"Of course," he continued, "this wouldn't be the case if you decided to tell the doctor to keep her alive."

I closed my eyes and sighed. "I can't do that, Matthias. You know I can't. I don't want this either, but it isn't our choice. It's hers."

"Of course you'd say that."

He turned around, and I grabbed his elbow. "I'm sorry, Matt. I really am, but this isn't my choice." My lower lip trembled. "Please don't shut me out like this."

He didn't bother turning around, instead jerking his arm out of my grip. "She's waiting for you in her room." Then, he walked to the back of the house. The patio door opened and slammed shut a few seconds later.

After knocking with a single knuckle on Helen's door, I

walked in and inhaled sharply when I took her in. I couldn't cry, not in front of her. But she looked so frail in that twin bed, her head pushed up by a tower of pillows. Her skin was paler than pale, almost greenish. Cheeks hollowed out, eyes half-mast.

I leaned down, tying my perfectly fine shoelace while taking in a big breath, then exhaling slowly. *You can do this, Addy.*

When I got back up, I gave her the sincerest smile I could muster, and she returned it, although it seemed to require a lot of effort from her. As I sat back down beside her, I took in her appearance again; she looked even sicker from up close. Her breathing was slow, ragged, and beads of sweat covered her forehead.

"Hey, A-Addy."

"Hey, Helen. I'll be right back." Getting up, I went to the bathroom to grab a rag that I wetted with cold water and draped on her forehead when I returned to the room.

"I'm s-s-so glad you came." Her speech was even more slurred than it usually was, and her voice was low and gritty.

"Me too. I'm glad you asked Matt to call me." And I really was. Having to bear the thought of Helen dying was hard enough, but imagining her leaving without saying goodbye first was impossible.

She choked on a breath before offering me a half-smile. "Have you two talked?"

I looked down at my bitten nails. "Um, no, not really. He's still mad at me about...everything."

"He'll g-get ov-v-ver it."

I didn't have it in me to tell her she was probably wrong, so I shrugged.

"I know my son, Addy. He is p-proud like no one else, but he also cares so m-much. And I can tell you he *cares* as much ab-about you as you *care* about h-him." She put emphasis on the word "care" and gave me a knowing wink when she was done. In normal circumstances, I would've found it funny, that she'd read us so well, but I didn't feel like laughing today. Her winks always made her look so jovial, so *alive*, but they didn't feel that way anymore.

A lump the size of a grapefruit took place in my throat, and I had to swallow hard against it. Helen's eyes closed for a moment, and I was about to leave when they opened again.

"Are you tired?" I asked. "I can go, let you rest."

The whine of her breathing resonated around me, like nails on a chalkboard. "No, not yet. I haven't said all I h-h-have to say." She swallowed roughly, and I grabbed the glass of water sitting on her bedside table, leaning the straw against her lips. Once she was done and I'd removed the glass, she gave me a subtle nod of the head, which I'm sure would've translated in a folding of her index finger in normal circumstances, inching me to get closer.

My ear was right below her mouth when she started talking again, her voice even softer than before. "You're the daughter I never had the chance to have."

At her words, a sob racked through my body, and I was glad she couldn't see my face.

"I don't know w-who I have to thank for it, but you sh-showing up at our door on that day in M-march? There's no other word f-f-for it than a blessing."

This time, I was sure she could hear my cries, and I didn't care anymore. I turned my face around, gazing down at her piercing blue eyes.

"And, I can't thank y-you enough for what you did for me. You g-gave me back control over my l-l-life, Addy." A tear fell from each of her eyes, forming two straight lines on her sharp cheekbones and sunken cheeks. "Take care of yourself, and t-take care of my boy too."

I closed my eyes as I nodded, whimpers coming out of my mouth. This was it. This was goodbye.

Her eyes were half-closed as I got up, fatigue clear in them.

Leaning down, I gave her forehead a chaste kiss, then turned around and left the room. As I crossed the kitchen, I saw Matthias' head lift, but I didn't stop for him. I got out the door as fast as I could, and once the first drop of rain fell on my cheek, I did the only thing that felt right. I ran.

MATTHIAS

*H*elen had been sleeping for the past three hours when she called for me faintly from her room. I'd gone in right after Adelaide had rushed out, but her eyes had been closed and her breathing slow.

I'd been tempted, when I'd come back inside and Adelaide was still there, to lean my head against the door and listen to their conversation, but I'd opted against it. My mother at least deserved privacy in her last moments.

Yet after seeing the way Adelaide had left, running with a hand on her mouth and tears streaming down her face, I'd regretted my decision. What could they have said? I knew they were close from the times I'd seen them together, but I might've underestimated the depth of their bond.

Helen's bedroom door squeaked as I pushed it open. "Do you need something?" I asked.

She blinked slowly, and I took it as a yes. Sitting on the leather chair beside her bed, I leaned forward and propped my hand on her forehead. It was hot and humid. "What can I do for you?"

Another slow blink, this time accompanied by a lift of her lips. "I need you t-to—" She broke into a coughing fit, her inhales sharp and rapid. Once she caught her breath, she continued. "I need you to lis-listen to me."

I stared at her with my lips pinched tight.

"F-forgive Addy."

My back hit the chair as I sighed. "It's not as simple as that."

"Yes, it is. If you want t-to be mad, be mad at m-me, but don't be m-mad at her for helping me."

"Helen, I don't... I don't really want to talk about *her* right now."

She wheezed a breath in. "But I do. I'm leaving, M-Matt, and I d-don't want you to have to face it al-alone."

"But you don't have to go." I didn't recognize my voice, whinier than ever. "You can always change your mind and stay with us longer."

The right corner of her lips rose as her eyes shone. "Don't be af-afraid of love, Matthias. Embrace it, and seize it while it's th-there."

Looking behind me, I inhaled a deep breath and let it out before facing her again, now biting my cheek. I still had time to make her change her mind. She wouldn't be leaving me. Not yet.

Her face paled even more as she tried but failed to cough again.

"Come c-closer, honey."

Blood oozed out where my teeth were tearing at my cheek. I swallowed, tasting iron as I grabbed her hand and leaned my chin down on the railing of her bed. While her face had turned ashen, her eyes were still strikingly blue. When I was younger, I used to tell her that her eyes reminded me of the water behind our house. Looking at her now, I found myself thinking the same.

"You're a g-good man, Matthias."

I interrupted her before she said anything else. "Don't say goodbye. Please, please don't say goodbye." My voice broke on the last word, and I bit my cheek even harder.

Her eyes sparkled with amusement. "I didn't say goodbye. I s-s-said you're a good man. And—" She looked up as her lips quivered. "And, getting to be y-your mother has been the g-g-greatest privilege of my life."

This was too much. I dug the nails of my free hand into my thigh while doing everything I could to control my breathing, in vain. Lifting the hand I was holding, I pressed it to my mouth as a tear leaked out of my eye. I wiped my cheek on my shoulder before giving her hand another kiss.

This was too hard. If I looked at her again, I knew this would be it. I'd wrap myself in my mother's arms and cry like a little boy. So, I got up, keeping my eyes everywhere but on her. "Get some sleep now. I'll see you tomorrow."

As I'm writing this letter, I'm feeling all kinds of things, if I'm being honest. A few hours ago, I learned the antibiotics weren't working, like I'd anticipated. I fear I won't have much energy to write later, especially considering I'm already more tired than I have ever been. I'll try to push through though, because I haven't told you everything I need to yet.

I know you took the news of my nearing death hard, but I actually want to reassure you. Yes, when I heard I had but a few days left, I was sad, at first. There would be so much I would miss. I even had an angry phase, which hasn't fully left yet. Why me? I've heard this question so many times before—from patients who'd received bad news or families being told their loved one had died—but never understood it like I did when I received my diagnosis, and even more when I received my prognosis. It seems you never stop learning and understanding things, even when death is close.

But that wasn't the reassuring part. The comfort I hope to give you comes from the fact that I'm ready, and knowing that I will die very soon brings me a sense of peace; I won't have to feel myself deteriorate and see how it hurts you anymore.

The calm I feel now, like a bird soaring over the ocean, is because I won't have to endure any more setbacks in my health. This wouldn't have been possible if I hadn't made the decision to let go and not fight against nature, so know that I haven't regretted my choice, even in the end.

Love,
Helen

23

ADELAIDE

$\mathcal{H}$elen died that night, less than twelve hours after I'd left her.

I didn't learn it through Matthias. No, he hadn't called me after it happened. As a matter of fact, we hadn't talked since that day. Not that I hadn't tried. I'd called him three times since Dora had told me Helen had passed away while she was sleeping, but my calls always went unanswered. He hadn't called after I'd left voicemails either.

Today, though, he wouldn't have a choice to see me. The date of Helen's funeral had been announced in the local news-paper, and I wouldn't miss it, even if it meant making Matthias pissed.

I straightened the last of my curls as I glanced in the mirror. I'd gotten dressed this morning in a simple black dress, something I thought Helen would have liked. She always did compliment me every time I dressed more girly. I opted out of mascara for today, not trusting my eyes to stay dry.

Surprisingly, after I'd learned the news, I hadn't fallen to the ground or cried. In a way, I'd almost felt relieved that she'd finally gotten that freedom she'd begged for. I hadn't stopped living either. As with my mother's death, I'd tried to get back on my feet as fast as possible. I'd looked for a new job and accompanied my father to his second psychotherapy appointment. I'd been…okay.

But today was a whole other game. I wasn't okay anymore. I'd woken up in a puddle of sweat, heart racing and stomach churning. It felt surreal to have to attend her funeral, even though I'd lived through the same thing three years ago, almost to the day. I should have gotten used to it by now.

I exhaled through pursed lips as I smoothed my dress over my thighs. I could get through this. When I'd come back here tonight, the worst would be over.

Three soft knocks came from the bathroom door. "I need to pee before we leave."

"Yeah, sorry." I opened the door right away, and my breath stalled in my chest as I took my little brother in his tiny black suit.

Louis was only seven, and it was already the second funeral he had to attend. At least, he didn't seem too affected by it. When I'd told him Ms. Helen had left for heaven, he'd said he was happy because she would be good company to Mommy.

Once Louis was finished with his business, my dad and I both grabbed one of his hands and walked to hop on the bus, which wasn't too crowded for a Saturday afternoon. I was thankful for it. I wouldn't have wanted to endure the looks of pity from other passengers taking in our all-black attire.

I realized as we made our way to the church that it was the one where Matthias and I had surprisingly happened upon each other. We'd laughed and danced and swooned that day. How far we'd gone from that point. It was only a few months ago, but it felt like it had taken place in another lifetime.

We took a seat in one of the pews closest to the back of the church, which was already almost full. Two ladies I'd never seen in my life were sobbing and hugging each other to my right. In front of me, a couple that might have been around Helen's age held each other's hands, their knuckles turning white. I had no idea Helen knew so many people, but thinking back on it, I should've known. I couldn't think of one person who would've crossed Helen's path and who wouldn't have felt impacted by her person.

The ceremony began not too long after we arrived. The priest got up and spoke about Helen, all generic compliments he probably repeated during every funeral he officiated. How she was appreciated by her community. How she did so much good around her. It was nice, even if it didn't feel personal to her.

We got up too. Sang some songs, repeated sermons, kneeled. It was fine. Everything was fine.

And then Matthias went to the front of the stage in a tailored black suit, his hair perfectly combed backward. I'd never been more grateful to be seated than at that moment. A simple look at the man who inhabited my head—even if I hadn't seen him in what felt like forever—and my knees buckled. His eyes roamed over the room, and when they found mine, they stuck there for a long moment. I'd stood there too, not so long ago, gazing at him while I sang. He now had the chance to do the same.

But before he started speaking, he broke the contact, looking down to the single sheet of paper he'd carried with him.

"My mother was the best person I ever had the chance to meet," he said. "She was good, and kind, and generous. She would've spent all of her time helping others if she could have. She was…"

His voice was clear and sharp. It wasn't laced with emotion, or hoarse from trying not to cry. Everything he said couldn't have been truer. And yet, it didn't feel like our Helen. Yes, she was all of those things, but she was also so much more.

She was a snorting laughter on a Sunday morning as we tried—and failed—to flip pancakes in a pan. She was stolen glances when we teased Matthias on things we knew would annoy him. She was hidden laughs over stupid lobster head-pieces, and smutty romance audiobooks, and boring podcasts, and wicked smiles with winks.

Matthias' voice surrounded me, but I couldn't catch what he was saying, with the thumping of my heart so loud it felt like all my vessels would burst. My gaze moved from Matthias to the urn sitting at the front of the church, accompanied by a picture of Helen that dated from a time when she was young and healthy.

My chest constricted as I stared at the urn, analyzing the soft flowery patterns engraved in the material, the chrome color that reflected the candles lit in the aisle. Helen was in there. She was gone.

She was gone. She was gone. She was gone.

The sentence rang in my head again and again until I couldn't breathe anymore. Until I felt like if I stayed here, I'd faint or throw up or explode in a sea of tears.

Without a second thought, I got up. Matthias' gaze lifted to me for a brief second, but I didn't hold it. Instead, I apologized to the man sitting beside me, and as soon as I was out of my pew, I ran outside.

MATTHIAS

"*T*hank you for coming."

I shook the hand of the last man to leave the house, a fake-ass smile on my lips. I couldn't have said who this old, bearded person was if my life depended on it. As soon as the door was closed, I leaned my back against it and closed my eyes. A sigh escaped my mouth at the thought that this fucking day was finally over.

After the burial, I'd come back home and shaken hands

with countless people, some who were close to my mother and some who had never come see her in the three years she'd been sick. I couldn't have been happier if I never had to hear the words 'I'm sorry for your loss' or 'she's in a better place now' again.

Everything had gone okay, I guessed. The ceremony was beautiful. It hadn't rained, the sun even making its appearance sometimes through the clouds. I'd kept myself under control, smiled even, to the people who'd tried to cheer me up with good memories they had with Helen.

Of course, the one thing that hadn't gone according to plan was Addy leaving the church in the middle of my speech, face ashen and eyes wide. And the worst part was, I knew precisely why she'd left.

I'd kept it safe. I'd said what people expected the deceased's son to say. I'd used the voice I'd been taught to apply when giving oral presentations in high school. Loud. Clear. Crisp. Addy hadn't liked it; of course, she hadn't. She knew as well as I did Helen would've told me to take the stick out of my ass and speak from the heart. But how could I do that without breaking down? I didn't trust myself, not with this. So, I'd given my beautiful speech without faltering from it, even when Addy had left the church in a hurry.

God, I need a drink.

As I made my way to the kitchen, I stopped in my tracks, like I'd hit an invisible wall.

There, on the floor, laid an item I'd watched my mother wear all her life. It was this ring, thick metal woven in the shape of a moon. It had been on the middle finger of her right hand for as long as I could remember.

My knees cracked as I retrieved it from the ground. It caught the light above me when I turned it between my fingers.

I'd always thought the ring was weird. Not that it was ugly; it was actually beautiful. I didn't know what made it feel so curious to me, except that it was...not my mother. Helen loved couture fashion and distinguished clothes, so it had always felt strange to see her wearing this simple, unadorned ring.

I'd always meant to ask her where she'd gotten it and what the story behind it was. She wouldn't have worn something like it if it didn't have a special significance for her. But I'd never asked her, and now I'd never know the answer.

I'd never know the answer.

She'd been there for me all my life. I could've asked her any time, yet I'd decided to wait until she was dead to ask. Because she was. Dead.

My mother was dead.

It hit me then, like a baseball bat to the head. I'd never see Helen again. I'd never hear her laugh at my jokes or get a whiff of her perfume when she passed by me. She was gone.

A fire erupted in my stomach, in my throat, and I had to let it out. I screamed with all I had, screamed for what I'd had and what I'd never have again. The sound was raw, so raw, as it came out of me. I screamed for Helen, who'd never get to go to another Lobster Festival. I screamed for Adelaide, who'd had to lose someone again. And I screamed for myself, now alone.

Except I wasn't, not really.

Pulling my phone out of my pocket, I dialed the number of the only person who might've been feeling the same way I was. I didn't care about what she'd done anymore. It felt so minimal all of a sudden, compared to the abysmal pain I was in.

As soon as the line connected, I exhaled in relief.

"Can you come here?"

As I'm feeling weaker than I ever have, chills running down my spine and phlegm drowning me from inside, the only thing I can think of is what you're going to have to go through in a few days, and it kills me to know I'll be the cause of your suffering. But the one silver lining I see in this is I know you'll have someone by your side, no matter what happens.

As always, I guess we can take this terrible situation and get a great Helen Advice out of it. So, here goes.

Surround yourself with good people. The ones who will be there to pick you up piece by broken piece when you go through hardships. The ones who will be by your side through thick and thin, through blazing heats and devastating blizzards. The ones who won't only be there for the birthday parties and the Fourth of July fireworks, but also for the funerals, for the doctor appointments, and for the days when you can't seem to pull yourself out of bed.

And, what makes my heart full is knowing that, whether you realize it or not, you have found some of those people already. Some new relationships might appear through the years, some old ones might taper off, but I know you'll never be alone. That is all I could've hoped for, and now my wish has been answered.

Love,

Helen

ADELAIDE

"*P*lease let him be okay," I repeated to myself like a mantra while climbing the front porch steps two by two. Matthias had hung up the phone before telling me what was going on. I'd only taken the time to bring Louis to Mrs. Zhu's before running to the bus stop. My dad had offered to look after him, but I wasn't feeling comfortable enough with the idea yet. Baby steps.

The sky was darkening above me, the sun right above the water level. There weren't any cars in the driveway, except Matt's Audi. All the visitors had probably left already.

After knocking on the door, I hugged myself, a shiver coursing through my body. Matt's voice had been indecipherable on the phone. How would he be when the door opened?

I got my answer a few seconds later. Matt looked at me with heavy eyes, his jaw set tight under his dark beard, his dark hair ruffled. The black dress shirt he'd been wearing at the funeral was rumpled, the bottom of it half tucked into his pants, half out.

I took a step closer, not trusting my voice to utter a word. From here, I could smell his cologne, light and musky and so incredibly male. For a second, I closed my eyes to inhale deeply, remembering a time when I'd been able to smell it almost every day. When I looked at him again, his face was impassable. No emotion was written in his eyes, no feeling etched in his face. But when I took another step closer, his bottom lip quivered.

Taking a final step toward him, I wrapped my arms around his body. That broke the dam holding the water in. His hands came fast on my back, his biceps circling my body so tightly I could barely breathe.

"It's okay, Matt. I'm here."

That was when I felt the first shudders of his chest against mine. He sobbed and sobbed as I traced large circles on his back, trying to keep my own tears at bay. No words were needed; we both knew exactly what the other was thinking.

I didn't know if this meant he'd forgiven me for what I'd done, but frankly, I didn't care. If he needed me tonight, then I'd be here for him. We could talk about it later. Tonight was bigger than us.

Keeping my arms around him, I pulled his body toward the living room, where we sat on the couch. His glossy strands brushed my neck when he leaned closer to me. I wrapped a hand in them, savoring their silkiness on my fingers.

His chest jerked again, and I hugged him even tighter.

"She's… She's not coming back," he whispered.

I closed my eyes and held my breath in when a tear fell down my cheek. Leaning my chin on his head, I dried my eyes on the back of my hands. Seeing him like this was almost unbearable. My Matt was a pillar in my life, a lighthouse in the storm. Seeing him break almost felt like all hope was lost. Still, it was better than the numbness he'd shown during his speech in the church. At least now I recognized the sensitive man I'd fallen in love with, and through him, I saw his mother whom I'd loved so dearly.

We stayed like this for a long time, our bodies intertwined as the light dimmed in the room, abandoning us in a darkness only disrupted by the radiance of the moon. Matt's sobs eventually calmed down, his breathing softening and his body relaxing.

After a while, my shoulders were stiff, and I moved a bit to try to find a comfortable position. With the silence in the room and the slow rhythm of his breaths, I'd imagined Matt had fallen asleep, but when his human pillow changed position, his eyes opened.

"You okay?" he asked.

I caressed his hair again. "Yeah, my arm was just getting a bit numb."

"Oh, sorry."

He jerked away from my body before I'd gotten the chance to tell him I didn't mind, that I actually wanted him to stay close to me. Once he was upright, his eyes searched the room before landing back on mine.

"You can go now," he whispered.

I jerked back.

"I mean, if you want. I'm okay now. I'm..." He scratched his cheek. "I'm sorry I called you." The breath that left his body seemed to be so, so heavy. "I'm sorry for everything."

My hand reached for his as his words shattered my heart and built it back up again. "Don't you *ever* apologize for needing me."

His gaze roamed over the dark living room, stopping over each piece of furniture. I held my breath. Eventually, he sighed. "The house felt so empty once everyone had left. I just didn't want to be alone tonight."

Oh, my poor Matthias. He was dressed like a professional man, but he'd never looked younger. I scooted closer to him. "Look at me."

Matt's face turned in my direction, but his eyes stayed on my jaw.

"I said," I uttered, hand moving to his cheek, "look at me."

Finally, he did.

"You are not alone." He flinched a little at my words, which increased the tension of my fingers on his cheek. "You will *never* be alone. Do you hear me?"

Matt's eyes glossed over.

"I'll be here for you no matter what." I'd done it before. I'd been Louis' pillar, then my dad's. I could be Matthias' too. It was what you did for the people you loved.

His face wore layers of pain, probably for many reasons. I wanted to tell him more, to show him just how much I loved him and meant every single word I'd said, but maybe that would overwhelm him more than anything else. Instead, I got closer to him and pulled him down so we were both lying on the couch. We adjusted our position so our bodies were intertwined.

Matthias released a sigh that sounded a lot like relief.

Comfort had a whole new meaning in my mind with my head on his hard chest, a leg wrapped around his, and his fingers tracing circles on my back. I snuggled my nose in his neck.

This was how it was supposed to be. Helen had said it from the beginning, and I realized then that she couldn't have been more right. Lying there with Matt after promising to never let him go, I knew it couldn't have been any other way. We'd fought this for long, but I couldn't anymore.

As sleep threatened to drag me away, I basked in this feeling of rightness. Repressing a yawn, I muttered, "Good night, Matt."

"Good night, Addy." He dusted a kiss on the crown of my hair and squeezed me tight. Almost too tight. I didn't think too much of it as I fell asleep.

*S*unlight drenched the living room when I opened my eyes. Yawning, I stretched on the couch, but didn't feel anyone beside me. I stroked the leather, realizing the other half of the couch was cold.

I opened my eyes, wondering where Matt could have gone. That's when I saw the note sitting beside my head.

I'm so sorry, but I have to let you go. Live your life. Don't worry about me.

Was it a mistake, this decision I made to follow the course of my disease and not fight more against it? Maybe. Maybe not. Whatever the right answer is, it's too late now, and there's nothing we can do about it.

I know this situation was hard on you, but if you could learn something from it, I'd say it was worth it. That makes the last Helen Advice, number nine: Always embrace your choices. The reason why you made them doesn't matter; at some point, you thought this was the right thing to do, and there's no wrong in admitting it.

Now, sometimes, it's possible those choices were mistakes. Everyone makes them, and that's okay. It's part of life. But even if they're mistakes that doesn't mean you shouldn't own up to them. I know I have said in a previous letter not to spend too much time ruminating over all the small faults you will commit in the future, but that doesn't mean you should never reflect on the bigger mistakes you make. Examine your choices, and if you have regrets, then be mature enough to apologize, to right your wrongs, to make things better.

Making mistakes is not the problem. Badly handling them is.

Own up to your choices.

Love,

Helen

25

ADELAIDE

"Thank you for the opportunity," I said before hanging up, dropping my phone next to me on the bench as I scratched the employer's name on my notepad. Louis squealed when he reached a peak of height on his swing, Josh yelling a "whoa" beside him.

Three weeks had gone by since Helen's passing, and I was still out of a job. Looking around me, I realized I was back in the exact same situation I was in six months ago. Nothing had changed in that time, yet everything had. I might've been sitting in the same park, scavenging for the same jobs, but I wasn't the same person. *I* had changed. I had loved and lost in more ways than I could count. But I had also found a strength within me I didn't know I had. I'd gone through so much and still made it out alive.

When my phone vibrated against the bench, my heart skipped a beat. I knew it wasn't *him*; he'd made it clear enough he didn't want anything to do with me. And he hadn't backed down from his words. After leaving his house two weeks ago, I'd hoped—expected even—to receive a call from him. We'd been to hell and back together; he couldn't reject me with seventeen words written on a post-it, without a single explanation. No, Matthias wouldn't do that to me.

But after all this time without any news, I figured yes, he very well could. Whoever I'd thought Matthias was, I'd been wrong. The amazing man I'd gotten to know during all those months wouldn't have done that to me.

That didn't change the fact that a tiny part of me still hoped I hadn't been wrong, that there was a simple explanation for this and *my* Matt would come back to me. So, every time my phone pinged with a notification or rang, I couldn't control the way my heart rate went through the roof.

My hope died down for an umpteenth time when I saw the unknown caller ID on my phone screen.

"Hello?" I tried to keep the deception out of my voice, but failed miserably.

An unknown male voice with a thick English accent answered. "Am I speaking to Miss Samson?"

A fold formed between my brows. "Yes, it's me."

The man cleared his throat. "Hi, my name is Conrad Callaway. I was Helen Philips' notary. I believe we met once."

Recognition flashed through my brain. "Yes, um yes, we did."

There was a moment of silence when he probably expected me to say more, but I was too surprised to think of anything.

"You're probably wondering why I'm calling." He waited a moment, and I wanted to scream from the suspense. "Well, a month or so ago, Helen sent something to my office that I was supposed to give you after she died."

I got up to my feet, blocking my other ear with a finger. "I'm sorry, you're saying Helen left something for *me*? Are you sure?"

"Sure as eggs is eggs." Mr. Callaway chuckled and cleared his throat when I stayed silent. "When can you pass by my office?"

I looked at the time on my phone before returning it to my ear. "I can be there in an hour or so?" I'd have to go drop Louis and Josh home first, but there was no way I wasn't getting this today.

"Delightful. See you very soon!"

I hung up before calling for the boys, who came running a second later. We headed back to our apartment complex, and right after asking Mrs. Zhu to watch them for a while, I walked the few blocks separating my home from Mr. Callaway's Portland office.

A bell rang above my head as I opened the door. The office was old, yet in perfect condition. Mahogany shelves filled with dusty books covered one wall, giving a comforting ambiance to the room. Before me, a brunette who looked to be in her early thirties sat behind a desk smiling.

"Hi," I said. "I'm supposed to meet with Mr. Callaway?"

She smiled. "Right away. Follow me."

I did as she asked, and we headed to our right, walking down a long hallway before reaching a closed door. The woman knocked before opening. "Someone's here for you."

Mr. Callaway turned in his chair to look at me. He was just as I remembered, white hair and a mustache that covered half his mouth. "Ms. Samson, come in!"

The door closed behind me as I sat on the leather chair in front of the desk. Mr. Callaway interlaced his fingers. "So, I won't keep you waiting. As I said, Helen left something that I had to give to you three weeks after her death." Pushing his chair back, he dipped under his desk and came back with a small red box in his hands.

"She sent what's inside the box by electronic mail a month ago. I took the freedom to print it."

I gulped when he handed me the box and traced it with the pad of my finger. Looking up at him, I asked, "Is that all?"

He nodded knowingly. I'm sure I wasn't the first person who wanted to get out of his office as fast as possible to look at what their lost ones had left for them in private.

I got up and was almost at the door when he called behind me, "Ms. Samson?" Turning around, I caught his sad smile. "I'm deeply sorry for your loss."

I answered with a tight-lipped dip of the head and ran back home. I dug through my memories to try to remember if she'd mention leaving anything to me, but I came up empty. And if she'd taken the time to send it, it must've been important. Helen wasn't one to do things without thinking them through first.

When I got home, I went straight to Louis' room and locked myself inside. I needed privacy for this. My legs were shaking as I sat on the bed, the box on my knees. I looked at it for a while, not finding the courage to open it yet. This was it, the one last thing Helen would ever give me.

Five minutes passed before I kicked myself in the butt. I was being ridiculous. If Helen had found the strength to leave something for me, even while she was living her last days, then the least I could do was look at it. So, after releasing a shaky breath, I removed the top of the box and looked inside.

Paper.

That was it. Paper. Well, a lot of paper, each sheet folded into thirds.

I grabbed the first page, sitting on top of the others. Unfolding it slowly, I read the words 'My Dear.' Right away, I squeezed my eyes shut and hugged the sheet of paper tight to my chest.

Letters. She'd written me letters.

I beamed, tears falling from my eyes at the simple thought of it. I still had more of her. She might not have been there to say the words out loud, but those were still her words.

And so I read. And read. And read.

I went through all of her letters, smiling at times, crying at others. She'd left me what she thought I would appreciate the most from her: her best advice and her favorite memories, things I already knew about her and others that were new to me. And she'd been right; she couldn't have left me anything better.

When I reached the last letter at the end of the stack, I felt a physical pain resembling the one that had struck me when I'd held her hand for the last time. This was it. Truly the last part of her I had left.

I opened it slowly and read, tasting salt from my tears. But when I reached the end of the letter, I smiled like I rarely had.

It wasn't over. Helen still had one last surprise in store for me.

My Dear,

This will be the last one of my letters. I hope you've enjoyed reading my words of wisdom. In these last few months with you, when my condition started to deteriorate, the only thing I could think of was that I wanted this to last forever. I wanted you to remember the time we'd spent together, to remember the great memories we'd made, and most of all, to remember me, both the good parts and the bad.

I wish we'd have had more time. But the time we did have was marvelous, and that's what I want to focus on.

If you're reading this, it means I'm gone, and not to be pretentious, but I know you must be having a hard time. So, I have one little thing I'd like to give you, in the hope it will dull the pain.

On August 20th, at 10 a.m., head to the lobster shack on Main Street. Your gift will wait for you there.

With all my love,

Helen

26

ADELAIDE

I woke up on the morning of August twentieth with a
tight knot in my stomach. I'd had to wait more than
a week for this, and it'd felt like pure torture. Helen and I had
never been to the meeting point together, so I had no idea if it
held any significance for her. Did she leave me another
package there? Would I get more of her?

The day was warm and humid, even for summer. As soon
as I left our apartment complex, I was thankful for the shorts
and tank top I'd decided to wear. I'd already given up on my
hair. It had a mind of its own because of the horrible humidity,
even after I'd tried taming it with my fingers.

I hopped out of the bus at 9:39 a.m., and according to my
phone, I had a twenty-minute walk to get to the lobster shack.
I wouldn't arrive early, but at least I wouldn't be late, which
was a personal achievement. I'd had difficulty leaving Louis
alone with our father in the apartment, but my dad
promised he was ready for it. The thought didn't calm my
nerves, but it forced me to at least give him the chance to prove
he had made some progress. If I wanted him to take some of
his responsibilities back at some point, I had to let him try, no
matter how much it stressed my protective big sister heart. I

texted him on my walk to make sure everything was going okay. He answered with a thumbs-up emoji. Better than nothing.

I reached the lobster shack at 9:54, panting. I glanced around me, but in reality, I had no idea what I was looking for. A message? A person? Since I was early, I sat on a bench beside the shack. I'd wait here, at least until ten. Grabbing Helen's letters from my purse, I read them again, looking for a clue of some sort, but came out short. Once done, I glanced through the crowd again, hoping that something—anything— would catch my eye. A breeze lifted my hair, and I reached to remove it from my view. Tucking the strands away, I looked up, and then—

Him.

Espresso eyes that softened every bit of tense muscle in my body. Hair that had once felt so soft against my skin. Lips that melted away every inch of ice that had covered my heart ever since he'd left me alone in his living room. It all shattered.

And suddenly, I remembered what it was like to love him. He had stolen the feeling when he had left in the night, but here he was, returning it to me.

I'd told myself I'd moved on—I'd had to after his clear dismissal—but my heart hadn't gotten the message, from the way it thudded erratically against my chest at the simple sight of him.

Matthias wore a long-sleeved navy cotton shirt and jeans, his beard longer than it was the last time I'd seen him. He was looking around him, similarly to how I'd done a few minutes before. And when our eyes connected, electricity coursed through my veins. No matter how hard I'd tried to get over him, it was clear I'd failed.

The way his mouth opened and his eyebrows drew together made me think of someone seeing a ghost. He'd probably thought he'd never have to see me again after his dismissal.

Jerk.

He stopped in his tracks and examined me from head to toe until his eyes narrowed on the stack of papers in my lap.

That got him to move again.

He walked in my direction with a firm step. When he reached me, he softly took the papers from my hands, apparently too surprised to even say hello.

He looked the first page over before demanding, "What... What are you doing with my letters?" A giant crease formed between his eyebrows.

"Your letters?" Getting up, I plucked the papers out of his hands. "You mean *my* letters?"

"No, I mean mine." He shook his head, muttering something to himself before looking away. The air was thick around us, like we were in our own little bubble of pent-up frustration. Well, it was frustration on my part at least. *He* didn't have anything to be frustrated about.

"I don't think you understand," I said. "Helen left these letters to me. Her notary called me a week ago." *You're not the one who gets to be pissed here*, I wanted to add.

His gaze traveled back and forth between my face and the letters in my hands, and after a few moments, his eyes widened. Then, he did the one thing I never would've suspected. He burst out laughing, looking up at the sky.

"She wrote us the same fucking letters," he whispered with an awe-inspired smile. "Decided to play matchmaker one last time."

Oh. Oh God.

I wanted to laugh like him, I really did. The thing was, it hurt like hell to think of Helen wanting us to be together, when he'd broken my heart mere weeks ago. He didn't want to be with me, no matter how much she would've liked him to.

Still, I had to admit, Helen was even more clever than I'd thought.

When he looked back down at me, his smile dimmed down, like he remembered how we—well, he—had left things off the last time we'd seen each other. Stuffing his hands in his pockets, he gazed at his shoes. "Would you... Um, would you like to grab a coffee or something, maybe? We could...talk."

I swallowed against the lump in my throat. The last thing I wanted to do was talk with him. He'd been so heartless with me, I didn't even know how to convey it into words. We'd shared an intimate moment, no matter how much he wanted to believe it didn't mean anything. We'd cuddled all night after he'd broken down in my arms. And the one thing he'd thought to do after all of it was dump me on a piece of paper. *Asshole.*

But I had to admit, the possibility to learn what had pushed him to do it was enticing. It might help me get closure, and hopefully make my heart move on the way my mind had started to.

"All right," I answered before overthinking it and telling him to go screw himself.

We walked in silence to a small coffee shop around the corner, neither one of us looking at the other. Once we'd ordered, we went back outside to stroll around the water bordering the shops.

After taking a sip from his cup, Matthias cleared his throat. "So, how've you been?"

I huffed and looked at my coffee to hide my eye-rolling. "I've been okay."

He stayed silent for a while when I didn't ask how he was doing in return, but he still didn't give up. "And how has Louis been? And your father?"

"Fine."

The summer sun blazing on us, coupled with the burning hot coffee sliding down my throat and Matthias' gaze on me, made my skin shine with a sheer coat of sweat. This was too much. I should've left as soon as I'd understood he was the surprise.

"Look, Addy—"

"Can we cut the crap and go straight to the point,

Matthias?" I stopped walking and turned in his direction. "What happened the night of the funeral?"

His eyes closed as he dragged a hand down his face. "Addy, I—"

"Don't 'Addy' me. Just tell me what the hell you were thinking, calling me to come to you and not even having the balls to look me in the eye and tell me you didn't want to be with me. Leaving a post-it note on the couch..." I kicked a rock, making it land in the water with a *ploc*. "What a cowardly thing to do."

He sighed. "I couldn't, okay?"

"What do you mean?" I felt like punching something. "Just be honest for once."

He threw his arms in front of him. "I couldn't stay because of you! I left *for* you, Addy."

"What in the world are you talking about?" He might've been even more messed up than I'd thought.

The hard mask he'd been wearing crumbled, revealing all kinds of emotions. "You told me you'd take care of me, but I couldn't do that to you. Not when you've had to take care of people your whole life. I wasn't going to be another burden to you."

My jaw fell to the ground. "But... But you wouldn't have been a burden to me, Matt." My voice was wobbly, filled with pain and fear and, despite everything, love.

His jaw moved back and forth as he inhaled. "You don't understand, Adelaide. I couldn't stand having you struggle even more. Not when I had a say in it." He exhaled shakily. "I'm a fucking mess, and I don't know how things will work out for me in the future, and I couldn't have us falling in love with each other only to break both our hearts later. You don't need any more pain."

I took a step back as I tried to catch my breath. Of all the reasons he could've given me, this was the last one I expected. It wasn't disinterest that had controlled his decision, but selflessness. He hadn't left me because he didn't want me; he'd left me because he thought I needed protection. From him.

The thing was, he didn't know it was too late to stop me from falling in love with him.

Even if I'd hoped he cared for me the way I did for him, his explanation didn't dull my pain. It actually heightened it, like oil on a fire. Crossing my arms, I stepped in front of him, stopping him in his tracks. "Was loving your mother and having her in your life worth the pain of losing her?"

He bit his cheek. "It's not the same thing."

"I asked you a simple question."

He swallowed. "Of course it was worth it."

"Then what's different? Why couldn't loving you be worth it for me?"

He took a step forward, taking a few strands of my hair between the pads of his thumb and index. "I can't handle possibly being the cause of more pain for you. I can deal with more pain for myself, but not for you. Never for you." His eyes watered, and he hissed a breath before looking toward the ocean.

My hand shot up, grabbing his wrist. "You can't shield me from pain, Matt. That's impossible. The only thing you *can* do is let me soak up as much joy as I can to make the pain worth it if it one day comes."My voice was raw, breaking over the last word.

My hair slipped from his hand as he brought his arm back beside his body. His gaze avoided mine when he said, "I'm sorry. I want to, so much, but I can't."

I closed my eyes as the pain registered in my body. I should've been used to it, with the number of times he'd already told me he couldn't have me in his life, but there was no such thing as getting used to Matthias' rejection.

I didn't say anything, only nodded as I bit my lip before giving him my back and walking away. But, the farther I got from him, the clearer it became I wasn't done. If I never saw him again, I needed to make sure I'd said everything I had to say before leaving. So, after five feet, I turned around, lip wobbling and legs shaking. He was still standing in the place I'd left him, immobile, watching me with a thousand emotions in his dark eyes.

"You know what the worst part of this is?" My voice broke down again, but I didn't care. I was going to be honest if it was the last thing I did. He didn't answer my question, although I hadn't expected him to. "I would've let you break my heart a thousand times over, just for the chance of getting more of the moments of pure happiness I felt when I was with you. If you'd just given me *something*, I would've given you *everything*."

With that, I turned around and left.

MATTHIAS

I watched her go.

Her frizzy hair blew around her face with the wind, but she didn't try to push it away. She let it go free, like she always did. She walked rapidly, as if she couldn't get away from me fast enough.

I understood.

And with her left my heart.

I believed everything she'd said before leaving, and that was part of the problem. I knew she would give me everything, but I didn't *want* her to. She couldn't keep offering herself away. I wouldn't ask her to give another piece of herself only to make sure I was okay.

Because that wasn't what love was. And if there was one thing I was sure of, it was that I was in love with her. So fucking in love, it hurt to breathe as I watched her leave.

Whether she wanted to believe it or not, I was doing this

for her. If it meant she'd be happier, then it didn't matter that letting her go killed some part of me.

Addy's the only thing that matters, I repeated over and over as I watched her walk away, my chest bleeding out on the pavement.

27

ADELAIDE

"*I* swear I'm okay, Stellz. You don't need to call me every single day," I muttered as I peeled a potato, my phone squeezed between my ear and shoulder.

"I know, I know. I just wish I could be there to hug it out with you. Oh, and to give him a good kick in the nuts."

I chuckled. "As much as I'd like to see that, I think it's better you stay in Montreal if you're still feeling that pissed."

"I'm rightfully pissed. He broke my best friend's heart. There's no worse crime."

Just as I was going to answer, I heard tiny footsteps make their way in my direction.

"Addy, do you think I can wear this tomorrow?"

Lifting my head from the potato I was peeling, I gasped. Louis was wearing his yellow t-shirt with red cars on it, coupled with green corduroy pants, blue socks, and his light-up shoes.

"Hey Stellz, gotta call you back. Fashion emergency happening here."

"All right. Just remember that you're a strong, independent woman who doesn't need no man. And that my nut-kicking services are always at your disposal."

250

"Okay, you crazy girl. Bye!"

Hanging up, I turned around and winced when I took in Louis' outfit once again.

"Lou, I don't think that's the best thing you can wear for your first day of third grade. It's a bit...eclectic, don't you think?"

A crease formed between his thin eyebrows. "What does eclectic mean?"

"Let's just say all the pieces you chose don't go well together. I'll help you once I'm done with dinner, all right?"

He nodded and took a step in my direction before wrapping his growing arms around my hips. "Thank you, Addy. You're the best sister in the world."

His words were like an embrace to my heart. Louis had the ability to tug at my heartstrings like no one else. I hugged him back. "You're the best brother too." When he let me go, I pointed in the direction of his room. "Now go change before you dip all your favorite clothes in mashed potatoes."

He left running right away, walking always a waste of time for him.

Back in total silence, I found it suffocating. I'd always needed music around me, but it had been even more crucial in the past few weeks. When I was stuck in silence, it was me and my thoughts, and that was something I wanted to avoid at all costs.

Turning on my playlist, music started playing through the speakers, filling the apartment with a crooner's voice. My father, who was sitting at the kitchen table, started swaying to the sound of the music while reading his newspaper. I'd been seeing changes in his demeanor, especially in the last week or so. The medication and therapy had slowly but surely transformed my father, making him somewhat alive again. He and Louis were what kept me going.

I returned to my potato peeling. I'd gotten more skilled in the kitchen recently, considering my new job. After spending a few weeks unemployed, I'd applied for the cook position I'd showed my dad this summer and got it right away. It wasn't my dream job, far from it, but it paid the bills and allowed me to keep my mind off everything I'd lost in the past month.

I couldn't think of Helen. It was an unwritten rule in our household, as well as in my head, to never mention her. I had to admit it felt wrong, like I wasn't honoring her memory, but that was the only way I'd found to prevent myself from breaking down at any time. Thinking of Helen only made me remember what it was like to be right where I belonged. How could I talk casually about her when the pain of her loss was still so fresh? Every time I tried to mention a good memory I had with her, it was like reopening a cut, over and over again. It was easier to ignore the last few months altogether.

There was also the fact that talking about her made me think of Matthias, which was the last thing I needed. That was another cut I didn't need to reopen. What I needed was to work and to function, so that's what I did.

Matthias hadn't tried to contact me since the day at the lobster shack. After a while, I'd ended up convincing myself I was thankful for it. If he didn't want to take the risk of being with me, then I didn't need him in my life, no matter how much I wanted him. And I did want him. But with each day that passed, I reminded myself—with Stella's help—that I was better off without him. I had enough on my plate, with Louis and my dad and work. Pining for someone unattainable wasn't what I needed, so him not calling was a good thing. Far from the eyes, far from the heart.

As I dropped the potatoes in the pot of boiling water, the music changed to the song I could never listen to without feeling heartbreak. Ben E. King sang about asking his lover to stand by his side, just like I'd asked Matthias.

And he'd told me no.

The sound of a chair scraping on the floor resonated behind me. I added salt to the water, all the while getting lost in the lyrics my mom used to love so much. The singer was right; nothing was better than having your loved one by your side.

I jumped when a hand landed on my shoulder. Turning around, I held my breath as my father stood behind me, his lips curled up. It had been so long since I'd seen him smile this sincerely, I looked him over again to make sure I hadn't imagined it. But hearing what he said next, I knew I hadn't.

"Would you like to dance, Addy?"

MATTHIAS

*W*hen the intensity of the piano was at its peak, I downed another drink.

Bach had always been able to drown my worries, making me lost in the intricacies of his notes. Today, though, his music didn't have any effect on me. If anything, it riled me up even more.

Red and orange leaves flew with the wind outside, creating a tempest of colors that I usually would have enjoyed. But today, the only thing they reminded me of was Adelaide's hair flowing around her face as she'd left me standing behind her.

It had been more than a month now. I should have been able to stop thinking about her a long time ago, so why the fuck hadn't I? Why was she invading each and every one of my thoughts, making it impossible to forget her? Why was I still imagining her sitting beside the fire pit when I looked outside, or picturing her spying on me while I played the piano when I crossed my study's threshold?

A knock sounded at the door. I crossed the hotel room, padding over its plush carpet, and opened to find Rosalie standing in the hallway, lips pursed and cheeks red. "I need a drink," she said.

Right as I opened the door wider, she headed for the mini-bar, which I'd already broached. The door closed with a bang that interrupted Bach's concerto for a second.

"What do you need a drink for?" I asked, refilling my glass with another two fingers of whiskey.

She sighed before leaning against the small granite countertop and taking a gulp of a clear liquid. "Ex-husband won't stop texting me. Apparently, he wants to get back together. As if he couldn't have thought about that before sleeping with that other girl."

"I'm sorry." We filled the silence with large gulps of our respective drinks. "Wait, how did you know I'd be drinking before coming here?"

She looked at me with an eyebrow raised. "Did you really think I wouldn't notice your sad eyes every time we fly together?"

I rolled my eyes but didn't find anything to retort with.

"What's that all about anyway? Girl problems?"

I made my way to the bed and sat on the edge of it. "Something like that, yeah."

"Wanna talk about it? I might be of good insight, you know." She pointed at her body with her index fingers, a smirk on her face.

What was the worst that could happen if I voiced my problems aloud? I certainly couldn't be more miserable than I already was, missing something I barely even had. So, I told her everything, from the pain that flooded me with Helen's death to my sort of break up with Addy.

When I was done, Rosalie narrowed her eyes at me and asked the easiest question I'd ever had to answer. "Do you love her?"

"With every fiber of my being."

"Then I still don't understand why you did it."

I sighed before raking a hand in my hair. "You don't understand because you don't know how much pain and struggle she's had to overcome in her life already. If you did, then you'd understand that I did her a service by taking myself out of her life."

Rosalie placed a finger on her chin, studying me before uttering, "Who do you think you are?"

I coughed, the liquor having gone down the wrong pipe. "Excuse me?"

She took three steps forward, coming to a stand in front of me and crossing her arms over her chest. "I said, who the fuck do you think you are?"

I placed my glass on the table beside me. "I don't understand what you mean."

"Why would you make decisions that involve her life and should be made by her and her alone?"

I shook my head. "You don't understand, I —"

"I understand very well that you decided what she could and couldn't handle instead of letting her choose for herself." She took another step forward. "So, I'm asking again, who do you think you are?"

I opened my mouth, but no word came out. When put that way, I did sound like an entitled asshole, but Rosalie didn't understand what it was like. Addy would do anything for the people around her, even if she was the one to pay for it in the end. I couldn't be responsible for that.

Yet, the more Rosalie's words spun around my head, the more sense they made.

In the face of my silence, she took a seat beside me and continued. "And even if you did do it to protect her heart, do you really think you've protected her from pain by letting her go?"

My brows furrowed as my eyes widened. "Well, in a way, I think —"

"Because from what I'm understanding," she interrupted, "you denied her when she is clearly in love with you. Do you think *that* didn't hurt her?"

My breath hitched in my throat. "Addy isn't in love with me," I answered, voice low and rough.

Rosalie huffed, looking at me like I was the biggest idiot in the entire world. "I've seen the way she looked at you. It was the same way you looked at her." She took another sip of her drink. "If that wasn't love, then I don't know what is."

Blood was pumping too loud in my ears. Knowing Addy might feel the same way I did made me both elated and terrified.

"Even if she did love me," I muttered, "it wouldn't change the fact that being with me could bring her more pain eventually."

Rosalie sighed. "So what if it did?"

I avoided her eyes. "You don't understand, she can't—"

"You think I didn't feel pain when I had to divorce my husband of ten years? Because I did. It hurt like a fucking bitch, but even in the darkest times, I never regretted the years I spent with him." She shook her head, her voice fiercer than I'd ever heard it. "He gave me so much happiness during our time together. It does hurt now, but those moments of happiness can never be taken away from me, and I'd never want to lose them, even if it meant I didn't have to feel pain anymore."

Again, I was left speechless.

"And," she added, as if she didn't believe her point had fully come across, "even if being with you is a risk to her heart, shouldn't she be the one to decide whether or not she wants to take that risk?"

That last question was the nail in the coffin of my resolution to stay away from Addy.

Because Rosalie *was* right, just like Addy had been.

The only thing you can do is let me soak up as much joy as I can to make the pain worth it if it one day comes.

That's where I'd gone wrong. I hadn't given her the opportunity to make the pain worth it if it did come. I'd given up on the one person who might've loved me as much as I loved them and who wanted to be in my life, simply because I was scared that she'd someday get hurt because of me.

If I hadn't been so scared, I could've been with her right now, instead of drunk and sad in a hotel room. Or at least, I could've given her the chance to decide whether she wanted to be with me or not.

With another gulp of whiskey, I decided I wouldn't be scared anymore.

28
MATTHIAS

*E*ver since the moment I'd decided to make things right with Addy, I hadn't been able to think about anything else. Not that she hadn't always been on my mind before, but now it was different. I needed to find a way to make her forgive me and want to be with me again. And this time, I wouldn't change my mind. I wouldn't give up, not for anything in the world, unless she told me she wanted me to. Because giving up would mean letting go of the one person who could make me happy.

Each day without her had been increasingly painful, like an infection to which I had no antidote. And as that infection grew, I saw again how right Rosalie had been; it was a certain game we played, life. A balancing act of pain and love. The things we loved most led to the most pain. Remove those things in an attempt of preservation, and the infection would spread twice as quickly. Our only hope was to hold onto love and hope the horrible disease stayed far behind.

There might not have been a way to protect Addy or me from future pain, but there was a way to work for our happiness. That was what I'd focus on from now on. It was what Helen would've wanted for me. For us.

The moment I got home after my work trip, I went to the place where I'd stacked Helen's letters and went through them again.

Fight, tooth and nail, for the people you love, she'd written once, as if she knew what I'd one day go through.

She'd wanted me to be with Addy from the beginning; had seen something even I had been too blind to see. Addy was the one for me.

Reading these letters would never be easy for me. Every time I went through them, I imagined my mother's lively voice and her laughs and smiles and cries at the appropriate places. It was a bittersweet feeling, to still have a part of her, all the while having to accept time and time again that she wouldn't be coming back.

Her letters taught me so much, about the world, but mostly about my mother. She'd been so many more things than I'd thought; had kept so much to herself. She'd loved a woman and had never told me. I didn't know why, but I was so glad she had now. When I'd read about her losing the person she loved, I'd felt more connected to Helen than ever before. I'd felt what she'd once felt and had wanted to sob for what she would never get the chance to have.

But *I* did have that chance. In my mind, it would have been dishonoring Helen to let the woman I loved go when I still had at least the chance to get her back. So, I'd do everything I could to win her heart again, both for my mom and for me.

ADELAIDE

For the life of me, I couldn't understand Matthias Philips.

I'd tried so many times, but I could never figure out what was truly going on in that head of his.

More specifically, why he'd try calling me again and again, weeks after he'd made it perfectly clear he didn't want to be involved in my life.

Groaning, I clicked the decline button on my phone, just like I had for the past three days.

It wasn't like he was calling me on repeat all day, only one call per day, but still. Why would he even try?

I guessed I could've answered and found out, but that couldn't lead to anything good for me.

In the last months, when I hadn't even so much as heard his name, I'd tried getting rid of my feelings for him, in vain. So, I'd done the only thing I could do about them; I'd stored them away, in a tiny box, with all the wonderful memories I'd made this summer. They were not gone, simply hidden from my everyday thoughts. But the first time I'd seen his name on my phone screen, the box had burst open without my approbation, flooding me with this profound love I hadn't acknowledged in a long while. And I hadn't liked it at all.

Four days later, and my chest still crushed my heart and lungs, making it hard to breathe until my ringtone stopped blaring around me. That was my problem: I *did* want to answer his call. More than anything in the world, I wished to hear his voice and speak with him like we used to. I still loved him, plain and simple. Despite everything I'd tried in the last days, my feelings hadn't been able to go back to their tiny box.

A text appeared on my screen.

Matthias Philips: I'm so sorry.

I read the simple message three times before deleting it.

It didn't matter that my feelings were still there, stronger than ever. I wouldn't cave in. The man had broken me twice; I wasn't stupid enough to put myself in a place where I could get rejected over and over again. I did love him, and if he'd wanted to commit — *really* commit —then I would've been with him in a heartbeat, but he wasn't there in his life. Maybe he'd never be. So, that could only mean one thing: Matthias Philips and I were done for good.

MATTHIAS

I was at a dead end.

Sighing, I let my head drop on the kitchen counter and grabbed Helen's golden ring, rolling it between my fingers. After weeks of examining and thinking, I'd finally figured out what its significance was to Helen. If only getting Addy back could've been this easy.

Behind me, Justin Bieber sang about needing his loved one all around him. I'd never related to the guy more.

I'd done what I could, and I couldn't think of a single thing that might make Addy listen to me and possibly change her mind. It wasn't like I could barge in her door and demand she take me back. That would make me look more like a stalker than a man in love.

But how could I give up on her? After knowing —*feeling* — what it could be like to be with her, I couldn't bear to move on. How could I go back to being with other women when I remembered what it was like to have her, to hold her in my arms and feel strands of soft, curly hair against my skin?

God, I'd been such a stupid asshole.

Think, Matthias. I couldn't let her go again.

I brought my hands to my hair. At that moment, more than ever before, I wished my mother were here to tell me what to do. She'd always been my watchtower, guiding me through life, with or without letting me know it. She'd been there for every girl problem and heartache I'd had in the past, and without her advice, it felt like I could never get it right. How I wished she'd left some kind of advice on this in her letters.

My hand stopped moving in my hair, my whole body freezing in place. *Had she?*

Getting up from the couch, I rushed toward my study, where I'd stored the letters. I skimmed over all of them once more, looking for a specific section that had suddenly popped into mind. When I found it, I read it over and over again.

Speak their language. And if you don't know what their language is, then find out. Ask the people who know them best, and do everything you can to understand them and be understood in return.

Suddenly, what I had to do next became crystal clear.

Returning to the living room to grab my phone, I dialed a number I'd used only once before. It connected after the fourth ring.

"What could you possibly want, asshole?"

I repressed a curse. Things were not looking good for me.

"Look, Stella, I know I hurt your best friend, but I really need your help right now."

There was a pregnant pause. "Give me one good reason to help you."

That was simple enough to answer. "Because I'm convinced I can make her happy. I might have screwed up a lot in the past, but I understand where I went wrong now." I swallowed. "I can't make the same mistakes because I don't think the same way anymore. I love her, and if she still wants to be with me, then that's what I want too." I released a shaky breath. "I can make her happy, Stella."

She didn't answer right away, and with each silent second that passed, my heart sank. She was my last chance, the one person who knew Addy better than anyone. If she didn't help me, I was done.

"Fine. I'll help you, but only because my girl has been a walking zombie ever since you let her go and I need my best friend back."

I exhaled harder than I ever had before, looking upward

and mouthing a 'thank you' to my mother who I could feel watching over me. All hope wasn't lost.

"As I said before," Stella explained, "you've abandoned her. Twice. All the sweet-talking in the world won't erase that fear in her head. No matter what you say, she still thinks you'll leave her every time your heart feels like it."

It was a punch in the stomach to know that was what she thought of me. Some asshole who'd use her again and again, never choosing her over everything else.

"You know," Stella said, "I don't think you've thought about it, but Addy has felt abandoned all her life. She lost her mother, then a part of her father, and your mother, and then you. She's used to it now, but that's also what she expects from everyone. And you haven't exactly proved her wrong, have you?"

I hated the protectiveness in Stella's voice, but only because I knew she was right. I couldn't believe I hadn't realized it before, but now that it was in front of me, I could see it so clearly, why she'd been refusing to answer my calls. And it was like a second punch to the stomach, that I'd contributed to this fear of hers.

With my silence, Stella continued, "Look, Matthias, I may give you hell, but that's only because I love Addy to death. I know you're not a bad person."

"What can I do to get her back, Stella? I can't lose her too." My voice cracked, and I took in a deep breath.

"You need to prove to her that you're in this for the long haul. She needs to be convinced that you won't leave her again, and you won't be able to do that without real proof of your intentions." A male voice spoke behind her, and she cussed. "Look, I gotta go now. I can't tell you what you need to do, but if anyone can break down her walls, I believe it's you."

She hung up on me.

Everything Stella had said made sense. Addy felt aban-doned, plain and simple. She wasn't sure if I truly loved her and wanted to give her my future, which was ridiculous; spending my whole life loving Addy wouldn't be long enough. But, it seemed like she didn't realize that.

Looking down at my phone, a small kindle of hope bloomed in my chest. Stella might not have known what I had to do next, but I did.

29

ADELAIDE

*T*he brisk air made me shiver as I opened the heavy wooden door, holding it open for Benjamin and Gabrielle. Once they got out, I let go and furrowed my hands in my pockets. Summer had passed us by, and before I'd realized it, our shorts and tank tops had been relegated to the back of our closets, replaced by long pants and sweaters.

"You were amazing tonight, Addy. That last song seemed really heartfelt."

I gave Gabrielle a half-smile. "Thanks, I thought it was good too."

The both of them waved and smiled before leaving toward the car they'd shared to come here, hand in hand. They were officially together now, and I was so happy for them. Although I had to admit, I hadn't even noticed something was going on between them until they'd told me. I'd had a lot on my mind in the past months, making me focus on myself and my problems more than on the people around me.

But that part of me was gone. I didn't want to be the person who didn't notice her friends were in love. I'd promised myself when they'd told me they were together that I wouldn't be like that anymore. The person I'd been during the summer —the flirty, lovesick Addy—was gone.

Shivering as the wind picked up, I walked faster toward the bus stop, tugging at the hood of my coat, and that's when I saw the last person who could possibly have been waiting for me.

My father was leaning against a tree, both hands in his pockets. I held my breath as I took him in, from his combed hair to his black jacket and old blue jeans. He looked so much like the father I used to know.

"Dad? What are you doing here?" I glanced around him. "Where's Louis?"

"He's with Mrs. Zhu." Pushing himself off the tree, he walked toward me. "I thought you and I could walk home together. Have a little talk."

My eyes narrowed. "Um, okay, sure."

We headed in the direction of our apartment. For a long minute, my father didn't utter a word, and the more silence stretched around us, the more suspicious I became. Was he okay?

"I'd like to tell you a story," he finally said.

What in the world was going on? This question must've been written on my face because he laughed when he turned to look at me. "Trust me, there's a reason for it."

Giving him the benefit of the doubt, I stayed silent and nodded. The chilly wind whipped around my face, but I somehow wasn't cold anymore.

"The beginning of my relationship with your mother was... up-and-down, to say the least."

My head whirled in his direction faster than lightning. "What? That's not possible."

He chuckled. "Oh, trust me, it is."

"But..." I shook my head. "But you always said your relationship was perfect. You met in high school and stayed together until the end."

He gave me an uneven smile. "Yes, that's in part true, but that doesn't mean it was perfect from the start."

Now I really wasn't following.

"When we met, I was a mess." He kicked a rock in front of him. "You see, the, um, depression I'm battling now isn't my first one."

My lips parted. How was this the first time I was hearing about this?

"Your mother, she was a force of nature, even then." Looking to the sky, he grinned before returning his eyes to me. "You remind me so much of her sometimes."

I blinked.

"I wanted her as soon as I spoke to her for the first time," he continued, "but it wasn't so simple. My feelings, they were all over the place, and I wasn't in the right state of mind to enter a healthy relationship."

My mind was running a mile a minute. The whole idea I had of them was turning out to be a big lie. At least in part.

My father scratched his neck. "Every time Marianne tried to get closer, I pushed her away. Not because I didn't want her, but because I didn't know *how* to love her." He exhaled with a smile. "But she never gave up on me. With each of my steps back, she took a step forward. She even said to me one day, word for word, 'I won't let you go, Richard. You take the time you need, but I'm not going anywhere.'" He laughed, his gaze now lost in space. "I remember it so clearly. She crossed her arms over her small body and stared at me until I had no choice but to listen to her."

This time, I grinned too. That did sound like my mother.

"She kept her word, you know." He looked down at his feet. "She encouraged me to go to therapy and she waited for me to be ready to be with her."

A lump had started to take place in my throat. I swallowed against it, one time, then another.

"I don't know where I'd be now if she'd given up on me

then, Addy." My father's steps slowed, until they stopped altogether. When he turned to face me, I wrapped my arms around my torso.

He examined me from head to toe before giving me his best dad smile. "I know you've been hurting, and if I'm right, it has something to do with a certain man who has stolen your heart."

I bit my inner cheek. "How do you know about that?"

He snickered. "I've observed you a lot in the past month. Heard snippets of phone conversations."

I rolled my eyes, which made him laugh again.

His face regained its seriousness before he said, "I know I haven't been the best dad in the last few years, but —"

"Dad," I interrupted.

He lifted a hand. "Let me finish, Addy. I know I haven't been the best dad, but I'm trying to be better, and it starts now, with this advice. If you think this man is the one, then don't give up on him."

I breathed out. "Dad, it's not that simple."

"Do you love him?"

I stared at him for a few seconds, fighting against the tears burning my eyes. Even if I wished it wasn't the case, the answer was more than clear in my head. My voice was wobbly as I said, "Yes."

He took my hand. "Then it *is* that simple."

A tear escaped and rolled down my cheek. My dad wiped it with his thumb. "Don't let him push you away if you think you should be together. Let him know that you can damn well make that decision for yourself. I never regretted that your mother did, and I know he could never regret you being in his life."

I choked on a sob when I understood he was right. Whether I liked it or not, it was Matthias my heart had chosen. I'd tried and tried to move on from him, but it was an impossible feat. I couldn't let go of him.

Stepping forward, I wrapped my arms around my father. "Thank you, Dad."

"I love you so much, Addy." He squeezed me tightly in return, exhaling against my hair.

I smiled in the crook of his neck. "I love you too."

30

ADELAIDE

"*T*his. Is. Perfect."

Louis beamed at me, another one of his front teeth now missing. His ladybug costume I'd sewn as best I could fit him like a glove. I'd imagined a seven-year-old boy would've wanted to dress up as a superhero or a monster for Halloween, but I'd been more than happy to make him this costume. He looked so adorable I felt like pinching his cheeks like an annoying old aunt.

"Are you ready to go?" I inquired while getting up from my chair at the kitchen table.

He nodded, already running to put his shoes on. My dad came out of his room a minute later, heading for his shoes as well. He looked tired, but at least he was coming with us. He had no idea how much his continuous effort meant to Louis and me.

As we stepped out of the apartment building, I headed to the left, where the higher-income apartments—the ones that were the most generous with candy bars—were located, but Louis pulled at the hem of my shirt. "I don't want to trick-or-treat here this year. We never get a lot of candy."

"Okaaay, so where do you want us to go?"

My dad answered in his place. "We were thinking of going to Cape Neddick."

My heart stuttered at the name of the town that now meant so much to me. I hadn't gone back there since the day at the lobster shack. And of course, thinking of Cape Neddick brought my mind to another subject I'd kept pushing off.

I hadn't called Matthias since my talk with my father two days ago. I wanted to, so much, but I couldn't. My mother had been stronger than I was; I wanted to put myself out there again, to tell him I loved him and to ask him to take that risk with me, but the thought of him telling me no paralyzed me. Every time I tried to call, my fingers froze, hovering over the keypad.

My face must have been pure shock because Louis added, "All the houses are huge there. They'll give so much candy!"

Right. This was for candy. Nothing else. We'd spend an hour there and then we could come back and I could return to ignoring what I had to do to make my heart full again.

Swallowing loudly, I said, "All right."

My father gave me a soft smile before walking toward the bus stop.

We went through the same forty-five minute ride I had taken on the day of my job interview, and even though it was months later, I was still the same jittery mess I'd been back then. Thankfully, my father was there to occupy Louis because while my body was present, my mind was in the Philips' house with Matthias and Helen.

Once we were out of the bus, Louis started walking in the direction of the beach houses, because of course he would. My father and I followed in silence, until suddenly, I heard something.

Music.

It was faint, but definitely there, coming from the beach where I'd gone with Matthias a few months back.

Louis started giggling like a crazy person, walking faster and faster toward the beach. What the heck?

As we got closer, I was finally able to recognize the song that was playing.

"Can't Help Falling in Love."

No. It couldn't be.

This time, I was the one heightening the pace, running until I was able to see the whole beach.

Standing there, facing the ocean, was a man I could never forget, even if I wanted to.

I spun on my heels. My father and Louis wore twin grins.

"You were in on this?" I asked, breathless.

"It was time, Addy," Louis said, his face suddenly wearing a very serious expression.

My dad nodded beside him, plunging his hands in his pockets. "It really was time."

Even with the crisp October wind, I started sweating. I wasn't ready. I hadn't prepared what I wanted to say to him.

And yet, by simply being close to him, it was like a weight had been taken off my shoulders. It was only in seeing him that I realized I didn't need more time to consider if I wanted to take a risk on Matthias. My heart was telling me all I needed to know. I loved him and I wanted him. It was worth the possible rejection. *He* was worth it.

My father stepped forward, wrapping his arms around me. Next to my ear, he whispered, "I wouldn't have brought you here if you'd told me you didn't want to be with him, but we both know you do." He took a step back, watching me as he added, "And if you want to go, just tell me and we'll leave and never look back."

I knew he was serious, but the simple thought of leaving made my stomach ache.

Straightening my back, I exhaled, my thoughts clear for the first time in days. "No, Dad, I don't want to leave."

Louis jumped up and down, clapping his hands together. My dad and I laughed, hugging him.

"Okay well, Louis and I will get to trick-or-treating. See you later," Dad stated before dropping a kiss on my forehead and leaving with my brother.

With one last exhale, I joined Matthias, my boots crunching against the humid sand. I'd never been to the beach during fall, but it was just as beautiful as in the summer.

Hearing me behind him, Matthias turned in my direction. The rising moon illuminated the soft smile on his gorgeous face, and I fell in love all over again. It had been so long. My blood roared in my veins, confirming I'd missed him even more than I'd realized.

His black bomber jacket fit him perfectly, just as his snug pants did. An unruly black lock fell over his forehead. The water was turbulent behind him, a good representation of all the thoughts racing through my head.

"Hey," I said in a breathless voice.

He grinned. "Hi. You look amazing, Addy."

I looked at my boots. "Thank you. You, uh, you look great too."

After a second of silence, we both said at the same time, "I need to talk to you about something."

We chuckled awkwardly, and I gestured with my hand for him to go first.

"I know you didn't want to talk to me," he said, "and I understand why, and I'm sorry for asking your dad and Louis to lure you here." He exhaled sharply. "I know I have no right to ask anything from you, but if you could hear me out, just this once, I'd really appreciate it. And if you don't want anything to do with me after, then I'll leave and you'll never have to see me again. Okay?"

How could I survive never seeing him again? If only he'd known how much my mind had changed in the last few days.

But he'd asked me to listen to him first, so I stayed silent and nodded.

He took a step forward and placed my hands in his, and it was like a bag had been taken off my head and I could finally breathe again.

His eyes never faltered from mine as he spoke. "Falling in love with you wasn't gradual. It hit me like a tidal wave."

I gasped, reflexively taking a step back, but he only followed me, keeping the same distance between our bodies.

"I woke up one morning and it hit me that if you ever walked out of my life, it would feel like losing a limb. You were an intricate part of my life, of my heart, and I was undeniably and whole-heartedly in love with you." He took another step forward, forcing me to look up. "And these past months without you…" He shook his head. "They've felt exactly like that, like I was missing a part of myself."

It was only when his thumb caressed my cheek that I realized I'd started crying. He gave me the warmest of smiles before continuing, "And you were right, it was a cowardly thing to do, to leave from fear of hurting you, of hurting me, and I'm so sorry for taking that choice away from you. It wasn't my place to do so." His voice was soft like velvet. "You can decide for yourself what you can and can't handle, and it might make me a bastard, but I'm really fucking hoping that you still decide I'm worth the risk."

A flood of tears streamed down my cheeks, but no words came out of my mouth. What could I say when he was telling me what I'd been waiting—*begging*—to hear for months?

Behind us, the song I'd sang for him at the wedding was still playing, the soft melody cocooning us in our own world. In my happy place.

He smiled again. "You told me once that you would've given me your heart to break a thousand times over to feel the happiness we felt together. Well, I'm only asking you to do it once more. And I swear if you do, you'll never have to fear it getting broken again. I'll give you everything, just like you said you would."

Then, he did the one thing I never could have imagined, even in my wildest dreams.

He kneeled.

Reaching in his coat pocket, he grabbed a tiny box, which he opened to me, presenting Helen's golden ring, a moon etched in the shiny metal. Simple, yet so elegant.

My mouth fell open, and Matthias lifted a hand in reassurance, chuckling. "Please don't freak out. This is a promise ring, not an engagement ring."

A storm of emotions must have been written on my face because he said, "It simply means I'll do all the groveling I need to do to make sure you know how much I love you. But in the end, I do want to marry you, Addy. I'll give you all the time in the world, but I'm not backing out of this. Not if you'll have me."

My hands covered my mouth, and I bent forward, tears of joy filling my eyes. I loved this man more than I had ever loved anyone before. He wasn't perfect, and he'd made mistakes, but in this instant, I couldn't imagine ever being with someone other than him. This was his proof that he loved me just the same, that he couldn't spend another moment of his life without me, either. In this ring, I saw his promise: no more back-and-forth, only eternal love.

"I never really knew why Helen wore this ring," he murmured, "and I only figured it out a few weeks ago." The box shook faintly. "When I was a little boy, she used to call me her little moon." He chuckled, looking at the ring. "That was my nickname. 'Come here, little moon,' she'd say before tucking me in bed. And, in the past months, when I missed you so bad it hurt, I looked at this ring over and over again, finally realizing that's exactly what you are to me. My little moon, brightening my path and pushing the darkness away from my life."

I couldn't speak, couldn't breathe, as sobs racked my body.

"Please accept this ring, Addy. Accept it, and I'll do whatever it takes to make my way to your heart again and keep it safe. I love you so, so much, and—"

I interrupted him by falling on my knees as well. Extending a shaking hand forward, I cupped his warm cheek. "Matt, how could you make your way back into my heart when you never left?"

His eyes closed for a moment. When they opened again, they were shiny. With a tentative smile, he said, "So I take it you accept the ring?"

After the conversation I'd had with my father, I knew I'd eventually try to make my way back to him, but this promise only solidified what I already knew: we were meant to be together.

I nodded vigorously, half-laughing, half-crying. "Yes. Yes, of course, I accept it. I love you so much, Matt."

Matthias' smile got even bigger as a lone teardrop fell from his eye. "Say it again."

I leaned forward and grinned against his lips. "I love you, Matthias Philips. I love you so much."

He locked his lips to mine, a quick kiss that held so much meaning.

My left hand was shaking as he put the ring on my fourth finger. I couldn't stop laughing, repeating to myself that this was real, that Matthias loved me and that we wouldn't part ways again.

When he was done, I crashed my lips onto his, so hard he fell on his back, bringing me onto the cold sand with him. Coming up for air, he breathed, "Addy."

Music was my first love, and yet there would never be a sound more beautiful than my name on Matthias' lips.

He framed my face with his hands, joining our lips once more. We kissed and kissed and kissed again, making up for the months apart we'd lost and preparing ourselves for our future.

And as I drowned in Matthias' embrace, I couldn't help but remember what Helen had written to us: *Fight, tooth and nail, for the people you love.*

That's what we'd done. We hadn't let go. We'd taken a risk on forever.

And once again, Helen had been right.

EPILOGUE

Two years later

ADELAIDE

"*J*esus, Addy, take a breath. You look like you're about to pass out."

I looked away from the mirror and glared at my best friend. "You're really not helping right now, Stellz."

She smirked before coming behind me, adjusting the veil in my hair. When it was in perfect position, she looked at me in the mirror from over my shoulder. "Are you having cold feet? Because if you are, you can just tell me and I'll get you right out of here."

I rolled my eyes, releasing a snort. The last thing on my mind was doubt about doing this. Matthias was the man of my dreams, the one I wanted to spend my life with. I was reminded of it every time our eyes crossed and my heart beat faster. Butterflies still swarmed my belly with every single one of his touches. "No need. I just..." Biting my lower lip, I traced the pattern of the ring I wore on my left hand. "I just wish some people could be here with us today."

I could imagine it so clearly, Helen and my mother sitting in the front pews of the church, watching me as I walked down the aisle.

Stella hugged me from behind. "I know."

I turned around and grabbed her hands. "At least I have you by my side."

Stella and I had gotten even closer in the last year and a half, if that was even possible. While we hadn't realized our schoolgirl dream of going to college together, we'd taken more time to see each other, either one of us driving — or flying, if Matthias was available — to see the other every chance we got.

In the last year, my dad had gotten better and better, to the point where he and Louis didn't need me at home with them anymore. I could've gone back to Montreal for school, but I couldn't bring myself to stay away from them for four years. So, I'd enrolled in college here in Maine, where Matthias and I could live in the house where we'd gotten to know each other, and I could see my family whenever I felt like it.

"Always," Stella answered, beaming, her golden-brown hair placed in the most intricate hairdo.

Looking up, I fanned myself. "You're making me cry on my wedding day."

She ran to get a box of tissues, patting one under my eyes. "Don't you dare ruin my artwork, bitch."

We laughed as a knock sounded at the door of Matthias' old room, which had been transformed into my bridal suite for the day. "Come in," I shouted as I glanced in the mirror again to make sure I didn't have blotched mascara everywhere.

The door opened slowly, and in came the last person I'd thought I'd be seeing on my wedding day.

"Mr. Callaway, hi! What a nice surprise!" If not nice, then at least strange. I hadn't seen Helen's notary since he'd given me the letters she'd left for me a bit more than two years ago.

"Good afternoon, Ms. Samson. It's very nice to see you too." He closed the door behind him, giving me a knowing smile. "I won't be very long. I only have to give you something."

Out of his wool jacket, he pulled a folded piece of paper. My heart thundered at the sight of it. It wasn't possible. Not another one.

"Helen had left me this one last thing to give to you, with precise instructions for it to be on the day of your wedding." My hand shook as I reached for the letter. "I wouldn't have come here for any of my clients, but Helen was a good friend of mine, and I know how much you and Matthias meant to her."

I couldn't look at him, my gaze focused on the letter in my trembling hands. How was this possible? At the same time, how could she not have done it? This was so *her* I would've laughed at her cleverness if not for the semi-trance I was in.

"Well, I'll leave you to it then. I wish you endless happiness, Ms. Samson."

I lifted my head just enough to mouth a thank you. If I spoke out loud, my makeup would be unsalvageable.

"I'll give you a moment," Stella said with a squeeze of my forearm before following Mr. Callaway out the door. Inhaling slowly, I took a seat on the bed before opening the letter. Right away, I imagined Helen's voice speaking to me.

My Dear,

How I wish I could've been there for you on this special day. Nothing would've made me happier than seeing the two of you get married.

My breath hitched as I read these sentences again and again.

It couldn't be. How could she have known? A sound

escaped my mouth, a mix of laugh and sob. After catching my breath as best I could, I continued reading.

I knew you would end up together the day I saw you meet. You had the perfect ratio of differences and resemblances, opposite enough to complete each other, but similar enough to see eye to eye. Whatever has led the two of you to be together, one thing's for sure: it was meant to be.

I would've loved to be there with you while you grow together, but I'm sure wherever I am, I can still see you. And I would bet my life I'll love getting to watch the people you'll become and the couple you'll form.

On this wedding day of yours, I wish you all the happiness in the world. And if on some days you can't find this happiness, then create it. Laugh, travel, cook, sing at the top of your lungs, and dance until your feet are blistered. Be kind to each other, and love like every day is your last.

Addy, Matthias, I would tell you to make me proud, but I know you already have.

With more love than you could ever imagine,
Helen

Stella's work of art was most definitely ruined by the time I was done with the letter. As I got ready to read it another time, the bedroom door jolted open right before my fiancé walked in. His tear-stained cheeks mirrored mine, just like the paper hanging from his hand. His black tuxedo fit him like a glove, and I didn't think he'd ever looked as handsome as he did at that moment.

"You're not supposed to be here, it's bad luck," I said with the least aplomb in the world. After reading Helen's last words to us, Matthias' presence was the only thing I needed, bad wedding mojo be damned.

He ignored my comment, walking in my direction and

grabbing my cheeks in his soft golden hands. "She knew. She knew all along it would be you and me here today."

I nodded as another set of tears fell from my eyes. An incredulous laugh escaped my mouth as I thought of all the times she'd set us up. "Her matchmaking skills worked out in the end. I'm sure she's really proud of that right now."

He chuckled, wiping my cheeks with his thumbs. "I love you so much. This is only one of the thousand signs that proved this was meant to be." With that, he kissed me, always making me feel like I did the first time. His teeth nipped at my lips in the way he knew would make me moan. I'd received millions of his kisses in all the time we'd spent together, yet I couldn't remember a single occasion they hadn't taken my breath away.

When he pulled away, his eyes were glinting in mischief. "Ready?" A simple question that held a hundred more. Ready to get married, to become his wife, to start our forever? And, to all these questions, I had the same easy answer.

"Ready."

ACKNOWLEDGMENTS

I don't even know where to start. So many people played a part in making this manuscript come to life, and in doing so, allowing me to make my dream come true.

First and foremost, I want to thank my amazing editor Tanya of The Word Maid for bringing this book to another level, and my incredible cover designer Murphy Rae for designing the cover of my dreams.

Next, I want to thank my amazing CP Darienne for reading this book as I was drafting it, with all the typos and the this/that errors and the inconsistencies. This book would certainly never have seen the light of day without you. I'm still in awe of the way you turned some of my sentences and ideas into literal works of art. You're an amazing writer and critic, but most importantly, a dear friend. I'm still not sure what brought the two of us to the CP match website at the same time, but whatever it is, I'm so, so grateful for it.

I also want to thank my other incredible CP, Rebecca. You had the guts to tell me everything that was wrong with this book, even knowing it would be hard to hear, because that's the kind of friend you are. This story and these characters wouldn't be nearly as good without your input, and for that, I can't thank you enough. Connecting with you was a true blessing, one I cherish every day we get to talk and exchange work and laugh. I never thought messaging someone on Twitter could change my life so much, but you're definitely the friend I didn't know I needed, and I'm so thankful for you.

Thank you to Jessica, who became one of my favorite people ever after I slid into her DMs this year like the creep I am. You never fail to make me laugh and tell me when my ideas or sentences suck, which I definitely need. Thank you for being the friend that you are.

Thank you to Gabrielle, my best friend and the person who read my book in a single sitting and gave me the encouragement I needed to decide to do something with this book. Gab, you have no idea how grateful I am for my parents to have named me the way they did.

To Lane, with her magical eagle eye.

To Michelle, who encouraged me all the way and was one of my biggest cheerleaders. I'm so thankful you're in my life.

To Birukti, who's a literal light in my life.

To my family, who've always been there for me and encouraged me to follow my dreams.

To my in-laws, who have taken me in like one of their own since the very beginning.

To my non-writing friends who've supported the hell out of me and asked to read my book even though they'd never read a contemporary romance before. You know who you are. I love you to pieces.

To my very own Louis, who loves me better than anyone ever could. I wake up every day more in love with you. Matthias might be dreamy, but he ain't got nothing on you.

And finally, to you, dear reader, who decided to take a chance on a new author. I don't know who you are, but the fact that you gave my story some of your time is the biggest compliment I could've ever asked for. Thank you, thank you, thank you.

TOPICS & QUESTIONS TO ENHANCE YOUR BOOK CLUB:

1. At the beginning of the book, Matthias doesn't trust Addy one bit and is extremely stiff with her. Do you think his behavior was appropriate? Would you have acted the same way if it was your parent instead of Helen? Or did you think his uneasiness was totally unnecessary?

2. Throughout her letters, Helen gives Matthias and Addy advice regarding all things life. Which one was your favorite? Which one did you relate to the most?

3. In chapter 27, Rosalie says the following when talking about her relationship with her ex-husband: "He gave me so much happiness during our time together. It does hurt now, but those moments of happiness can never be taken away from me, and I'd never want to lose them, even if it meant I didn't have to feel pain anymore." Do you agree with what she says? Have you ever thought the same thing about a past relationship?

4. When Helen asks Addy to become her legal caretaker and to keep it a secret from Matthias, Addy agrees, even knowing it

would hurt Matthias eventually. Do you agree with her decision to keep the secret until the time came, even though she had entered an intimate relationship with him? Would you have done the same? If not, what would you have done differently?

5. Medical aid in dying has been a burning subject in the past years, and is now legal in eleven states in America, including the state of Maine. Why do you think Helen decided not to choose this method? Do you believe there is a difference between medical aid in dying and letting the disease follow its course, knowing it will soon cause death?

6. Throughout the last months of her life, Helen wrote letters to Addy and Matthias, and we learn in chapter 26 that she decided to write the same letters to both of them. Why do you think that is?

7. The idea of control is explored in different examples throughout the book. Which character's way to express their need for control did you most relate to?

8. After the Samsons' mom dies, their dad becomes sick, stops functioning, and leaves most responsibilities to Addy, to a point where she becomes Louis' main parent figure. During some hard moments in her life, Addy shows frustration toward her situation. Do you think it's reasonable for her to be mad at her father, even though he is sick? What would you have done in her situation? Was deciding to pick up his responsibilities in the hope he would eventually fall back on his feet the right solution?

9. In chapter 18, after Addy says to Matthias, "God, I could kiss you right now," she hears him whisper something back. What do you think he said?

10. If you were making a movie of this book, who would you cast as Addy, Matthias, Louis, and Helen?

ABOUT THE AUTHOR

N.S. Perkins lives the best of both worlds, being a part-time romance author and full-time medical student. She has always been an avid reader, preferring to stay curled up with a good book in her bed rather than going out. Although her first love was the fantasy genre, she soon realized what she loved most about those stories were the romance parts. When she read her first romance novel, she fell in love, and has been basking in this love ever since.

When she's not writing or studying, N.S. loves to try new restaurants, dream about the next beach she'll be visiting, and creep the cutest dogs in the parks around her house. She lives in Montreal with her partner.

Made in United States
North Haven, CT
02 November 2021

10794688R00164